EAST END

1
HEAR NO EVIL

USA TODAY BESTSELLING AUTHOR

NANA MALONE

East End

Edited by Angie Ramey
Proof Editing by Michele Ficht
Published in the United States of America

EAST
END

PROLOGUE

East

She was faster than she looked. What the fuck?

The woman darted out of the private room and into the bar. I followed as quickly as I could, but I had to avoid tripping over Livy. I practically jumped over a chair, and narrowly avoided the hostess, so she had a lead of several feet on me.

I was out of the backroom in the VIP area like a shot. And the woman in front of me turned back, her eyes slightly widening when she saw that I was approaching.

She grabbed one of the busboys by the collar and shoved him toward me, then she sprinted.

No way was she going to be fast enough.

I spun around him, avoided a table with a couple on a date, then scooted around the pair of blondes who eyed me appreciatively.

Note to self: Come back for them later.

Then I bolted out the door.

I saw her running to the right, long legs eating pavement. Oh, she was a runner. Awesome. I was too. London Marathon, five years running. Former track athlete. This was going to be a Sunday jog.

She quickly darted across the street, and I followed suit, ignoring the cars blaring their horns at us.

As she crossed the park, she started to lose some of her steam, which was when I picked up speed.

Up the hill, her legs stopped working for her and started working against her.

She slowed, and that gave me just enough advantage to put on a burst of speed and catch up to her. I grabbed her by the back of her shirt, yanking her back. "Nah, uh-uh-uh-uh. You don't get to take pictures of me and my friends and not at least tell us your name." I was irritated that I was huffing and puffing.

Jesus Christ, she was fast.

"I know all about you and your friends, the kind of men you are."

As I spoke to her, I felt along her arm. Then I spread my hands across her waist, lifted her top, and pulled the wire. She grabbed for it, but I kept it just out of reach. "Uh-huh, this is the camera, isn't it?"

What I didn't account for was her quick thinking, and her knee came straight for my balls. I turned my leg just in time to catch her knee on the side of my thigh. It still hurt like a son of a bitch. "What the fuck? Who are you?" I didn't let her go, and she continued to struggle. I held on to her, and I grabbed and tried to pull the camera free one handed, but it wouldn't come off.

"Let me go." She struggled in my grip.

"No, not until you tell me who you are and who you work for. I'm not going to hurt you, but I can't let you run loose. So who are you?"

"Someone who's going to see all of you burn."

"Bold words for a captive woman."

"Oh, you think I'm your captive, do you?"

She elbowed me, and I doubled over. "Jesus fucking Christ."

2

She tried to twist free, and when my hands slipped, I hooked into her belt instead, and she fell on the ground with me. I rolled on top of her. "Stop moving. I don't want to hurt you."

I tried to yank the camera from her body. "I just want the camera. You can't take pictures. I don't know who you are, or what you want, or what story you think you saw, but it's not happening. Not today."

"I will end you."

"I'm sorry sweetheart, but aren't I the one on top of you?"

Then a jolt hit me. Right in the center of my chest, and I felt like I had been punched by Thor's fucking hammer. I jerked back, convulsing. She rolled me off easily then. "I told you, you can't hurt me. People like you aren't going to hurt me again."

She stood over me, and I could see that the messy brown hair she had tied at the nape of her neck was a wig. It was askew at the front. Her hair was darker. Chestnut maybe? It was hard to tell in the dark.

Fuck. Why couldn't I move? My teeth started to chatter, and I jumped. *Fuck.*

Then she reached down to my hand. I tried desperately to hold on to the camera, and we fought for it. What was a valiant fight in my head, to her was my laughingly feeble attempt to hang on, because she plucked it easily out of my hand.

"You, East Hale, are going down. I won't stop until I crumble your house of cards. Do you understand me?" She leaned close, and the scent of honeysuckle filled my senses, making my mouth water.

But then my mouth was filled with the taste of metal, and my teeth rattled. Then along with not being able to fucking move, I couldn't breathe either. It was like her scent wrapped around me, enticing me, and then when it was too late, choking me.

I wasn't sure how long I laid there seizing. God, had she used a Taser on me?

That was how Bridge found me, on my back in the grass, my eyes open, my body coiled and tight. He was panting from the run. "Christ, both of you are fucking fleet-footed. I saw her hit you when I was across the street. Are you okay, mate?"

I blinked up at him and groaned. "Fuck me."

With a cheeky smile he said, "East, we've talked about this. You're not my type. I like you as a mate."

"Fuck you."

He grinned. "I see you're getting back to fighting form. You'll be all right. What did she hit you with?"

That buzzing in my head and my teeth had to mean she'd hit me with a fucking Taser. She came prepared with a Taser. Why?

Bridge pulled me to a sitting position, and I dragged in slow, steady breaths. "Fuck, that hurts."

"Is it actually pain or tingles?"

I groaned. "I guess more tingles. My teeth, God, they feel awful."

"Yeah, that's a lot of voltage. I think you should get checked out by the doc."

I shook my head. "I'll have the staff doctor come to the penthouse. I'm sure it's fine, but fuck me, who was that woman?"

"Well, you're the one who went after her. And you caught her. She didn't tell you anything?"

I studied my friend in the darkness, the moonlight making his jet-black hair appear slightly bluish. I opened my palm, displaying the SD card I'd stolen out of the camera. "I am Elite, remember? I have some tricks up my sleeve."

Bridge squatted down next to me and took the SD card out of my hand, studying it. "How long will it take before she finds out her SD card is missing?"

"I'm not sure, but it could be a day. But I'm sure that I'll have everything off of that thing tonight."

"Of course, you will."

I glanced around, staring into the darkness, wondering if she had turned back to watch her theoretical kill.

"I don't know who you are princess, but I will find out, and then you and I are going to have a very long chat about why you don't tase strangers."

Nyla

My legs ached. My lungs burned. But still, I forced my arms to keep pumping.

If your arms moved quickly, then your legs moved quickly. Neural coupling, right? It was some long-ago advice from a running coach, but I was going to rely on it to survive.

I'd miscalculated. I'd thought tonight would be easy. I should have probably predicted this outcome. I just didn't want it to be a failure.

You almost got caught.

Run. Run. Run. Run.

I darted down an alleyway despite the lack of illumination. I could only hope nothing unseen waited to trip me. The safe passage was on the other side. Amelia had a car waiting, and all I had to do was make it to her.

I didn't hear footsteps behind me. I didn't hear anyone chasing after me. I didn't know if they were giving chase, or if they were coming, but that one guy… Hale. *East bloody Hale.* He had followed me out of the restaurant.

The real question was if he'd recognized me or not. No one

should have. The disguise I'd worn was a good one. My partner, Amelia, was a whiz with prosthetics.

I kept going but slowed my steps as I stripped off the black hoodie I'd been wearing, pulling the arms through and reversing it so the red inner lining became the outer layer. I thrust my arms into the sleeves again and snapped it on. As I sped up again, I spat out the filaments used to plump out my cheeks. Then I peeled off the latex I'd used to fashion a nose for myself and tossed it at the nearest bin.

I yanked the wig off my head and shoved it in my pocket because I didn't want to leave it where it might be found.

Listen, no one is following you.

I wasn't dumb enough to believe that. I'd been trained too well. I knew someone could be following whether I detected them or not. I knew it wasn't safe to stop and check my clothing. I might have been tagged with a listening device even as I ran.

The dark alleyway narrowed between the Marks and Sparks and the Cock and Crow pub, the late-night revelers and bustling traffic noise shielded by the buildings. Christ, I wanted to take a breather.

No! Don't stop. Rest later.

This was my I-shat-the-bed egress route, and I needed to stick to the plan.

I ran and ignored the pounding of my heart, the screaming of my lungs, the weight in my legs. *Ignore it, just run. Safety first. Worry later.*

I raced to the end of the alley, not even looking around me to see what might be waiting for me. Everything posed potential danger. Getting my body safe was the first thing I needed to do. My kidney ached from where I'd taken the hit. My shoulder throbbed from where I'd fallen. But I'd catalog the injuries and worry about those consequences later.

My partner, Amelia Jansen, jerked her head up as I stumbled into the car. "Jesus fucking Christ, Nyla, what the hell is wrong with you?"

"Drive," I managed to grind out.

In a flash, the MINI Cooper's tires spun, and then she shifted like a Formula One driver, swerving into traffic. Fighting the burn in my lungs and panting as I spoke, I gasped, "I think I was followed."

Amelia's eyes went wide. "You're serious?"

I groaned. "Unfortunately." Then I put my finger to my lips, indicating she should be quiet as I peeled off my jacket and then flung it out the window as we passed a bin.

My tank top went next as I tugged it over my head and pitched it, then I contorted and shimmied out of the black stretch bottoms I'd worn. Amelia rapidly blinked over at me, but she kept swerving like she was auditioning for *The Italian Job*.

I kept expecting to hear the shrill chirp of sirens, but there was nothing other than the bustle and honk of taxis, revelers and tourists.

Were we even being followed?

You can't take that risk.

Amelia slowed as we approached an alley and in the dimness between two streetlamps, the rest of my clothes went out the window.

She lifted a brow and asked, "Are you clear?"

I nodded. "I think so. Let me check the camera."

Delicately, I ran my fingers over all the edges of the camera that I'd been using to take pictures. I looked for anything out of order, out of place. "I think we're good. But let me just grab the SD card."

She groaned. "Thank God that camera is intact. The requisition paperwork was going to be a nightmare."

"I wish I could say of course it's in one piece, but it was touchy for a minute there. Bastard almost smashed it." After a careful search, I hadn't found any listening devices. With a sigh of relief, I flipped open the SD card holder and muttered a curse under my breath.

"What's wrong?" Amelia asked.

"Motherfucker."

"What? Talk to me, Ny. What's happened?"

"He took it." I held up the camera and showed her the empty SD card slot.

She frowned. "Shit."

Plowing my hands through my hair, I tried to fight off the impending panic.

If you panic, you are out of the game. Breathe.

I forced myself to drag in a long deep breath, hold it, and then release it slowly by counts. "I went into the restaurant as planned. While I was serving, I was in there twice before they even noticed anything. But this fucking camera, one of them saw it. And then he chased me. I ran. God, I didn't think anyone would follow or that he'd be that fast, quite frankly."

"You didn't take evasive maneuvers?"

I choked out a laugh. "Are you fucking kidding me? I ran for my life. Yeah, I took evasive maneuvers. He was just faster than I expected."

Amelia took up my hand. "Relax, take another deep breath."

My brain offered up helpful images of me fighting that arsehole. He was supposed to be a lazy billionaire. But oh no. The twat had fight skills. Actual martial arts fight skills. He had fucking surprised me.

I had done my research on the London Lords, as they called themselves. I was looking for proof of their secret society. There had been whispers, rumors. Filthy rich men who were the real

London power brokers, and I knew in my gut the London Lords were part of it.

I had studied their movements, where they went, who they talked to, who their friends were. I'd just needed evidence, but all my evidence was fucking gone.

"Okay, I went in there. I took my pictures. I was trying to identify all the players, and fuck, there were some people I didn't recognize in the room. And then he saw me and chased me, and we had a fucking fight in the park. He was good, Amelia. Jesus Christ, like skills you read about, he was that good."

"So what, are you hurt?"

Even as I shook my head no, I rubbed my shoulder where I'd taken the brunt of my fall, but it was my kidney that hurt the worst. "Not in a real way. I don't think he was trying to hurt me. Lucky couple of punches." *Bullshit. He had you dead to rights.*

"You were so lucky, Ny. If he'd managed to subdue you, if you'd been caught, it would have been both of our asses. That wasn't a sanctioned operation."

Did she have so little faith in me? "I never would have given your name."

She rolled her eyes. "Process of elimination. I'm your best mate, and we're almost always attached at the hip." She had a point there. With a frustrated sigh, she took the exit toward Camberwell and my townhouse. "How did he get the drop on you? That disguise should have worked."

I shifted in my seat with a wince. "He was, at the very least, as good as I am. And he didn't get the drop on me; he was lucky."

Amelia slid a glance at me. "What are we going to do?"

I looked at the camera. "I'm not sure yet, but I'm not giving up until we manage to pin something on the London Lords."

"If anyone can do it, it'll be you."

I fucking prayed she was right because I'd lost this

opportunity tonight. Cocked it right up. I only knew the London Lords as Bennett James Covington, East Hale, and Bridge Edgerton. They had another friend, Drew Wilcox. I didn't know much about him. Wife, family, that was it. Covington had recently gained a fiancée. Edgerton also had a fiancée. They'd been engaged for two years but still had made no move to get married. That was all I had.

No sufficient proof and now no surveillance photos either.

"We know they're involved in something larger. They are tied to the Van Linsted case. We just need to prove it."

She was right. When I'd met Ben Covington earlier in the year, my instincts told me something was up with him. The more I pulled that thread, the more questions I had.

Then my case mysteriously had been tied up, with an additional high-profile case tossed in. I'd gotten credit for both busts. But I knew what they were. A pay-off of sorts. Ben Covington didn't want me looking into him and his friends... and I needed to know why.

ONE

East

What the hell?

That woman. First, she was a hell of a fighter. Second, she was quick. She moved like she had proper training. She managed to put me on my ass.

I hadn't even bothered to go back to the restaurant. After Bridge had picked my ass up off the ground, I headed back to the penthouse. There was no way I could let it go.

She'd been taking pictures of us.

Exactly what did she see?

We were discreet.

Or so you think.

I scrubbed a hand down my face. Chances were, she hadn't heard anything she shouldn't have. But all of us together, that was a risk. And with Interpol sniffing around after the Van Linsteds were arrested, it was a big risk.

I didn't have any moral problems with what we'd done to Bram Van Linsted. After all the shit their family had pulled, the cheating, the lying, the abusing and trafficking of women, we had zero qualms about them getting exactly what they deserved.

Even if what they deserved was not the result of their direct crimes, we still put them in jail for a very long time. What I did have qualms about was getting caught before we finished getting vengeance for Toby. There were more people in the Elite that deserved punishment. And if we got pinched, they wouldn't get what they deserved. If we got caught, they would remain free.

So I had to care quite a bit that a random woman was photographing us.

She could be a reporter.

That was true. But there was something familiar about her. *Why did I know her?* Dark auburn hair, perky nose that was slightly too big for her face, full lips that looked like they were permanently curved into a smile.

Her cheekbones had been all wrong though. It was like she had these great features, but the arrangement was all wrong. Why was that?

I strode into my penthouse, full of piss and vinegar, ready to hit something.

As I marched to my bank of computers screens, I forced myself to take deep, even breaths. Wasn't that what the long-ago therapist had said for me to do when I felt the anger coming for me? For the rage threatening to take hold, take deep breaths to suppress it. Remind myself that I was not in control of everything, and I couldn't control it all. Usually, it helped. Usually, I could calm myself enough to think, but in that moment, I wanted to know what she wanted, why she was watching us, and I was in search-and-destroy mode.

With a vicious tug, I almost ripped my Ozwald Boateng suit jacket when I yanked it off.

I jerked my tie loose, so I no longer felt like I had a noose around my neck. And then I flopped onto my couch, broken and exhausted.

The rush of calm was instant, followed by a little tingle of anticipation.

The hacking had started as a result of a little too much alone time. As a teenager, life at home had been complete shit. When I wasn't shipped off to boarding school, my parents were mostly absent, and if they were present, they were either cold and distant or angry-chatting most of the time. Granted, most of it was directed at AJ.

And like most teens, I'd taken to doing whatever I could to block it out. I'd avoided going home. And when I was at home, I was tapping away on my computers. Of course, I'd gone poking around in probably a whole hell of a lot of places I shouldn't. But side note, it gave me an excellent skill set that I loved. It gave me that high, that buzz. The thing that alcohol and drugs had never given me.

The only thing that rivaled that sweet numbness was sex. But that wasn't the kind of relief I needed tonight. I needed to know who the hell that woman was and what she wanted.

I wasn't so far gone that I didn't check on my pet project first. The security system I'd put in place at Belinda Lloyd's place was holding, and she seemed safe. She hadn't hit any panic calls. And I'd put facial recognition into each camera. If her abusive ex showed up, the police would be notified. All was good there. There was nothing to do.

With a few quick keystrokes and taps, I was plugged into CCTV for the South Bank area. I pulled up the camera feeds right around the restaurant, and then I sat back as I watched.

"Where are you, little minx?"

The camera caught her coming out the side door, and then a hulking shadow falling in behind her. That was me. And she took off running. She moved like an athlete. No flailing arms, good form. With a slight lean forward, she pushed off of her legs like she spent a lot of time running, not as a weekender but as someone who had been trained properly. Her arms were the driver. They weren't sloppy. She knew what she was doing, and she darted and moved like she knew exactly where to go. Like she had plotted her escape route. And then I lost her.

I switched over to where I knew we'd ended up in the park, then I leaned forward, watching her movements, the way she ducked hits and blows. I watched myself fight, knowing full well I'd held back because, well, she was a woman and I hadn't wanted to hurt her.

Because it didn't matter what the hell was going on with you, you didn't put your hands on women. It as an easy enough rule to follow most of the time.

But this one had been hitting like she meant it, and she'd landed a couple of good blows. Absently, I rubbed my ribs thinking about it. She had knocked me flat on my ass, so that was going into the books, and I was pretty sure Bridge would never let me live that down, but whatever.

One of the cameras from the nearby bar caught a view of her face. There was something on her cheek. It looked like a cut on her skin, maybe?

I tried zooming in, but there was only so much CCTV cameras could do. I growled. I watched the fight over the camera and my easy slip where I took her SD card. Then I watched her knock me on my ass with that Taser. *Excellent.*

To my chagrin, I was half hard. Jesus fucking Christ, what the fuck was wrong with me?

I was no masochist. Whips and chains, unlike what Rihanna and Britney said, did *not* usually excite me. But somehow, I'd gotten my ass handed to me by this woman, and the memory of it made me hard. But that would be another conversation for another therapist on another day. She took off, running east out of the park. So, where was she?

Another few quick taps on the keyboard took me into the feeds for the likely exit points. I picked one, searched all the cams, but there was no sign of her. Finally, it was when I looked south that I saw her. She'd doubled-back around. God, she was smart. She'd come prepared.

With a determined frown, I leaned forward until I finally caught her. She was in the alley behind some bars, panting, holding her ribs. Fuck me. Had I hurt her? The wash of shame was quick. The nausea seemed to follow too. I didn't care how badly she seemed to want to hurt me or the London Lords. It didn't sit well that I'd injured her.

She reached up to her face. That piece of skin that I'd noticed on her cheek, where I worried that I'd hurt her, she dug fingers into it and pulled. I sucked in a sharp breath as I watched her peel away the skin and cheek that had seemed too full for her facial frame and the nose that seemed a little bit off. The action at first made my gut clench.

Ridley Scott, one of your aliens is free.

But then I had a clear picture of who I was dealing with.

The face revealed was like a punch to the balls. My dick, instead of deflating, the motherfucker went full steel. The woman from the park was none other than Nyla Kincade. The woman hell bent on being a thorn in the side of the London Lords.

We had too many secrets to keep. Ten years ago our brothers in the Elite had caused the death of our friend.

The four of us were hell-bent on revenge. And no one was going to keep us from that.

We'd already taken down Bram Van Linsted. We had two dominos left to topple. Garreth Jameson and James Middleton. And we had no intention of stopping until they were gone, dead, and buried.

But it seemed that intrepid little Interpol agent was coming for us. I should be concerned. Instead, every cell in my body wanted to scream, 'Game on.'

A text drew my attention when it beeped.

Unknown: *I know what you want. And I can help you get it. But first the London Lords will help me.*

East: *Who the hell is this?*

Unknown: *Francois Theroux. I'm the man who will help you get revenge.*

⚬

East

After a sleepless night, I was still unsettled by that little mishap with Agent Kincade.

Mishap? Is that what we're calling it? She kicked your arse.

What the fuck was that shit even? Why had I followed her? To what, confront her? But instead, I'd been the one who ended up on my ass.

I scrubbed my hand down my face. Nyla Kincade was a threat, not just to me, but to my family and our carefully constructed plan. I needed to get my shit together.

I'd spent half the morning in a zombie haze. I'd nearly missed two standing meetings. Spilled coffee on myself. Zoned out in a planning meeting on the design for a new boutique hotel in Australia.

By lunch time, my assistant, Belinda, paused in my doorway, looking concerned. "Uh, Mr. Hale, I just wanted to remind you that it's Friday and I'll be leaving early for Tommy's recital at school."

Recital? What was she on about? Why was she reminding me of the day? I knew what bloody day it was.

Do you? You had the date wrong in your earlier meeting.

Right. "Yeah. Of course. Thank you for the reminder. And how many times do I have to tell you to call me East?"

"Habit, sir," she said with a small smile as she quickly reminded me of my other meetings and told me she'd set alerts for them. She tugged at her sleeves nervously, but it was no use. I could see the hints of bruises.

She whirled around but not before reminding me, "You have a meeting in three minutes."

"Yep, got it. And Belinda?"

She lifted her brows. "Yes?"

"You're doing great."

"Thank you, Mr, erm, East."

She swung the door closed, but before it could click shut, Drew burst in. "What's the matter with you? You look like shit."

"Cheers to you too, mate."

He shrugged. "Calling it like I see it. You look like me when wee Alice was born."

I winced. "No one can look that bad."

"Twat," he muttered.

I shook my head as if that small movement was going to exorcise Nyla from my brain.

Good luck with that.

Ben and Bridge came strolling into my office right behind Drew, and I figured I should just rip the bandage off. "Last night, the woman I chased out of the restaurant was none other than Agent Nyla Kincade."

Bridge whipped around, Drew cursed, and Ben just stared at me before saying, "Come again?"

"I know none of you are deaf. I tracked her movements after our little fight in the park." I pulled up a map on one of my monitors and showed them her route. "She went this way, removed her disguise, and was picked up by a MINI Cooper right here." I showed them the point on the map.

"Fucking hell." Ben ran his hands through his too-long blond hair. "Why can't this woman leave well enough alone?"

"Not sure, but she's a hell of a fighter. I took her SD card off of her, and I'm decrypting everything now."

Bridge stalked over. "What the fuck does this mean? We gave her a plum case. That should have made her back off."

I shrugged. "I think our best course of action is for me to approach the section chief and implore her to back off."

Ben rubbed his jaw. "You want to take on Agent Kincade?"

Fuck yes. We had a score to settle. But no way was Ben going to give me the all clear if I said that. "It just makes sense. She's already come after you and Liv, Ben. Bridge and Drew have families, so there's no need to put them in the crosshairs. Let me deal with her."

He crossed his arms and studied me closely. "Fair enough. Don't approach her directly. It only makes her fight harder. She's tenacious. See how far you get with the section chief."

"Yeah, will do." I sighed and pulled out my phone. "There is something else."

Bridge scrubbed a hand down his face. "Maybe we should quit while we're ahead."

"Sorry, mate." I handed the phone to Ben.

He read the messages and frowned. "Who the fuck is Francois Theroux?"

"I've done some preliminary digging. Theroux, he's no light-fingered bugger. He's a world-class thief. Stolen millions. And he's at the very top of several international top-ten capture lists."

Bridge whistled low.

Ben sighed. "So this is real? What does he want from us?"

"No idea, and that's the problem. I don't know how seriously we take it. Anyone who knows of his crimes could easily be jerking us about, pretending to be him." I glanced around at the lads. "What do you want to do?"

Drew rubbed his jaw. "What's our exposure? Do we have to do anything?"

I frowned. "Well, my inclination is to seek and destroy anything that could hurt us. But we need to do some research first. We need someone who would know Theroux and his methodology."

Ben sighed. "Lucas."

I shrugged. "Our erstwhile prince." Lucas Winston might be a prince of the Winston Isles, but he was also a thief. *Former* thief. And he had helped us bring down Bram Van Linsted and his father, Marcus.

When we'd learned that Bram had a hand in our mate Toby's death ten years ago, it was a blow, but not a surprise. Lucas had helped with the plan for revenge, and I knew he'd be in to help us again. "If anything, he can tell us the intangibles. Like reputation, temperament. At least what the rumors are. They'll help us predict how this Theroux character will act."

Drew stroked his chin. "There's got to be more we can do. Can we trace the text? This is too much to be a coincidence."

"Not that easy. I already tried a trace. The encryption is next level. It can be done, but it will take time." He was right about this feeling too coincidental. "The text makes me nervous too. Could also be from someone looking to make us spin our wheels since we took Van Linsted off the board."

Ten years ago, Bram Van Linsted, whose father had been the Director Prime and headed the Elite for well over thirty years, had played an integral part in the death of our friend Toby. A couple months ago when we learned what they'd done, we'd made a vow for payback. One that now extended to Garreth Jameson and Francis Middleton since we'd exacted our revenge on the Van Linsteds.

This new threat, this was something different, something Lucas might have an understanding of.

Ben cleared his throat. "East, keep digging. I'll call Lucas. Drew, you can speak to the Five. Theroux knew exactly how to get access to East, so he knows who we are. Find out if he's one of us. The Five would know."

The Five were The Elite's checks and balances. They were meant to be the least corrupted of our organization. Which was apparently a tall order.

Drew nodded. "Yeah, okay, I'm on it."

Bridge nodded. "I'll work some old contacts, see if I can dig anything up."

It was Drew who asked the obvious question. "How exposed are we?"

That was the crux of things. Theroux had burrowed into our fortress of goddamn solitude like it was a gossamer thin veil. He had our number, and he claimed to know exactly what we were planning. I shook my head. "I don't know yet."

"I don't like it," Ben murmured. "For now, we wait and watch. And we get Agent Kincade off our backs."

Bridge rubbed at the stubble on his jaw. "We're on a tightrope, lads. We need to tread carefully."

Ben nodded. "We do. And we will. Starting with getting Nyla Kincade off our scent."

"I'm on it. She won't be a problem." And she wouldn't be. I knew just how to deal with her.

TWO

East

Agent Roger Kincade was a bear of a man. He was tall, about six feet, and broad. Wide. Fit for his age. He looked athletic. I'd put him at 55, maybe. But he had shrewd, hawkish eyes that told me he missed nothing. I had picked the Windsor Club for a reason. It screamed old money. It screamed authoritarian. It screamed 'my club is better than your club.' It was meant to shock and awe with its dark paneled wood and genuine gold fixtures.

It was one of the oldest buildings in London. But for all the austerity, there was also a genuine sense of warmth.

Even though he was only a guest, Roger Kincade was greeted like an old friend at the door. I'd picked a vantage point where I could see him walk in. The valet was accommodating, kind, already had his coffee order and asked him if he would like hot towels. Then he was shown directly to my table.

When he arrived, I stood and gave him a smile that should have fallen somewhere between no nonsense and open pleasure. I knew his daughter had gotten her tenacity from somewhere, so I knew he wasn't a man I should play with.

"Section Chief Kincade, it's a pleasure to meet you."

I shook his hand. His grip was firm but not really tight. He was direct, looked me in the eye, and I could see he was a straight shooter.

"I appreciate you taking the time to meet with me this afternoon."

"Well, it didn't seem that I had any choice," he said as he pinned me with a level stare.

"Of course you did. I understand you're busy."

"Mr. Hale, what is it exactly that I can do for you?"

Of course, he was straight to the point, direct to the pot of gold. All right then.

I sat back and watched as he took a bite of the scone that had been brought along with his coffee. The man nearly moaned but managed to school his face after a couple of sips of the Italian roast I knew he preferred. When he cocked his head, a small smile tightened his lips.

"I'll give it to you. You sure know how to treat a guest."

"Well, we try. I won't waste your time. I'm here about your daughter, Nyla, Agent Kincade. She's been looking into our organization. And we need her to stop."

He lifted a brow. "Are we going to name this organization?"

I gave him a small smile. "Don't be coy. You're in the loop because you're a section chief of Interpol. And your boss's boss's boss, I believe those are the levels, is a member. I could have gone over your head and dropped this request way up the chain of command. But I have a good deal of respect for your daughter. She's smart, intuitive, tenacious. Jesus Christ, is she tenacious. I need you to impart to her that when it comes to the Elite, she's barking up the wrong tree. There's nothing illegal, or immoral for that matter, happening within the Elite."

"So what, I'm just supposed to put her on the bench?"

"Redirect her efforts, perhaps. I won't go into the reasons for why you would want to comply with this request. I understand that your predecessor picked his battles."

Roger sat back then and folded his hands in his lap. "Lord Hale—"

I put up my hand to interrupt him gently.

"Please. You can just call me East or Mr. Hale. Lord Hale is my father."

"All right, Mr. Hale, then. I don't really care about your organization. You lot run around being London power brokers or whatever, and it doesn't affect me or influence me. I don't care. And I want to make it perfectly clear that I don't care how many times you invite me to the fancy inner circle. If you do something illegal, I will stop you. As long as there's nothing illegal happening, I don't care what you do. You can keep your organization secret. But, if I find out that you're stepping your toe out of line, I'm going to take the leash off Nyla, and I guarantee you, I have sixty more agents just like her."

"Excellent, Roger, that's what I wanted to hear. Now, if you don't mind, reassign Agent Kincade to something, anything else so that she can focus less on our organization and move forward."

His gaze studied mine for a long moment. Assessing, as if trying to see what my angle was, what else I wanted. "And if I don't comply?"

I shrugged. "That's up to your boss's boss's boss to decide. I won't threaten you. I won't threaten your daughter. That's not what I'm here for. I'm in essence asking for a favor. From a citizen who has done nothing wrong. I just don't want your daughter picking at things she has no business picking at only to find that, while nothing illegal is happening, she's unearthing centuries of long-buried secrets. And that knowledge could be potentially dangerous to her."

Nyla

I'd taken great care with my makeup that morning. It had been a little tricky to cover up the bruise along my cheek, but I just wore my hair down, styling it artfully to cover up most of the bruise and then taking care of the rest with makeup, so I didn't have to get too heavy-handed.

What I couldn't cover up was how I winced every time I had to walk. When I'd fallen, I'd taken a bump to my head, which was the kind of pain that most people only read about. Bone deep and jarring with every damn step. I couldn't even stand to wear heels, so I'd slipped on some flats. But flats hardly felt like the body armor I was going to need. Obviously, it was a tough day because it was new assignments day. And my father, well, he wasn't inclined to give me any choice pickings. God forbid he looked like he was playing favorites.

I dragged open the heavy glass door to the London Interpol Offices, ready to do the whole scan and swipe thing to get past security when I caught sight of the group gathered in the lobby and skidded to a halt.

My stupid fuckwit ex, Denning Sinclair, also known as the man who had stolen my job as Associate Section Chief, was playing prolonged tonsil hockey with his new love... whom Amelia had dubbed 'the teenager' on account of her being so damn young. She was some kind of graduate student. Just what I needed today.

The person who came behind me through the door cursed as he bumped into me, and I was shoved forward by his momentum.

"Oi. Watch where you're standing."

"Sorry." I kept my voice low, because God help me if Denning heard me.

He had his hand on her ass, and I felt like I was going to throw up a little bit in my mouth.

But you don't want him anymore, right?

I pulled my hair up, scraping it back off of my forehead and dragging it up into a bun at the top of my head. Then I remembered I had a bruise to cover, so I couldn't even do the whole nonchalant, I-don't-care hairstyle thing. I tugged my hair back down. It was better I not get asked why I was bruised. I'd done a decent job with the makeup, but my father would see through that.

God, you're a mess.

I could do this. I could walk by them and give no shits. Not a single one. This was not going to hurt at all.

Lies.

Luckily, the lobby was crowded. People were milling about, deliveries coming in, couriers going out. It should be easy to mix into the crowd. So I tried that. Join the throng, make it past the barricades, ID out, swipe, swipe, hand over my bag for gate check and—

"Nyla?"

I forced out a slow, steady breath. "Sir." I spat the word out like an epithet. The fact that he insisted on all of us calling him sir was such bullshit. A year ago, he'd been one of us.

Apparently, he'd been able to separate himself from his octopus of a girlfriend. I didn't know how he'd managed it.

"Why are you in such a rush? Are you going somewhere?" His gaze narrowed, and he scanned my face. "What's wrong with you?"

I injected a note of sarcasm into my voice. "No greeting, just 'What's wrong with you?'" I rolled my eyes. "Try this instead. Good morning. Now, you just repeat that."

He sighed. "You don't have to be so sensitive."

"Not the word I'd use, *sir*." I swiped my way through the barrier, collected my purse from the other side of security, and swung it over my shoulder. I wanted to remind him of the HR seminar on employee relations and how microaggressions were a no-no. But I was already exhausted.

He scowled at me. "You know full well that's not what I—"

A sing-song voice came from behind Denning. "You're Nyla, right?"

I held my breath. Today was shaping up to be all kinds of shitty. I squinted at the lithe brunette. "Yep. That's me."

She patted her chest. "I'm Hazel. Denning has told me so much about you."

The hell he had. "Somehow I doubt that."

"Oh no, he has, really." Her smile was bright and saccharine. "He talks about his entire team. He's so proud to lead all of you."

I had to get the hell out of here. "Well, that's nice. If you'll—"

"Actually, before you go, I want to make sure you'll be at dinner at our place at the end of the month. I sent an email, but I never heard back."

I'd filed that email in my trash. "I'm so sorry. I'm just so busy. I won't be able to attend."

Hazel's smile went tight. "I have to insist. Why don't you email me with a better date and time after you've thought about it?"

"Sure, I'll do that." *Never gonna happen*. She was out of her mind, because there was no way I was going to subject myself to that.

I turned and left them where they stood in the lobby, not even knowing what Denning wanted to talk to me about, but certain I wouldn't want to give a shit. I went to my office first, dropped off my bag, and made a cup of tea, all before the morning briefing.

When I finally sat in my usual chair at the briefing, Amelia took a seat next to me before sliding over a glazed doughnut in my direction. "Here, eat this. Chances are, you haven't eaten."

"Yeah, that's me. Constant diet of tequila and bad decisions."

She rolled her eyes. "Eat."

I took a little piece of the doughnut and nearly moaned in ecstasy as the sugar dissolved on my tongue.

At the head of the table, my father stood to his full height. His mostly dark auburn hair, rich and full, caught the overhead lights and reflected reddish glints.

People always did a double take when we were together and wondered how, with my olive skin and darker hair, we were father and daughter. He always just said I looked like my mother.

Although, I didn't really. My mother had been stunningly beautiful with her dark hair, her big eyes, and her soft pouty mouth.

Denning took his usual position across from me, and the rest of the team filed in. Dad gave each of them a withering glare for being late, since he considered being on time late.

"All right, team, let's get our status updates out of the way and then move on to team assignments."

Amelia leaned over. "Here we go."

Amelia and I had been trying to get our own dedicated cases for well over a year. We both had the proper experience. We both were general badasses, if we did say so ourselves. And we were both ambitious. The funny thing was that, even though my father had a few female special agents, there were some whispered rumblings that they always got the shit cases.

I'd never agreed with that. The father I knew wouldn't do

that. He wasn't a misogynist. But recently, I'd been starting to wonder.

Dad called for the status checks. Around the table we went. Denning had been working on a drug case that was just now coming to an end. They had found the perpetrators in Ibiza. But somehow, Denning had to be there for several weeks trying to suss the guy out. Ibiza wasn't *that* big.

Finally, my father reached me. His gaze just roamed over me, narrowing slightly as he looked at my cheek. Was the bruise visible?

I stared back, fighting the instinct to reach up and touch my face. "Nyla, why don't you tell the team where we are on your assignment."

Amelia and I both shifted in our seats. The shitty thing was I was back at square one with few leads. "Well, we're still waiting for an update on the jewelry heist. Right now, I can't get anyone to report anything stolen out of Grimwald Authenticators. Even though I know for certain something happened there that night. The cameras were taken out in precise fashion, as if done deliberately and not by malfunction, so we're still digging."

For the last year, I'd been on the hunt for a ring of jewelry thieves. It had led me down a path of human traffickers, whom I'd caught, but I'd never solved the diamond heist. And my theory was why I was currently sporting a bruise and taking the arse kicking.

"Leads?"

It didn't matter what I knew my father was going to say, I had to try. I pulled out photos of this year's Gem Gala. "I'd like to take a run at Prince Lucas Winston. He was at the Gem Gala. He *and* his sister, but still neither he nor his sister, a prince and princess, had anything stolen.?" I left out his connection to the London Lords on purpose.

My father shook his head. "No. You already spoke to Jessa Ainsley, yes?"

"Well, yes, but I think he could be helpful if you just let me talk to him. We're running out of leads."

"You are a very good agent, Nyla. Find another angle to work."

I sat forward, struggling with my emotions and the need to keep my voice even. "All due respect, sir, he's tied in with the London Lords, and they are up to something. The moment I started sniffing around them as part of my investigation, I was given a huge case. It's basic redirection. What don't they want me to look at? I just need time. All my instincts are flaring."

My father planted his hands on the table. "Then perhaps you can offer me some proof of wrongdoing? Why the prince?"

Because he was connected to the London Lords. I swallowed and bought myself some time. "He and his sister are clearly in the middle of this. He's part of the distraction from the London Lords. And he's a known associate of one Tony Angelo, who we know is wanted for grand larceny, assault, burglary and a host of other crimes."

Denning piped up sarcastically with, "And let's not forget he's been seen standing next to the London Lords in a photo. *Clearly* an admission of guilt."

I scowled at him. "That's not what I'm saying, but it's worth —"

My father put up his hand and then shook his head. "Sorry, Nyla, find another way. Besides, the same people that you've been going after helped you close a human trafficking ring. And you got all the credit for that. But right now, you are getting a new assignment. I will not have you poking at these people unless you have something tangible. A prince for Christ's sake." He rolled his eyes. "You have no hard evidence."

"I'm telling you they gave me a distraction because they don't want me watching them."

"Drop it." He then turned his attention to the rest of the team as we continued going around the circle. When he got back to Denning, he gave him a nod.

Denning stood like my father had. As if he had rights and privileges above any of the rest of us. "Meanwhile, I've been hot on the case of Francois Theroux. There are whispers that he's possibly turned up in Spain, so I'll be putting together a small task force to do some reconnaissance and chase him down."

God, he was so transparent. Francois Theroux was my father's white whale. He had been chasing that man for nearly thirty years.

He and my father apparently had gotten in some cat-and-mouse chase before I was born. To hear my father tell it, he had been so close.

And then Theroux had slipped out of his hands. And since then, every two or three years, Theroux would resurface, and my father would get spun out chasing him. I had often wondered if I could catch Theroux, would my father take me seriously? Would he see me for once? Value me? I wished. But instead of me, he was letting Denning take the Theroux case.

I hated how he played favorites with Denning. Granted, I had made the mistake of dating him. My father had warned me that it wouldn't work out.

He had been right, of course. But nothing smarted like having my ex being chummy with my father and him having a new girlfriend and flaunting said new girlfriend in my face after telling me I was 'too much.' Not that I cared.

At the end of the meeting, Amelia rushed after me as I marched to my office. "Hey, wait up. Please tell me that your hurry is in fact because you have zero intention on giving up."

She knew me too well. "You know I never say die." In my office I slapped down my new case file paperwork and plopped into my chair in full slouch. "I just have to find proof of the impossible and prove that the men behind it are doing illegal things. You got a magic wand I can borrow? I could really use it."

She closed my door quietly and leaned against it. "No. But I met my mum for an early breakfast, and she dropped an interesting tidbit about the Bridgeport hospital charity event tonight. She mentioned that there would be several wealthy eligible men in attendance. In particular, *East Hale.*"

I pushed myself up to sit straighter. "Amelia, I could fucking kiss you."

"Make it good, gorgeous. It's been a while since anyone did it properly. Probably why my mother insisted I go tonight."

"I'm always good," I said with a wink.

"Let's hope so. You have a thief to catch."

I certainly did.

THREE

East

Hours after meeting with Nyla's father, I still had her on the brain. And maybe that's why I'd been more than happy to volunteer for auction duty.

I still wasn't sure what to make of the older Agent Kincade. From my research, I knew he'd comply. But how he would handle Nyla was what worried me.

You have an Interpol agent up your ass, and you're worried that he might crush her spirit?

Where the fuck was my sense of self-preservation? I'd spent too much time pulling up everything I could find on agent Nyla Kincade. If she was coming after us, the least I could do was be well informed. But there was a chance she'd heed her father's advice, and for now, I hoped the situation was contained.

If by contained you mean reliving that fight you had with her over and over again, then sure, contained is the right word.

No matter what I found out about Nyla Kincade, I wouldn't be sharing my new low-key obsession to know what she smelled like or what her laugh sounded like.

"Right now we have a Pan Elise painting. Opening bid

is £30,000." I forced my attention back to the excuse that had brought me there, just half a block from the Interpol offices.

Lucky for me, my mother couldn't attend the auction because she had a prior engagement, and my sister was in Monaco. As the acting curator of the Du Mont family collection, she really *should* be here. But her wife was six months into a difficult pregnancy, so it was better if she didn't have to travel back to London.

So the job was mine.

The painting wasn't really right for our family collection. But that didn't mean that *I* didn't want it. It would go well in my personal collection with its bold colors and light touch if AJ didn't want it.

To the far right, a bloke sat with his back turned to me. He had short dark hair, a suit, and a blue shirt, and I couldn't see him well enough to figure out who it was because of the way we were seated sort of amphitheater style.

I raised my paddle for fifty, he raised it for sixty.

I knew that the artist was up-and-coming. I'd seen her exhibit in London a little over a year ago, and she was making a name for herself with bright strokes and flashing colors. And I knew her style was completely wrong for the family collection, so what the hell was I doing?

I raised my paddle again automatically, the hum of competition flowing under my skin.

The auctioneer called off numbers back and forth as we did silent battle with our paddles.

Who the fuck was that? And why wouldn't he just say die?

The painting was probably worth maybe eighty thousand. The artist was becoming a hot commodity, but honestly, this kind of bidding for an up-and-comer was ridiculous. But still, I couldn't stop myself.

Because I hated to lose. I hadn't gotten where I was by letting anybody win, and I certainly wasn't going to lose now. The funny thing was I hadn't even originally wanted to come to the auction. I'd begged off, told AJ to come down herself. Begged my mother to cancel her charity engagement. But now, it seemed like a good distraction.

The auctioneer called for a hundred and fifty thousand, and I raised my paddle. I should have just done this on the phone.

But you're checking in on your girlfriend.

Fine. What I was doing was scoping out the Interpol building, which was just down the street. I could have said no to this today or done it on the phone, but when I noted the location, I decided to do a little reconnaissance. Not that I had plans of ever walking in through the front door, but it paid to be prepared.

It was just smart to know where all the cameras were.

Besides, thoughts of Nyla Kincade had caused me a sleepless night, and because of the idea that I might catch a glimpse of her, I may have jumped at the chance to be there in person.

One hundred seventy-five. I raised my paddle, frustrated that my competitor would not back down. Who was he?

That question was answered when he turned to his companion just to his left and murmured something, laughing, and then turned back to sneer at me.

His face. I knew exactly who he was. And a whole stream of feelings roared in as I raised my fucking paddle again.

Garreth Jameson. That twat. We'd gone to Eton together, though I barely thought much of him then. We were even peripherally friends most of the time until everything changed. After what he'd done, I vowed that one day I would kill him.

At the time I'd made that vow, it had been one of those

things that you say but you only sort of mean. But now that I was a grown adult, had skills, power, and money, I meant it in a very real sense.

Bored, I sighed and raised my paddle before speaking clearly. "£200,000."

A hush fell over the auction. Jameson turned back to me, sneering once more, and I met his gaze, giving him a smug grin. He scowled and put his paddle down. "Yeah, that's right, you git." I mumbled to myself. "I won this time."

It went on like that for the remainder of the auction. Me bidding on pieces I did not want merely for the joy of making him bid over his likely maximum. Driving up the price, sitting back in mock disappointment when I would lose out on pieces. Nodding in acquiescence as he got overly priced garbage.

One day, you really do need to grow up.

Yes, one day. Just not fucking today.

When it got to the pieces that I was there for specifically for our family collection, my bidding was modest but well within range. I knew exactly what they were worth and this time, I wasn't playing with my money. I was playing with Du Mont money. Of which my mother, being the last in the line of Du Monts, had plenty.

But I also knew she was very particular about her art. What she was and was not willing to spend on. There would be some pieces that would be kept in our family vault and some that would be on display in the museum in Monaco. When one of those came on the auction block, Jameson raised his paddle, throwing out the maximum sum my mother was willing to pay. I frowned. That son of a bitch. My palm itched to raise the paddle and force the price up.

Not your money. Stop it.

No, it wasn't my money, but what if I supplemented it?

Stop it. You've already spent £500,000 today. Don't be ridiculous.

That money was a drop in the bucket, honestly. But considering I hadn't intended to spend it when I'd left my penthouse earlier, it probably said something about how I felt about Garreth Jameson.

I kept my paddle down.

Jameson turned, his brows lifted in surprise. I shrugged, indicating, 'Well, you win some, you lose some.' I knew for a fact that he would try and offload the piece soon. The Jameson family had a reputable art collection of their own, but it was nothing like that of the Du Monts. This piece certainly wasn't going to fit, and since his father controlled the collection, the old man would be livid about his purchase.

I acquired the other two pieces below our maximum price, which I could be happy about, and my mother would be thrilled. I was just sending a text to AJ after the auction and had gone to arrange for delivery when Jameson approached. "Oh, tough one today. I didn't think that the Hales stooped to turning up in person to do their own auctions."

"And what are you doing here? You could easily have had a representative do it."

"Since I am a bit of an artist myself, I like to see the pieces personally. I'm not a pretender, you know?"

I raised an eyebrow at that. "Oh, I didn't realize you were still painting. I thought after, you know, that forgery thing that you got caught up in, you'd stopped."

His brows snapped down. There had been a forgery scandal some years ago. Paintings by a moderately unknown artist, complete with authenticity paperwork, had started floating around. Each piece not going for any more than £10,000, which is really what they were worth. But there were murmurings, rumblings, that they were forgeries.

They weren't really worth paying attention to, but I remembered the scandal for the Jameson family because Garreth had been caught in the fray as having some mild acquaintance with the forgers. Those in tighter circles had murmured that *he* had forged some pieces himself.

While a talented painter, he lacked imagination in his own work, but he had the skill to copy well enough. It was a skill that, in and of itself, was amazing. He just lacked vision.

He nodded, giving me that standard rich-git smile. How many times had I given that smile? The one that we were all bred to give. The one we were all taught. We learned it by watching our fathers do it in social situations. Ninety percent smugness, five percent disdain, and five percent contempt. It made my hands itch to hit him.

"Well, congratulations," he muttered.

I nodded. "Congratulations to you too. I didn't think the Elise would fit your collection from what I've known of it, but way to branch out. Good for you."

Even though that smug smile remained in place, I could see the slight furrow of his brow. He was not good at hiding his emotions.

As I turned to leave, he said, "It's been a long time since I've seen AJ. She was one of my favorite people."

Time stopped as my brain locked into the fact that he had the nerve to speak my sister's name after what he did to her.

I might not be able to use my burn against another member of the Elite, but I could certainly throttle this worthless wanker.

A burn was a complete social, financial, personal annihilation of someone. And no matter what, another member of the Elite couldn't save them. Short of murder, you could do anything to ruin them. We each were inducted with one burn available to us. But Elite members were exempt from a burn.

I took a step toward him, and then I felt a soft hand on my arm. My gaze flickered to the right, Charlotte Bryce, the auction director, smiled up at me. "Mr. Hale, if you would just come with me, I have arranged for delivery of your pieces. Just tell me which ones go where."

I settled my gaze back to Jameson, and he gave me a head nod, though smugness and malice were reflected in his eyes as I said, "I'll be seeing you again, mate."

He grinned. "Yeah, you certainly will."

What was supposed to happen was that I turn and follow Charlotte, but my brain was having none of that. Instead I indulged in the fantasy of beating the snot out of him, right there. From our years in the Elite, I knew hand to hand wasn't his specialty. He'd rather taken to fencing.

I could take him.

I could. I really could. But I needed to get my shit under control. Vengeance would be much sweeter if I made him squirm first. So, I forced myself to unclench my fists, then I turned and walked away.

Jameson might think he'd won that round, but we were coming for him. He had a lot to answer for.

East

To catch a thief, you needed to be a thief. Prince Lucas of the Winston Isles had taught me that.

So for the evening, amongst the glitz and glamour, I was exactly that. International thief. No, international *spy*. A regular James Bond.

You wish.

"East? Mate, are you focused?"

I frowned as Ben's voice pinged in my earpiece. "Hush, I know what I'm doing."

Bridge's voice was wry. "Are you sure about that? Maybe we should ask your last girlfriend."

I bit back my scowl as I took a sip of the champagne. "Would you two knobs shut it so I can get this done?"

Bridge's chuckle was low. "You know, I quite like being the one in the van. This is easy. Twist a few knobs, glance at a few monitors. Why are you always whining about how it's not easy to be in the van?"

"I swear to God, Bridge, if you touch any of my shit, I will kill you." I loved my mates, but my gear, those computers... They were like my children.

"Oh relax, I'm not going to break your precious machines."

Ben's voice was gruff. "Both of you, focus. The sooner this is done, the sooner we all get to move on."

I placed my champagne glass on the tray of a passing waiter. It was showtime.

We'd all drawn straws as to who would be next in line to deal with the Elite, the one to deal the next blow. It was between Drew and me. And as Drew wasn't attending the gala tonight on account of fatherhood duties, where both Jameson and Middleton would be, I was the lucky git.

When we were barely more than kids, we'd all joined the fastest path to fortune and power. Some of us had to learn hard lessons along that path.

For starters, the three of us, the London Lords, could have made it without the Elite. Membership had its benefits, but we'd been determined not to use those benefits if we could help it. They came with too many strings.

To make matters worse, our so-called brothers were behind

the death of our friend. So, tonight was about payback. And she was one hell of a feisty bitch.

The aim was to clone their phones. Once we could listen in, we'd get leverage. And once we had leverage… It was game over for them. Ben, as Director Prime, needed to be above reproach. And someone needed to be in the van to make sure the data came through. Someone also needed to be able to handle the coding tech if it glitched. We'd already tried this once, and not only did it not work that time, but it had taken way too long. So we were using a new tech now. One that required me, someone a little more technologically savvy, to make it happen.

"Just get it done, East. It's easy. You plant the device, remove it after five minutes, then do it again."

"I notice you're not the one doing the switch."

I adjusted my cufflinks peeking out of the sleeves of my Tom Ford tuxedo. The Bridgeport Hospital Charity Gala was a yearly event. All members of the Elite attended, and the guest list was a who's-who of London society, as well as some of the rich and famous worldwide. It was the charity of all charities to be seen at. Everyone wanted their name on the placard to say they supported whatever the hell the cause was this week.

Not actually because they cared, but because they wanted the ability to preen and show off.

And I hated the lot of them.

"We have incoming."

I stilled while trying to look nonchalant. "What's the problem?"

Ben muttered, "Your father is coming straight for you on your five o'clock."

I swallowed my groan but still headed for my mark. I would deal with the old man later. Now was not the time. "Yeah, fine." I picked my route. One that seemed unintentional as I deftly avoided him in the crowd.

I twirled around a waiter here and sidestepped a socialite there. A smile and a dancing flirt with a model across the way. By the time I made it to Garreth, he was speaking to a tall brunette woman. She had a wide smile and a familiar look to her. I knew her from somewhere.

Garreth's grin was on me. "Hale, twice in one day? I'm starting to think you're stalking me. Enjoying yourself?"

That was the thing about the Elite. You could spend your entire life loathing people, and some of them still thought you liked them, despite the undercurrent of hatred. The overt kind where you traded barbs and attempted stabbings, and the subtle kind, where you were both aware of your mutual loathing but kept most of it internal. And then there was the covert form, where one of you loathed the other, but the other was utterly clueless.

Jameson and I were the overt kind. But in public, we could pretend to be gentlemen. "Jameson." He took my hand to shake.

Play the part. Act the part. Be the part.

I could not kill the man in a room full of people.

To most of the people in this room, I was one of them. Son of Lord Richard Hale. Cream of the Elite crop. A member of my family had been part of the Elite since the beginning. Outsiders assumed that I was entrenched in it. But truth be told, I hated the Elite just as much as Ben did. Just as much as Bridge did. We each had our reasons. "Yeah, mate, good, good. Just making the rounds."

As we chatted amiably, I felt the prickle of awareness. My father was coming. I needed to get this done quickly. I turned to the brunette. "I see you have beautiful company this evening."

Her smile was sardonic. "You don't remember me, do you?"

In my ear, Bridge chuckled. "What? A woman has left your bed unsatisfied, East? Say it isn't so."

When I was out of this stupid party, I was going to throttle him. "I am so sorry. I don't remember you."

The thing was, I knew exactly who had been in my bed. I selected women who met specific criteria. I knew them all. Every single thing about them. And no, I wasn't a stalker. I just liked to know who I had around me. It took only one time of being lacerated to learn a lesson, and I had no intention of learning that particular lesson again.

"I'm Janina Harrison. We met at the Wescott Benefit a few months ago. You never did call me."

Christ. "Oh my goodness, Janina." I had no idea who she was, but I knew enough to play the part. "You will have to forgive me. Of course, I intended to call. But... business. We were opening a new hotel. I was focused on that. But I am more than happy to call you this time."

She lifted an elegant brow. "Somehow, I don't believe you."

Jameson gave a hearty laugh. "Looks like she has your number, Hale."

What I needed was for her to ask for someone else's number and leave me alone so I could plant the fucking device.

From behind me, I could hear my father talking to someone.

I needed to do this quickly because talking to my father would be its own special kind of headache.

As a waiter passed, I held my breath and waited for just the right timing, then I deliberately stuck out my foot in a quick manner. He jostled his tray and saved the half drinks, but then one toppled and splashed Janina.

Her squeal was immediate. "Oh my God, watch where you're going."

I offered a silent apology to the waiter as I left him to fend for himself. I then reached for my handkerchief and handed it to Janina. "Oh, look at that. Is that red wine? It's going to stain."

She frowned. "Um, yeah, I'll go have a look. I'll be right back."

As she scurried off, I turned my attention back to Garreth. He was also dabbing at his tuxedo. "Jesus, the staff they hired for this event leaves a lot to be desired."

I reached inside my pocket and grabbed the device. It was small enough that he wouldn't notice. All I had to do was place it.

From behind me, my father called out, "East, is that you?"

That was bullshit. He knew it was me.

I took a step toward Garreth and tapped him on the shoulder to distract him. I slid my hand inside his jacket, placed the device, and pulled my hand free as I pressed my other hand firmly to his shoulder. When I turned, he was already nodding to my father, pleasantly distracted.

I muttered into my com, "Start the transfer."

"Fucking finally. You took longer than Ben the first time."

"I swear to God, I will kick your ass."

Bridge only chuckled.

Ben's voice came next. "All right, let me arrange a distraction for your father."

I sighed. "No, I have to deal with him."

Garreth and my father exchanged pleasantries, and I forced myself to nod at my father.

"Where have you been, lad? I was hoping to speak with you, especially now that one of your own is currently our Director Prime. There are a few initiatives that I'd love to talk through with you."

Of course, you would have something to further your own agenda. When did my father ever not think about himself?

"Well, we're right here."

The old man looked uncomfortable, as if he were desperate

43

for privacy. I knew better than to let Garreth slip out of my sight, but the old man looked like he wasn't going to let it go. He wanted some alone time, and he wanted it now. "East, I'd like to speak to you alone for a minute."

Garreth tapped me on the shoulder. "Mate, I see Davis over there. I have a question for him about a player. I'll catch you later."

Fuck. Fuck. Fuck. I had no control of the situation. If he left and found the device before we recovered it, we were blown. But Ben was on it, it seemed. "You deal with the old man. I'll run interference with Garreth. East, just plant the next one on Middleton, and I'll do the same thing."

Bridge's voice was clear. "All right, we have thirty seconds before we're done. Ben, you take over. East, try to shake the old man so you can plant the second device."

"Yup, on it."

My father leaned forward. "What was that?"

There was more swearing from Bridge. Then he said. "Fuck it. I'm coming in. Data from the first device is transmitting smoothly."

Dammit. I didn't need his help. I could get this done.

Can you? The old man isn't going to let this go.

"What I said, Dad, was that we have nothing to talk about. I have zero desire to engage with you. If you want to bring me to the table to take my place as a Hale, then you know what you need to do. Until then, we're done."

He frowned. "East, I know things had been tense between us for some time, obviously. But I thought now that Covington had been named Director Prime, your feelings would have eased a little."

I forced a tight smile. "What does Ben being the Director Prime have to do with anything? He's my best mate. He *should* be Director Prime. He's the only one who's going to lead us in the right direction. It doesn't change how I feel about you."

He winced.

The vote for a new Director Prime had been filled with tension. The most powerful man in all of Britain, if not the world. And that was now Ben, so of course, everybody would want a piece of him. And they were going to do it by getting as close to Ben as they could.

"Look, things have been difficult between us, but it's time to put that aside. I'd like to talk to Ben about—"

"Dad, I'm not going ease a path for you. If you want to talk to Ben, then talk to Ben. I have more important things to do."

He frowned at me. "You really plan to hold a grudge?"

I shrugged. "Yes. I am going to hold a grudge. That's how this works. I will do my damn level best to destroy you. So let me be clear in case, somehow, it's not. *You* severed any relationship we had a long time ago. And there is no recovering from that until you decide to repair the damage that you've done." I then turned and walked away. I had another device to plant.

FOUR

East

Where the hell had Middleton gone? I could have sworn I saw—

Instead of Middleton, a dark-haired woman crossed my path. She wore vermillion red, and her dress dipped in the back, displaying an expanse of skin. I turned toward her to get a better look. Was that—

"Eyes on the prize, mate."

I snapped back to attention at the sound of Bridge's voice.

When our gazes met, he grinned at me. "My eyes are on the damn prize. I got caught up with the old man. Where's Middleton?"

"You can relax. I tagged him already. Ben will collect that device too."

"Shit." I hated being the weak link.

"All good." He nodded his head in the direction of the brunette. "You got distracted, mate."

"Shut it. I can do more than one thing at a time."

He smirked as he sipped his scotch. "Sure you can. That's why you're staring after that woman with your tongue hanging out of your mouth."

In a perfect world, he would have withered under the look I shot him. "I am not. It's part of the facade."

My best mate grinned at me. "Sure. I get it. You're just getting into character."

"Exactly. Matter of fact—" Another beautiful brunette approaching us made me stop in mid-thought. "Emma! What are you doing here? Shouldn't you be somewhere having fun?"

She gave me a warm smile, and I enveloped her in a tight hug. Emma Varma was sort of our adopted little sister. Her brother Toby had been part of the squad. Back in the day, the five of us had big plans to take over the world.

But then he'd died.

No, he was killed. There's a difference.

There was in fact a difference, and Toby's death was why we were here tonight. For vengeance. For blood. For justice.

She pulled back. "Well, don't you look nice in a tux?"

"I look good in anything." I said, winking at her.

She rolled her eyes at me. "Of course you do."

She turned her attention to Bridge, but there was no welcoming smile for him. I couldn't quite explain it, but the two of them looked like they were sending heat lasers at each other, daring one another to eviscerate.

"Bridge." Her voice was tight as she addressed him.

"I thought you went back to the States for your new job."

I watched with rapt attention as she squared her shoulders and pushed out her chest. What in the ever-loving-Prada fuck was going on here? It was like I was watching some weird praying mantis mating dance. I wanted to shout at Bridge that he was out of his depth and that he'd get his head bitten off. But for the two of them in that moment, I didn't exist.

They were locked in this weird hate/eye-fuck situation.

"Thank you so much for taking interest in my job, but after

the Van Linsted thing, Mum just wanted me close to home. So I put in for a transfer. I'm home now. Guess you'd better get used to seeing me around."

"You should go back. I'll look after your mum."

Emma laughed at that. "You're ridiculous. Still playing power broker. It must really burn that you have zero power over me."

He took a step toward her, but she'd already tuned him out. "So what are you lot up to? I know it's not to write a fat check. I saw you sniffing around Jameson and Middleton, and I want in."

The hell? No way, no how. "Don't know what you're on about," I muttered then took a sip of scotch.

"You can't bullshit me, East. I can see it in your eyes. You trust me and want me to know. And let's not forget that I got you the video that was the catalyst that set us all on this path. Don't shut me out."

She wasn't wrong. "There's nothing to tell, Ems. Bridge and I have something to do. We'll catch you later, yeah?"

She blocked our path of escape. Bridge's body went tight and rigid as he came into contact with her. When he spoke, his voice was pure ice. "Stay out of it, Emma."

"Or what? You're going to toss me over your shoulder and drag me out of here? Let's not forget one simple thing; you need me. I'll be around when you finally figure out you can't leave me out of this." Then she stepped aside and stalked into the crowd.

Bridge glowered after her, looking very much like he was considering clubbing her over the head.

"Well, I'm empty. Join me at the bar?"

He was still looking toward the direction Emma had sauntered when he mumbled, "I'm going to go check on Mina."

And by check on, he meant shag out his frustrations. But Bridge's fucked-up relationship was none of my business unless Mina forced my hand. She claimed to love him, so it was better to leave well enough alone.

Suddenly my phone chimed. So did Bridge's. We both pulled them out of our inside pockets, and I frowned as I stared at the text lighting my screen.

Unknown: *If you want Garreth Jameson to pay, be out on the balcony in 5 minutes.*

Bridge held up his phone as I met his gaze. "Same tosser? Is it Theroux?"

I scowled at his phone. "Looks that way," I muttered as I searched the crowd for Ben. "Let's get to the balcony."

He lifted a brow. "It's unlike you to be so trusting."

He was right. Outside of my mates, I trusted no one, let alone a couple of random texts. But I wanted information. Any scrap of information offered was a clue to better understanding.

I didn't even have time to formulate my thoughts before Ben headed in our direction, his long stride rapidly eating up the distance. He held up his phone face out and gave it a little shake. "You get the same one?"

Bridge and I nodded, surreptitiously scanning our surroundings. The message directed us out to the balcony, so I looked up at Ben. "We're doing this?"

He frowned then gave us a curt nod. "Let's go see what this arsehole wants. And then maybe ask how he knows us or what we're looking for."

Bridge rubbed his jaw. "I don't like it."

"But do you have a better plan?"

Bridge said nothing, so we headed around the bar to the stairwell that led to the balcony.

Once on the balcony, only Ben received a text with a video.

The video zoomed in on the profile of a man in shadow. He was seated next to a painting that caught my breath. If I were a betting man, I'd have said that it was a Miles Kruger.

But my family had all known Krugers in our collection. My

great-grandmother, Ruth Du Mont, had been a wealthy Jewish heiress married to a German businessman. At the start of the war, he smuggled her to safety in America, then did what he could to secure her inheritance. He bought art and safeguarded the pieces her family had handed down. He didn't survive, but when the war was over, unlike so many, she had the things he'd been able to safeguard for her.

She eventually remarried a British doctor, and she and her new husband had spent years completing the collection her first husband had started for her.

Over the years, my mother's trust had been able to acquire every original piece of art that had belonged to her family, including the Miles Kruger pieces.

But it was said there was a missing one. One that hadn't been seen since the war.

I let out a long breath. "Is that fucking time-stamped?"

Ben nodded, pointing at the corner. "The newspaper, when you zoom in on it, that's today's date."

"That has to be a forgery," I mumbled. No fucking way did he have the lost Kruger.

Ben shrugged. "I mean, your family has the definitive collection of Krugers. You would know—or your mother would."

I shook my head. "My sister would, because she's the curator of the collection. But the collection's in a museum in Monaco. It has been for the last fifteen years."

Christ. If that was a genuine Kruger...

The man leaned forward, partially obscured in shadows. From what I could tell, he was apparently white, older, as he had some sagging in the jaw area. But it was still a strong chin with a slight cleft.

"I'm sure you're wondering who I am," he began in a strong voice laced with a touch of a French accent. "But that's not important. What's important is what I'm offering. You and I have a common interest. And we can help each other."

The man shifted in his seat, and my eyes stayed glued to the painting behind him. That couldn't be real. It just couldn't.

He continued. "As I said when I reached out to Mr. Hale, I am aware of your Garreth Jameson problem. And I'm willing to assist. Given the need for secrecy, I'll need to secure your full cooperation before we can move on."

Bridge lifted a brow. "What, he thinks we work for him now?"

The man's lips lifted into a smile. "I know what you're thinking, Covington. Or perhaps Edgerton. You hate to be controlled most of all. No, you don't work for me. But we can help each other if you are amenable. We'll draw up terms." He paused. "However, if you are not amenable, unfortunately, this video will go out to the authorities."

The screen went dark for a second, and then I could see motion. The building was familiar. We'd robbed it a couple of months ago. Suddenly I could see men scurrying like ants out of the building, heading to different exit points.

What the fuck was this? I'd scrubbed all CCTV feeds from the surrounding buildings that night. All security. Everything.

This is a drone.

Fuck. I'd cocked it up.

How were you supposed to check for a private drone?

The video sped up until it showed Ben and Bridge at the van, and Ben ripped off his balaclava.

"Shit." Ben's muttered curse was soft.

The man continued. "I know Mr. Hale is thinking that he was lax on security. I assure you, you were not. I'm just *very* good. And I like knowing who I'm doing business with. If you assist me, I will give you what you want by using this." He pointed at the painting. "Mr. Hale knows that Garreth Jameson and his family would do anything to get their hands on this. I'm willing to use it to give you what you want."

Ben ran his hands through his hair. "Who the fuck is he, and how does he know so much?"

The man leaned forward then. "Forgive me for not introducing myself. My name is Francois Theroux. You have one week to give me an answer."

I was trying to figure out how much of a hoax this was. Who had that kind of access? Who could listen in on our conversations? Then the man sat forward and allowed us to see him clear as day.

A thick shock of white hair, well-tamed and styled, swirled atop his head. His face, though years older, was classically handsome. Strong jaw. Cleft chin. Roman nose that looked like it had been broken at some point in his past. There was an air of refinement to him.

Then the video went black.

Ben asked, "Any of you know this arsehole and why he thinks he'll get away with blackmail?"

I shook my head. "The photos I have of Theroux are of him as a younger man. But it's a close enough match. That's definitely him."

Bridge frowned. "Are we supposed to know him?"

Ben scowled down at his phone. "Alright then. We are going to find out everything there is to know about Francois Theroux."

"On it," I muttered. I trusted nobody as a general rule, so a helping hand was going to be met with suspicion. One that was trying to blackmail us was even more reason to be cautious.

East

An hour later, I found the woman in the red dress leaning against the bar. The red silk of her dress showed off strong back muscles and a fantastic ass, leaving me to speculate if she had any knickers on.

The approach was easy. Familiar. I knew this dance and knew it well. Approach, banter, shag in the first semiprivate place we could find, walk away. As I approached, anticipation danced over my skin. As I drew nearer, I hesitated a moment. That scent. Honeysuckle? Her dress screamed sex, but her scent was pure tempting intoxication.

Why was it so damn familiar? "You make a hell of a statement in that dress."

She turned slowly, hazel eyes landing on mine as she shifted her shawl and clutch to the bar. "I certainly hope so. It's bait."

I momentarily choked on my last breath as I stared at her. "Agent Nyla Kincade." Just saying her name had my cock going rock hard. Flashes of our last encounter made me want to drag her out of the gala to check for fucking bruises… and then kiss them all away.

What. The. Fuck.

Listen, you tosser. She is the enemy and will happily stick you and your mates in the nick.

Her grin went wide. "Mr. Hale. Fancy running into you again."

Think, you knob. I needed to play this delicately. What the hell was she doing here? And why, instead of me unsettling her, was she here in my sandbox unsettling me?

I needed to be careful, tread lightly. After all, she was coming after me and my friends. "I've never seen you at one of these charity galas before. I didn't think they were your speed, Agent Kincade. But now that I know they are, they will be infinitely more entertaining."

"Of course, you'd be aware of every single woman who comes to these things. Your reputation precedes you." Her gaze swept over me and I felt like my skin was on fire. Was she playing with me? Did she think it was a good idea to poke the rock-hard bull right now?

"So, you've been asking about me? Should I be worried you'll get out your cuffs? Though that might be all manner of fun." I went for one of the most charming smiles in my arsenal. One that was a guaranteed ice-melter. But still, all I got back from her was some bemusement.

Her gaze narrowed as it slid over me from head to toe. "I do love my cuffs. And I don't doubt you'd enjoy the feel of the cold steel against your skin." She sipped her champagne then. "But I'm not here for you. I happen to love a good cause."

She wanted to play games. She was here to tempt me, but for what reason? Into making a mistake? I wasn't going to play.

But you want to.

I had already had a chat with her section chief, so she was walking on thin ice. Playing a game she didn't know the rules of and one I was quite looking forward to. Turning my smile into a smirk, I lowered my voice and leaned forward. "I must say, you're an excellent fighter and surprisingly quick. Well done with the Taser. I still have the taste of metal in my mouth. The next time we tussle though, I dare hope there will be significantly less clothing."

I spent a good deal of time watching people. Nyla Kincade was a pro. Her expression remained cool and placid, save a quick blink and slight purse of her lips. "I'm sorry. I don't know what you're on about."

I leaned close, inhaling deep. "Oh, but I know you do. I tracked you as you darted through the South Bank." The bartender slid a scotch across the bar to me, and I lifted my glass to take a sip. "The quick change, the prosthetics. You are very, very good. But I think I was most impressed with your hand-to-hand skills. I have to tell you, Agent Kincade, you left some bruises. I should probably discuss with my therapist just how arousing I found that, but that's neither here nor there."

"Your kinks are none of my business."

"Oh, but they could be." My blood hummed, even though I should be afraid, worried. At the very least wary. She met my gaze and lifted her chin. Christ, I wanted to taste her. "I should be worried about you, Agent Kincade. How's the eye? The make-up job is excellent. It's hard to see the bruising. I am sorry. I didn't mean to hurt you."

"Again. Not me. You're mistaking me for some kind of badass. I wish I could meet this woman and have her teach me her ways. But alas, I'm not who you think I am."

The humming had found its way to my brain, short circuiting it. Because instead of trying to get answers, all I wanted was to take another deep whiff. Find out if she smelled like sweet honeysuckle all over her body. My guess was yes.

"I think you're very naughty and have found yourself in way over your head. All you have to do is tell me what you were hoping to achieve, and I'll give you back your SD card, unwiped. Honestly, there wasn't anything good on it, but you worked so hard to sneak in and disguise yourself. Hell, I might even give it to you if you say please just right."

She leaned into me and the last remaining ability I had to think vanished in favor of my cock acting all kinds of inappropriately.

"Mr. Hale."

"Hmmm?"

"Feel free to hold your breath. See how long you can last. I dare you. You might as well, because I'm never going to give you what you want."

❦

Nyla

First of all, up close and personal East Hale was make-you-stupid handsome. He smelled like something piney and clean. And it was debilitating. I was lucky I had functioning brain cells around him. The other times we'd met had been fleeting, and he hadn't been so... close. And well, the last time I was focused on not getting caught. But now, with his low voice and sandalwood cologne helping to amplify his potent masculine swagger, it was a wonder I could speak.

He also has you dead to rights.

How the fuck had he tracked my movements? I'd had that route mapped out. There were very few cameras. And how did he have access to CCTV? He wasn't law enforcement or intelligence services.

I'd come here play nice and back off like I'd been ordered to.

You came to pretend.

Okay, fine. I'd come to pretend. I'd also come to tag him with a listening device. I had zero intention of walking away from the London Lords, despite my father's direct orders. I would get my proof, and then my father would have no choice but to listen to what I had to show him about East Hale. Well, him or one of his friends. He was just the first one who took notice. I hadn't been lying when I said the dress was bait. He had me. He knew he had me. The question was how I was going to play this. I could continue to deny it, or I could own it. Then we would be two warriors facing off.

With a deep breath I met his gaze. "How's your shoulder? Did I hurt you?"

His eyes went wide, and his broad smile lit his face. "You're certainly ballsy. I really thought you would continue to deny it."

I sighed and polished off my champagne. "What's the point? You saw me."

"That I did." His gaze narrowed on me as he watched me warily. "You are a naughty little thing." His heat was like a caress. "So what are you doing here?"

I sidled up to him, patting his jacket with my right hand. "Well, I was instructed to apologize. So I came here to do that."

His grin was quick and devilish. "Bullshit."

Absolutely bullshit. I'd touched him very specifically to distract him as I reached into his opposite lapel and planted the bug. I might not have my father's support, but if I came with hard proof, he couldn't deny me. And East Hale was going to give it to me.

My smile dimmed somewhat as he studied my face carefully. I'd covered the bruise with makeup, but there were still some remnants of the deep purple from when I'd fallen with him the night before.

He raised his hand for a moment, and I thought he was going to caress my cheek, but he only moved a strand of my hair out of my face.

I frowned at him. "You should probably wait until I give permission before you enter my personal space."

His answering smile was lopsided. "Noted. Does this include when you beg me?"

I lifted a brow. "Oh, I don't beg."

An intense smolder entered his eyes even as the smile remained. "Something tells me I would enjoy making you beg."

I shook my head. "Oh God, save me from arrogant men. If I went my whole life and never once met another arrogant man, I swear to God, I would be a very happy woman."

This was fun. Why was this fun? He was quick-witted. Charming. So beautiful it hurt to look at him. Those green eyes of his were bright and intelligent. Without a doubt, they saw everything. And those lips. God, those lips.

"So what are you really doing here? I don't believe your attempt at an apology. I'd like the truth. You were willing to fight for what you actually wanted. So tell me, Miss Kincade, why are you *really* here?"

Don't fall for it. You'll get stung.

"Well, Mr. Hale, this has been lovely, but I have to get going." I put forth my shiniest smile. "I have a date waiting for me."

He lifted a brow as I passed him, and his fingertips brushed my elbow, the delicious shivery sensation pausing my forward motion without him exerting much force. It was more a sensation of being able to feel the waves of dominance he emitted. "Who's your date?"

I grinned at him. "Wouldn't you love to know?"

"I would, actually." His gaze held me in place. "I have the feeling you'd enjoy yourself more with me. Leave with me. We have so much to talk about. We can even have dinner."

"And if I told you I don't do dinner?"

"You have to eat some time." He lifted a brow and cocked his head, an easy flirtatious smile playing on his lips. "How about breakfast?"

"I don't eat breakfast with men I barely know."

The smile widened into a cocksure grin. "Then get to know me. I have the distinct impression that I could change your opinion about the London Lords if you got to know me."

I shook my head. "Sorry, but I have to go."

He finally let me pass, and I breathed a soft sigh of relief. Being close to him felt dangerous somehow. Like I was playing roulette with my life. My heart hammered against my ribs. My breathing was far too shallow. The hairs along my arms stood on end as if alerting me to some impending doom. But it was just East Hale watching me.

I wasn't afraid of him. That wasn't the right emotion. But I was just too aware of him being too aware of me.

Your father is going to kill you.

Admittedly, this was a risk. I knew what I'd been told. But I also knew what my gut was telling me. I knew something was up. All I needed was proof. And I was going to get it. If the bug yielded nothing, then I'd stop.

Do you think you can?

I tried to make my way through the crowd, around the women in their elegant evening gowns and the men in their shiny oxfords and tuxedos. I'd almost made it to the door when my phone rang. "Jesus Christ, Amelia, now is not the time."

"Oh, this isn't Amelia." The voice on the line was deep. Husky. Lazy, like a drawl, but accented. French? Maybe Portuguese, but I wasn't super familiar with that accent.

"Who is this?"

"It's someone who wants to see you succeed."

"Look, I have my hands full with creepers and arseholes. You have the wrong number, and you should know that you're calling an Interpol agent. So if you were trying to harass me or anything of that sort, you will be sorely disappointed."

"I know exactly who I'm speaking to. Agent Nyla Rebecca

Kincade. All you have ever wanted in your life is to please your father. I am about to give you that opportunity."

Icicles formed in the lazy rivers of my blood as it traveled through my veins and arteries. "Who the hell am I speaking to?" I quickly glanced at my phone before replacing it at my ear. Had I been hacked? Was this some idiot hacker's way of attempting to get money from me? I had none to give. I was paid civil servant wages.

"Oh, perhaps you'll forgive me. It's been so long since I've spoken to a beautiful woman."

"Right you eegit, this conversation is about to be—"

"How would you like the biggest arrest of your career, Agent Kincade? Francois Theroux."

I choked out a laugh. "You're not serious."

"I am, in fact, very serious." There was something so melodic and soothing about the voice.

"Everyone on the planet has looked for Theroux, and you want me to believe that you can find him. Also, you could just have him pay you off. Why turn him in? Why would you do that?"

"I have my reasons."

"I don't believe you."

"I understand your trepidation."

I wove through the crowd. "What's in it for you?"

There was a momentary pause. "There is plenty of time of time for that. I'll be in touch. Think your answer through very carefully."

"So you're going to dangle a carrot and not tell me what the stick is or what human I'm going to have to sacrifice? Who the hell are you?"

His chuckle was low and melodic. "It seems I can rectify the first part of your hesitance. My name is Francois Theroux. Welcome to my game. Chat soon, Agent Kincade.

Then the line went dead.

Holy.

Fucking.

Shit.

I scowled at my phone. As I stared, a text came up from a blocked number and it contained one image.

A man only partially in shadow sat forward. While his hair was all white, his face was handsome and barely lined. Strong jaw. Cleft chin. A nose that was the definition of Roman, and full lips.

Everything about his countenance screamed gentleman.

I knew exactly who he was. *Francois Theroux.* And on the table next to him sat the newspaper. I zoomed in and then my breath caught and lodged in my throat.

That was today's date. He wasn't lying. I'd just spoken to Francois fucking Theroux.

The hairs on the back of my neck tingled, and as I turned slowly around, my gaze collided with East's. What was it about that man? Even as I turned from him in the crowd, eager to get as far away from him as possible, I could still feel the heat of him behind me. The pull toward him. I tried to keep my eyes on the prize as I focused on the exit and getting the hell out of there.

But I underestimated him. Out of the banquet hall, I made a right down the hallway, and he just came out of nowhere, tugging me into a little alcove next to the restrooms. "Agent Kincade."

I jerked my body straight, desperate to get his hand off of me so I could avoid that zinging pulse of electricity. He released me easily, but we were still close. Too damn close. I felt his heat wrapping around me like a warm cocoon, promising stress release and safety, and many, many orgasms.

I shook my head a little to try and clear the fog. "What is it you want, Mr. Hale?"

The corner of his lips tipped into a wry smile. "So formal. Mr. Hale, or Lord Hale, is generally my father. My friends call me East."

"Are we friends? Is that what this is?"

"I don't know what this is. I feel like once you fight someone you have a window into their soul. I think we got off on the wrong foot. Maybe we can start over?"

I swallowed hard, trying to get a clean crisp breath that wasn't pine and leather and didn't make my head spin. "I just—I don't know. I find you lacking."

This time, he treated me to a full-blown grin. Christ, I was so screwed. Because with that easy smile and that peek of dimple in his naturally tanned skin, I was dumbfounded. Unable to breathe, unable to move. That was his true secret weapon. The smile stunned you. And then he went for the strike.

I forced my chin to tilt up. "Again, let me ask you, Mr. Hale, is there something you need?"

He chuckled softly. "Honestly, when you took off running, I didn't think we were done. I had to come and find you and talk to you at least. Clarify things. And I also wanted to return the shawl you left at the bar and see you to the door."

"There's no need for that. We didn't come together."

"And isn't that a crying shame?"

I should have moved away. I really should have, but there he was. He didn't even need to take a step toward me to crowd me. Just him standing there all tall and taking up space was all it took. He stole my breath right out of my lungs. "You know, Mr. Hale, I've met your friend."

"Which one? I have lots of friends." He cocked his head innocently.

"Oh, you know which one," I said. "Mr. Covington, like yourself, presents a pretty picture. And his girlfriend... Well,

I guess, his fiancée now, I actually kind of like her. She's sassy. Direct. Takes no shit. I think they're a good match."

He nodded slowly. "I agree. But that's their story. Don't try and evade, Agent Kincade, how about us? Don't you think we should pick up where we left off? For a start, will you come to their wedding with me?"

I blinked rapidly and jerked back. "What?"

"I've asked you on a date. Generally, how it works is one person asks the other one to accompany them. You know, to something like dinner or a movie or in this case a wedding. Which are boring, quite frankly. But I figure, since my friends are getting married, I could use a date. I don't usually take real dates to something so personal, because well, you never know what's going to happen with the bridesmaids. But since I know the bridesmaids pretty well this time, I think a date is in order."

"So, you're inviting me because you can't shag the bridesmaids this time? Is that what I'm getting?"

He shrugged. "It's as good a reason as any. Besides, you're beautiful. But I think you know that already."

I shrugged that off. My father had told me my whole life that beauty was in the eye of the beholder. And one day, someone was going to behold me that didn't find me beautiful, so I had better be smart. I had better be cunning. I had better use all the tools in my toolshed and not just my face or my body.

I hadn't really understood as a child. Mostly, back then, I'd just wanted my father to tell me I was pretty. It wasn't until I became an adult that I really realized why he couldn't say it. It was because I looked like *her*.

Exactly like my mother. And he must have still been mourning her. It probably hurt him to see me every day. But that was neither here nor there. Hearing East Hale tell me that

I was beautiful did something to my insides. And if that something meant making my panties wet, then ding, ding, ding.

I licked my lips. "That's very kind of you to say, but looks don't matter."

"You're right. Looks don't matter. Some of the most beautiful people have the ugliest souls. But that's not the case with you, is it, Nyla Kincade?"

I cocked my head. The way he said my name sounded like something warm and sexy and throaty. Especially when he added that husky rasp to it. He made me want to peel off my panties and give them to him.

Stop it. Focus. Get the hell out of here because right now, Amelia is listening on the goddamn com device, and she's getting all of this.

If my embarrassment over the fact that my best friend listening in wasn't enough, the fact that I wasn't really wearing any panties probably should have been my next clue.

"Well, Mr. Hale, while this has been quite interesting, I'm afraid I have to leave right about now. I have more important things to get to."

As I turned, he gently reached for my elbow and flipped me back. "Oh, not so fast. I did ask you on a date. And from the look in your eyes and the way you licked your lips when you looked at me, I know you want to say yes. But I really rather prefer to hear the words."

Words. He wanted words. Which words?

See, that was the problem with men as good-looking as him. They made you lose your train of thought. I focused on the only thing that I could manage, my shawl in his hands. I reached out and took it back, wanting to wrap it around my shoulders again. "I'll take that."

He lifted a brow. "Is that a no?"

"Why are you asking *me*, Mr. Hale? Clearly, I am not the

kind of woman you'd normally ask out on a date, so I guess I'm just curious. What is it you want from me?"

He moved then. Closing the space between us, blocking out the passersby in the quiet hallway of the venue.

"What do I want? With you, I'm not quite sure yet." He leaned forward ever so slightly. Then he breathed deep.

I blinked rapidly. "What?"

"Your scent, it intoxicates me. There's a light floral in it. But mostly you smell like honeysuckle in the summer breeze. What is that perfume?"

I swallowed hard. For the last five years, I'd been using the same perfume every day. It was the slightest hint, and he'd gotten it right. Honeysuckle. God, what was wrong with me?

Step away from that beautiful man. It's safer that way. Amelia is listening.

I told myself I was going to step back out of his gentle grasp. I was going to walk away because this was a dangerous game, and I was not supposed to be there. But still, there I was, taunting, waving the red cape in front of the bull, trying to get answers, unable to make sense of anything. This was probably what my father was talking about. My impulsivity. I didn't always think these things through.

But how was I supposed to know what to expect from East fucking Hale? Or Bridge Edgerton? They were the kind of men that could melt your panties from their sheer hotness. And while Bridge Edgerton was the kind of broody, dark, good-looking, sexy man, there was something about the way East smiled. That fucking dimple. No man should have dimples. Honestly. They should be reserved for children and women because men would use them for evil. Like what he was doing right now.

"Miss Kincade, if you tell me you don't want to go to the

wedding with me, I am more than happy to let you go. I don't pursue women who aren't interested. But I keep waiting for an answer, and you keep not giving me one."

Answer. He wants an answer. Right. To the question. Just tell him now.

I tilted my chin. "Now, you and I both know you don't really want to take me to a wedding."

"Your answer isn't telling me what I want. I feel like I need to lay it out because clearly, you're having a little brain glitch in that pretty little head of yours."

Oh, son of a bitch. He turned that grin on full blast, and there were two goddamn dimples.

Knickers down! Knickers down!

You're not wearing any.

No. No, I wasn't. That warm pulsing rush between my thighs was going to make them sticky. I shifted on my feet, pressing my thighs together in the hopes that despite the tightness of my dress, he was not going to notice any embarrassing spots.

Jesus Christ, next time wear fucking panties.

"Go on, say no. I'll walk away. Just say the words, Nyla."

I wished to God he would stop saying my name that way. Like we were in bed and it was a hushed whisper that was half-reverence, half-curse.

"I—"

I couldn't finish what I was saying because he leaned ever so closely and then tucked his body against mine, and I felt the full press of his muscles through that outstanding suit. "Say the words, Nyla. Say, 'No, East. I don't want to go. I don't want to attend the wedding with you.'"

"You recognize I'm an Interpol agent who plans on bringing you down?"

His grin was slow. Sexy. Determined. "And what will you do

when there's nothing to find? Will you regret wasting time we could have been shagging?"

"Honestly, I—"

And then his lips pressed to mine, and his tongue swooped in, licked into my mouth, and God help me, I moaned.

The sound was low. Throaty. Desperate.

Oh hell.

He kissed like he moved. With a command and a distinct lack of patience. But there was also a surprise in his kiss. A gentleness. A coaxing that was at war with his pure power.

He dipped down further, his big hand slid into my hair and angled my head by sliding his fingers along the base of my neck and into my hair, tugging ever so gently and turning my head as he stroked his sure tongue into my mouth.

I couldn't help it, my hips sought out his with a jerk. The motion made him growl deep and press into me. The sound of his low rumble made my knees week and my skin too hot. Like it was stretched all over my body.

Heat and slick moisture pooled at the juncture of my thighs. The slickness was accompanied by this throbbing ache. Hell, I was quite certain there was a wet spot on my dress.

With one kiss, a stroke of his tongue, the press of his body and a gentle rocking of our bodies together, and I was so screwed. I wanted him. More than I'd ever wanted anyone in my life. I tore my lips from his and staggered back. Well, as much as the dress and the wall would allow. My gaze snapped back to his. "I have to go."

He nodded slowly and then stepped back. "I'll take that as a yes, Agent Kincade."

When I was a step further away from him, I could breathe a little bit better, and I could think. "I'll have you know, Mr. Hale, I will not be going anywhere with you. I don't date men I'm investigating. I don't date men who are clearly trouble. I don't date men who are on a power trip."

"I'm not on a power trip. You can't be on a power trip when you have it already."

I had no choice but to run. I called it self-preservation. It wasn't until I was outside running down the stairs, sucking in deep gulps of air, that I realized I'd dropped my shawl again. I considered going back for it, but hell no. The further away from East Hale I could get, the better.

Even better, if I could prove what he and the London Lords were up to, I would never have to worry about him again. Men like him were dangerous. Men like him were to be avoided at all cost.

FIVE

East

"Let's set a few ground rules." I greeted the tiny-statured dynamo with the dark curling hair who had just crossed the threshold into my penthouse. "You poke around my system; I'll poke around your system. You touch something you shouldn't touch, and I'm going to mess with your database. If you make commentary about my code, we're done here."

Standing just inside the door, Telly Brinx made a show of scanning the room then grinned up at me, her wild dark hair flowing about her shoulders like a fountain. "Nice penthouse. I guess the hotel thing pays off."

Telly Brinx had the distinction of running Brinx Technologies, being best friend to Ben's fiancée, Livy, being a sometimes-excellent hacker and my all-the-time nemesis.

Normally, I would solve our little Theroux problem by myself, draw it out. Take my time to prolong the pleasure. But the man had upped the ante, so he needed to be dealt with swiftly. Ariel Winston was also an option to help, and as she was pseudo family I could ask, but we'd been playing phone tag since she was in Australia with her footballer prince of a husband. So unfortunately, it was Telly or no one.

I scowled, unwilling to buy into her distraction. "Did you hear me?"

Telly waved her hand in a dismissive gesture. "Oh relax, I'm here to play nice."

When we had been dealing with the Van Linsted situation a few months ago, she'd come in handy. And for something like this, to find the unfindable, I knew I was going to need more hands and more processing power.

She perused the living room, going over to the bank of computers I had against the wall. "Ooh, these are sexy." But she really cooed when she pointed at my NETLA processing center. "Jesus Christ. This is one of the fastest processing cores in the world."

"I know," I muttered smugly.

"This thing costs a fortune. You realize whole corporations don't even have one of these, right?"

I shrugged. "I know."

She turned around. "So just like that? Daddy Warbucks that you are, you can just buy one of these?"

I shrugged. "Well, yeah. If you're nice I'll even let you touch it."

She laughed. "I like that you just so nonchalantly say that. Of course, you can buy one. Fine, Mr. Billionaire, what do you need?"

"Well, you're not going to believe this, but I need to find a fucking needle in a haystack."

"Okay, what are you trying to find?"

"*Who.*"

Telly frowned and crossed her arms. "What's going on? When Livy said you needed my help, she didn't say why. So I need to know what you need my help *with* exactly. I can't find a needle if I don't even know if it's silver, black, or gold. You need to be specific."

I had trust issues. I knew that. But Telly had been instrumental in our plot and plan a few months ago. And I needed her now. Because while I could look, two brains were better than one. And

I wanted to be certain. "All right, well, for starters, the boys and I got a video message."

"Right. Okay, Liv showed it to me this morning. Can I see your phone? I want to make sure I've seen the whole thing."

I took out my phone and played the video for her. For the duration, she stood there and watched it. When it was done, she nodded slowly and then proceeded to laugh. "Oh my God. What, is this a thing with you billionaires? Always with the crazy hijinks?"

"Can you help or not?"

"Ugh, gosh, don't get your knickers in a twist. I got you. So, you want to find out about this Francois Theroux?"

"Yes. Who he is and everything you can find out about him. I'll be working on how to clear the footage he has of us, uh, behaving badly."

She grinned. "Is that what we're calling it? Okay, but I don't need my hacking skills to tell you about Theroux." She scooped up some of the crudité I'd laid out and popped it in her mouth. "Hell, I'll be back home with the fiancée in no time."

I indicated the couch, and she plopped down on it, sending her inky dark hair bouncing over her shoulders. "I can tell you everything about Theroux. Well, not *everything,* because obviously, I don't know who he actually is, but I was obsessed with heists as a teenager."

I lifted my brows. "Heists?"

"Yeah. Trust me, I know this stuff. You think you and the lads are gangsters, but you've got nothing on this bloke." Settling in, she picked up a throw pillow and held it against her chest as she leaned forward in animated fashion. "Look, Theroux is one of the best thieves in the world. He's legendary. He's stolen things from under people's noses without anybody even realizing they were gone. No alarms. No police. No nothing. If he is poking at you lot, he's probably bored."

That got my attention, and I sat up straight. "What do you mean, bored?"

"Okay, look. If everything they say is correct about him… He's what, maybe sixty? He probably can't heist things anymore because he's older. Probably less mobile. And I haven't heard anything about a good Theroux heist in a while. He always claims his heists, you know. Maybe he's just tired, or bored, or… whatever, I don't know. But the point is, he has been pretty quiet for the last five years at least."

"You think this guy could be an imposter?"

"I mean, that guy kind of looks like he could be Theroux. He's the right age. We can run him through a facial app, but it's likely that's *not* Theroux but an actor. Chances are he's dicking with you. But if he says he has the painting, a missing painting at that, an important one, and he wants you to come and get it, it's an invitation from Francois Theroux. You can't ignore it."

"I fully intend to ignore it."

"Well, you can if you want. But there's a reason he's sending it to you. He could get a lot showier with his request, and maybe that is *not* what the London Lords need right now, considering there was just a whole, you know, heist and coup d'état. You don't want him connecting the dots, yeah?"

I frowned. "Right. So what do you suggest we do, then?"

Telly shrugged. "I don't know. I'm not going to tell you to mess with him. But I do think that maybe he wants to wage a battle with someone. The problem is you don't want to get involved in that."

No. No, we did not. "Can we at least trace where the video came from?"

"Sure. We can find out where the last relay was sent from, but I promise you he won't be there."

I ran my hands through my hair. "Then what the fuck am I supposed to do, Tell?"

"I don't know." She tossed the pillow aside. "Have you considered actually taking him up on his offer and helping him with whatever it is he wants?"

"I feel like it should be clear and apparent that we're not taking some random thief's bait."

"Okay, let me ask, then. Why would you even consider it?"

"Because he's offered Jameson on a platter. And he threatened to expose the Van Linsted heist if we don't comply."

She whistled low. "Jesus. Well the bait is tempting. The blackmail I'm less fond of. And you can almost guarantee Theroux has baited other people as well."

I leaned forward in my seat and planted my elbows on my knees. "What do you mean, a guarantee?"

"Guys like this, they live for the chase. You want the best on your team because he undoubtedly will bring his A game. What does he want from you specifically?"

I had to fight my natural instincts. What I wanted to do was keep things close to the vest until I knew more, but to find those things out, I needed her help.

"He's not told us yet."

Her delicate brows furrowed. "What, so this is some kind of blind-faith blackmail?"

"See, the operative word there being blackmail."

"So what's the play?"

That was a very good question. One I wasn't sure of the answer to just yet. "Well for starters, the goal stays the same. Jameson is our target, so I need to gather more intel. Getting distracted is a bad idea. And Theroux is no friend of ours, so we need to keep an eye on him as well."

"We might also try to see if Lucas knows Theroux. Honor among thieves and all that."

"Yeah, we talked about that, and Ben is going to call him."

She shrugged. "Just doing my part. See? That was easy. And we didn't even have to bust out any of your fancy processors. Just good old-fashioned brain power."

"Well, thank you." I tipped my imaginary hat. "Looks like we'll be needing more of your brain power, because I have every intention of catching Theroux."

"Oh my God, do you understand how many law enforcement officers have tried that?"

"Does that matter? He's messing with our business. He claims to have the lost Kruger painting." I shrugged. "I don't like it. I want answers."

"You might have to get used to the fact that you're not going to get them. Theroux's a ghost. I don't think for a minute that we will figure out who he is unless hc allows it."

I gave her a wolfish smile. "And I think you underestimate me."

☙

Nyla

My father had always been inventive when describing my personality. He liked to use words like *impulsive, bulldog, one-track mind*. Words he never used to describe me were *liar* or *disloyal*.

I did have a tendency to get myself into trouble though, and I wouldn't let things go until I had a clear answer. And if I didn't have a clear answer, that meant the fight continued.

But even I wasn't so stupid as to try and hold back the information about the mysterious phone call from my father. I always did the right thing. Even if it was to my detriment.

Which was why as I peered through file after file on my jewelry theft ring, I couldn't stop thinking about the call.

I was so focused on what to do, even though I knew the answer to that, that I almost missed a glaring lead. I sat up, quickly adjusting my reading glasses. Most of my leads thus far had been dead ends, but this one could give me something to unravel.

Three years earlier, the Royal Museum in Monaco had encountered a nearly perfect heist that involved replacing the originals with forgeries before a major exhibit featuring part of a new collection sent to them on loan from the Tillson family. Leonard Tillson was a tech billionaire who had been buying up art like it was his job. He'd acquired pieces at auction and loaned them to the museum to display, only to discover that several pieces of his collection were forgeries, despite pristine authentication records.

I scanned the file for the name of the curator of the museum. I needed to speak to them. I knew the museum being in Monaco could be a logistical problem, but maybe, if I was lucky, they would have a London acquisitions agent I could speak with.

They did. But the moment I saw the name, my body had a two-pronged response. First my stomach fell. Or maybe it flipped. And my heart started to race. Of all the art experts in all the world… East flipping Hale.

How was he involved with the museum? I knew his family were philanthropists and he was a rich sod, so of course I assumed they must have art. But what was his connection to the Royal Museum in Monaco?

This is your chance to find out more about him.

Yes. Exactly. And since he was a direct connection to my case, I didn't have to be hands off.

Not like you want to be.

No. I wasn't going to muck up my life by continuing to fantasize about a man I knew to be bad news. I had enough problems.

For better or worse, you're going to need to talk to him, so get it together.

So what if he'd given me the best kiss I'd had maybe ever? So what if I could still feel the ghost of his lips over mine? So what if I kept trying to figure out exactly what his scent was? None of that mattered. I was a professional. And I never gave up.

No way was I going to listen to my lady parts. And even if I did scratch an itch, I could still remain detached.

Liar.

Not that I would.

My father passed my office, and my gaze automatically went to my phone. I knew what I had to do, despite my nerves. I had to be prepared for him to give this lead to Denning. My gut twisted at that thought, but I tried to remind myself it didn't matter. There was no way I could hold onto the information.

I held my breath as I knocked on his office door. He glanced up, and I noticed for the first time just how pronounced the lines around his face were. "What's up, Nyla?"

I took a deep breath as I stepped in. "Can I ask you a question, Dad?"

"Does this have to do with the London Lords or anyone from the Winston Isles?"

He studied me warily, likely wondering what fresh hell I was going to bring his way. I knew that expression. It was the *Nyla, stay in your lane* face, the *Nyla, why are you causing trouble* face, and also the, *Nyla, why can't you just play by the rules* face. Oh yes, I knew that face well.

And I hated seeing it. In that moment I knew what would happen. I knew if I told him about the call that I wouldn't get to investigate. I wouldn't be the recipient of warm, excited energy.

So I didn't tell him. Instead I said, "I have a lead in my case. I need to speak to the curator of the Royal Museum in Monaco or their representative." I cleared my throat before continuing. "Their London representative is East Hale."

I let his name hang in the air and said nothing, letting the thick blanket of tension swirl around us until my father broke the silence. "I told you to steer clear."

"And I'm following orders for once." Except for last night. "But they had pieces in a loaned collection stolen and replaced with forgeries, similar to several of the thefts in my jewelry theft case. I really do need to speak with him."

His glower was worse than the time we were in Rome and I *borrowed* the car to go to a party with friends. "Do you really think it's in your best interest to circumvent a direct order?"

"That's not what I'm doing. You can check for yourself. East Hale really is the London contact. I will stay very far away from anything to do with Grimwald Authenticators, but I do need to ask about the collection for the museum."

We stared at each other for a long moment.

He frowned at me and sat back in his chair, the sun catching the red in his dark hair just so. "Nyla, I don't have time for games."

"No games, Dad. I'm just trying to do my job. This is my first step before heading to Monaco, but I can skip it if you prefer." There was no way he would want me to go to Monaco without proper due diligence.

"You are on a very short leash, Nyla."

I sighed with relief I didn't necessarily feel. "Believe me, I know."

When I was done with my father, I went to dot my Is and cross my Ts. There would be no avoiding Denning. As my direct superior, he needed to know about what I'd found. I walked down the hall and around the corner, past the cubicles, and to the office in the center of the hallway. I knocked gently, and his assistant, Lisa, let me in. Denning was on the phone, but I marched in anyway, with Lisa chasing after me. I turned to her with a tight smile. "Lisa, it's fine. I'm not here about relationship things. It's actually about work."

Lisa's face flushed. "Jesus Christ, Nyla, I'm so sorry. But you know how he is."

"Oh, I do. And I guarantee you, I want nothing to do with him unless I have to. This is an I-have-to moment."

She gave me a sad smile and backed off. When Denning hung up the phone, he scowled at me. "Is there a reason you're in my office?"

"Actually, yes. You think I'd volunteer to be in here otherwise?"

He rolled his eyes. "What do you want?"

"Well, I wish I could say I came in here to tell you what a wanker you are, but that will have to wait for another day."

His gaze narrowed at me, and I could tell that he was on the verge of reading me the riot act. But then I smiled beatifically at him. "I've had a break in the case, and I need to speak with the Royal Museum of Monaco's London agent, East Hale." I quickly relayed the information I had. "Dad already approved it."

He scowled then. "Jesus Christ, Nyla, what the fuck? You went over my bloody head?"

"Is that what this is really about?" No amount of shaking my head was going to shake my irritation. "No, I merely informed my father of something. That's all. Then he gave me the go ahead. If you don't like it, take it up with him." I left out the part about me keeping the information about Theroux from both of them.

I wasn't going to keep the text a secret for long. I just wanted to look into it first.

Sure you do. So what happens if you get another mysterious text?

Wasn't that the question of the hour.

SIX

East

This was going nowhere. After nearly a week, Nyla was still clouding my brain and I couldn't bloody well think.

The four of us had been arguing about the Tottenham and Man United game for well over an hour. Drew and Ben were barely talking because things had gotten a little heated over the new top player that had originally been on the Man United youth leagues. Then Bridge had said something sassy about Ben's choice of player, and it had become a powder keg. But the tension we were feeling had nothing to do with the game. The muttered curses were the result of us walking the tightrope of hero vs. antihero for the last week.

And then we made the mistake of attempting to work.

Ben was testy when he asked Drew. "Any news from the Five?"

Drew shook his head. "They know nothing about Theroux. They wanted to know if we have exposure. I deflected. I'm sure they were unconvinced."

Deep inside, the shadows inside my mind suggested that if the Five didn't know Theroux, then we were truly flying blind.

Ben cursed before turning attention to Bridge. "Did you fare better?"

Bridge shook his head. "No. None of the fences I know, even those with high end clientele have a line on him. Everyone agrees. He is not your average thief. He's likely using a broker. Or he looks the part and can get away with private sales. I'll also note that despite the company he keeps, there hasn't been a single kill."

Ben expelled a long breath of air. "East, tell me something good."

All I had for him was disappointment. "Sorry mate. Chaka Khan I'm not. Telly and I could find nothing. The closest he came to leaving a trail was early in his career thirty years ago when Roger Kincade almost had him. Kincade winged him with a bullet, but he still vanished into the ether. His DNA is on file though."

Ben crossed his arms and started to pace. "So what, he has us by the bollocks and now he runs us? Controls us?"

Bridge coughed. "The fuck he does."

"I'm working on tracking him. It'll take time. We might have to take it a step further and see what he asks for."

"I don't fucking like it," Bridge ground out.

"None of us *like* it, mate, but we are where we are."

Bridge's jaw ticked. Something was up with him. I felt it, but there was no getting it out of him until he was good and ready to talk.

"At least tell me you are somewhere with Agent Kincade," Ben said.

And by somewhere he doesn't mean fantasizing about her every night while you wank off and sniff her shawl.

Fucking hell, I did that *one* time. Once... okay twice. It had been almost a week since the hospital benefit, and it was like the woman had poisoned me with her kiss. Injected me with her essence so that now I couldn't fucking breathe without thinking about her.

Well maybe you shouldn't have kissed her.

My dick twitched with his tacit disagreement. *Christ.*

I cleared my throat. "I've dealt with her father. She won't be a problem." *You mean you* hope *she won't be a problem.*

Bridge raised a brow but said nothing. But I could see him trying to ferret out what I was hiding. Ben was clearly distracted because he could usually see through me better than anyone.

"I've also got surveillance set up on her, so I'm watching."

Drew smirked. "I'll bet you're watching."

I normally didn't give a shit when they ribbed me about my voyeuristic tendencies, but now it felt somehow inappropriate.

Because really, what was a little light cyber-stalking between friends? If she was coming after us, I needed to know everything about her. Right down to what perfume she wore. That information led to an adequate profile.

Or maybe you needed to know the scent that has been haunting you.

"I have tapped into the CCTV cameras across from her flat. I have a camera in her flat, but I'm leaving it inactive for now. I have one at her desk at work as well as a separate bug. Again, I'll leave that camera off unless we need it. I didn't want to be too intrusive."

Which was unusual. I could be intrusive as hell. I liked being intrusive.

Bridge rubbed his jaw. "Maybe Telly should have a look at the beautiful agent to make sure she's backed off since you seem distracted."

"Telly?" I jerked back as if I'd been slapped. "Low blow, mate. You know she's my hacker nemesis."

"Yes, but does she know you two are nemesi? Nemeses? How the fuck do you say the plural of nemesis?" Ben muttered under his breath.

I narrowed my gaze at my *former* best mate. "Et tu, Bennett?"

He merely shrugged. "Mates, I feel exposed and you lot know full well we have targets on our backs. The sooner we can get a handle on one of these guys the better. Our work isn't done."

The Van Linsteds had tied themselves into a nice little knot. Jameson was headed that way himself with his shady business dealings and his father's obsession with art. There was so much potential for corruption, and that could help us out along the way.

Middleton appeared clean, but I knew he wasn't. His hands had been sullied ten years ago; his family was just better at hiding it. They were professionals at spinning narratives in their crisis management agency, after all.

If nothing else his family had been covering up for his sins.

Bridge nodded. "If East can't find something, it's well hidden, or he's lost his touch and we'll need more time. It's better to be as surgical as possible, and we will. After all, we are the London Lords. Well, Ben is half a lord now since he gave his balls to Liv."

Ben cleared his throat. "Seriously, mates, I'm right here. Big hairy brass ones perfectly intact, thanks."

I rolled my eyes. "Would everyone just shut the fuck up? All of you. I know that you think I can just punch a couple of numbers and yeah, I'll Hogwarts my way into something good. We need something we can *use*. Something that will stick. And right now, we don't have it. Unless our not-so-illustrious leader wants to dig into Elite inner workings."

Jameson was a twat. And if I had to, I was going to use Theroux to get him just where we wanted him.

Ben met my gaze. "Grousing and shit talking aside, we know you'll get what we need. If Jameson is the one we can get dirt on, then he's the one we'll take down first. We'll make it work."

"What we have is a start. We'll need more. I need access to his computer, which means getting into his office. The old man's birthday is this coming weekend. Distaste or not, we'll be invited. Ben is the most powerful man in the entire world. We are his entourage. And we are the London Lords. No one can touch us."

Except Theroux.

Bridge stroked his jaw. "First of all, I'm nobody's entourage. But also, there are two sides to every coin. As powerful as we are, there are others who would do anything for that power. We need to be careful."

"That we do," mumbled Ben. "Oh, before I go, East didn't you say your mother had the name of some designer for Livy for her wedding dress?"

"Oh yeah. It's in my wallet. Let me grab that for you." I shoved away from my bank of monitors over to the entryway where I normally left it, but it wasn't there.

With a frown, I checked the closet in case I'd left it in my trench from yesterday when it was pouring down. Still no luck. I eventually found it next to my nightstand. Riffling through it while I walked, I found the business card I was looking for. My mother, she really did like to keep it old school.

My feet halted when I found something else. A tiny square film on the inside sleeve. I peered at the little patch. It looked like a computer chip.

Son of a bitch. *She'd bugged me.*

Grinding my teeth, I returned to the living room and gave Ben the card. When everyone left, I grabbed one of my laptops and pulled up my favorite scene, the CCTV camera from the parking tower across from Nyla Kincade's flat.

As I tapped in the coordinates, I rubbed the smooth silkiness of her shawl that she'd dropped between the fingers of my left hand.

You have a problem.

Yes, I did. And the problem's name was Nyla Kincade. Bringing her shawl up to my nose, I took a quick whiff and that heady combination of need and irritation lingered in my blood, sending me to the edge of desire. I watched her. I had never trained the camera on her bedroom, never looked in there, but the sight from her living room was what I focused on. And that was somehow more intimate. I watched her as she cooked and then plopped on her couch to watch TV. My favorite was her in her unicorn fitted pajamas. But that night, she wasn't wearing her unicorn fitted pajamas. She strolled out of her bedroom in the tiniest pair of shorts I'd ever seen.

What I wanted to do was pick her up and put her over my knee, but a phone call would have to do.

Her words were quiet as she answered. "Hello?"

"Agent Kincade. You've been very naughty."

Instead of hanging up on me, which she probably should have, she sighed. "East Hale. To what do I owe this very late phone call? Did you mistake my phone number for a phone sex line?"

"I can get women to talk dirty to me any time I like."

Her chuckle was low. "I'll bet you can."

"For such a naughty little thing, I'd have thought you'd be more contrite."

She strolled past her windows, hips sashaying as she went. All the blood in my rational brain rushed to my dick. "You are going to have to be more specific. This has been that kind of day.

Did I scratch your precious car? Perhaps I made your day more difficult. And if you are going to tear me a new one, I would advise you maybe take a number. The line for that can get quite long, you see."

I frowned at that. She'd had a hard day?

Not that it matters to you in the least.

Nope, it didn't matter. But still, I didn't want to make her day worse.

"I'm sorry you've had a shitty day. I have an idea or two of things that might cheer you up."

Her chuckle was soft. Lilting. "Oh, I'm sure you do. But alas, that's not going to happen. I don't kiss arrogant men."

"Now, don't add lying to your day's transgressions."

"What is it you want, Mr. Hale?"

"Well, Agent Kincade, I would like your assistance. It seems that someone has bugged me."

There was a beat of silence. "That's probably something you should take to the police."

"Aren't you the police?"

"I'm Interpol; my cases are different. If you like I can provide you with the number—"

"That won't be necessary. But thank you for being so helpful. I think I'll speak to your section chief again. I met him once. He seems like a reasonable sort."

More silence.

That was okay, she knew I had her. If she wanted to play cat and mouse, I wanted her to be very clear on who was the predator and who was the prey. "I have to say, I'm impressed. It was at the hospital gala, right? When I was so busy falling into your eyes and you were flirting with me."

That earned me a scoff. "Please, when I flirt, you'll know."

A smile teased my lips. The more she defied me and fought

back, the harder I became. "I know Interpol plays by a different set of rules, but you ought to play by the rules of the country you are stationed in, and illegal bugging is a big no-no."

"Good thing I would never do such a thing. I'm a good little agent."

Fuck, I was so hard.

As if she could read the direction of my thoughts, she perked up. "Also, Mr. Hale, dare I ask, how have you gotten hold of my phone number?"

"Ingenuity."

"Right. *Ingenuity.*"

"I decided to call you to tell you that whatever you think you're doing, you're in way over your head. You need to back off."

"That's the thing, Mr. Hale. I have a tendency not to give up on anything. I mean, of course, that's *if* I was interested in you. Which I'm not."

I chuckled then even as I rubbed the soft silk of her shawl and inhaled. "You are intriguing, Agent Kincade. So let me help you out. Why don't you tell me what it is you want from me, and I'll tell you if I can give it to you or not."

She'd disappeared from my camera feed, and I could hear rustling, as if she was moving around in her bed. "Mr. Hale, I promise that you don't have anything I want."

"Are you sure about that? I think you're intrigued by me. I think you can feel the hum between us. I think that after that kiss, you could still taste me. Hell, I would wager you can still taste me right now. You know that low pulsing between your thighs? The one that you've been trying to ignore? The one that you've been telling yourself isn't good for you? That's because of me. *I* make you feel that way. And it really, really is a shame that you thought you could get away with bugging me. Because

I've made a decision, and I don't intend to be fair." I rubbed the silk of her shawl with my fingers again, the faint hint of honeysuckle making me ache.

"First of all, Mr. Hale, I want to remind you that you're talking to an Interpol agent. Second of all, I'm not afraid of you. I have dealt with bigger and badder men. And I put them in jail too. You poke at me, and I'll poke at you."

"Oooh, kinky. Should I remind you that you fired the first shot?"

There was another beat of silence. "You can't prove that I bugged you, so it's a stalemate."

"That's the best part. I don't need proof. You're the one who's afflicted with that burn, not me. So since it's open season, I should probably mention to you that I really, really like the shorts you're wearing."

There was a hitch in her breath, and I could hear her swallow. "What?"

"They're cute. And also, you should probably close the blinds of your flat. A T-shirt that says, 'Woke up fine as hell' and boy shorts? While I appreciate the view, I will say, so does half of London."

She came back into the living room and whipped around, searching for me somewhere on the street. "You arsehole."

"If you say so."

"You want my address? I can give it to you. Come find me anytime."

I liked her. She was fire and spunk, and just a bit shy of crazy. And I wanted her. And that was a real big fucking problem.

The real question was, what was I going to do about her attempt to tap us? Because if she tapped my fucking wallet and I hadn't been paying attention, what else had she gotten her hands on? "Sleep tight, Agent Kincade. We'll be speaking again soon."

SEVEN

East

"Are you sure you know what you're doing?" I mumbled.

Bridge's voice was mellow as he chuckled. "Yeah, I pressed the knobs and buttons, hoping I'd get it right. Right?"

A feeling of unease settled over me. "Jesus fucking Christ, all you have to do is look at the cameras and make sure no one's in this hallway. How hard can that be?"

I could hear the sounds of the birthday party in the background as Ben chimed in. "Bridge, stop fucking with him. East, I know you're used to being in the van, but Bridge can manage it. Besides, you're the one that has the expertise to hack into the computer and get any information we need. So suck it up, buttercup."

"I will have you know that I was the one who actually did a stint in clandestine services."

I could hear Bridge groan. "Yeah, and you never let us forget it, mate."

More sounds from the party filtered through the comms, and Drew chimed in, sounding nervous. "Can we just get this show on the road? You're making me nervous."

Ben chuckled then. "Easy, Drew. This is the simple part. We do nothing and look innocent. East does the breaking in. When he arrives to the party late, we make it seem like he was here all along. It's not that hard."

Drew mumbled something along the lines of, "Speak for yourself."

Something was going on with him. As a general rule, I didn't play lookie-loo on my mates. We had a trust barrier. I didn't poke around in their lives, and no one asked questions when I poked around in other people's lives. But there was something going on with Drew for sure, so I might have to break that rule.

"Look, Bridge, don't fucking touch anything. Just tell me when someone comes down this hallway."

"Yeah, yeah. Sure, which hallway?"

I was going to kill him. He was in my SUV playing around with my equipment.

That sounds dirty.

Well, it felt like a personal violation. "Tell me you're not serious."

Bridge sighed. "I'm not a moron. I also did a stint in the clandestine services. I just don't like the spy information stuff."

"Fine, just make sure the hallway's clear."

I went to the supply closet. I had walked in with my mates as usual. Had a glass of champagne. Talked to several people. Flirted, all the while winding my way around to the south hallway near the servants' quarters where I turned on the infrared blockers that had been tucked into my tuxedo.

No one had even noticed that I was filling out my tuxedo a little more today. Although one woman had run her hand over my chest and asked me to dance, but she noticed nothing different about me.

But yeah, I looked like I'd packed on about fifteen pounds of muscle, mostly because I needed the tux to go over my *other* out-fit. The one that was going let me steal the information, sneak it out of the party, and then return and change clothes.

I looked at my watch timer, waiting for the thirty-second countdown.

Right on cue, Bridge began the countdown, so I at least knew he was paying attention.

Ben's voice was low. "Affirmative."

Drew chimed in. "Affirmative."

And we were a go. Black mask on, camera's down, lights low, I had five minutes. That's all it would take. As expected, there was no one in the hallway. It was smooth, almost *too* smooth and easy. My mask was pulled down. If a guard should happen to not be in position and come wandering, I knew where my exits were. I just had to follow the plan.

I knew exactly where the senior Jameson's office was. All of us had spent enough time in each of these mansions owned by the older Elite members as teenagers to know our way around. So many parties, so many graduations, so many ceremonies.

With an easy decryption of the keypad located outside Jameson's office, I located the laptop with ease. He'd also done me the favor of not shutting down or logging out. I couldn't help but shake my head. Had they never heard of cyber security? Copying of the files was easy. *Far too easy.*

Paranoid, I checked the signal jammer attached to my hip. The little red light was on, so any transmitting devices in this room wouldn't transmit. So why was I so on edge?

Three minutes. I checked the computer. The decryption was complete, and the files had been copied. Thank fucking Christ.

I pulled out the flash drive, eased out the door, and quietly closed it behind me. I was moving briskly down the hall when I heard a feminine voice. "Hey, who the hell are you?"

I froze. I knew that voice. Despite my best instincts, I turned to look over my shoulder, and even though I still had my mask on, her eyes went wide, almost as if she knew exactly who I was. I had two choices: try and talk my way out of there or run.

I chose to run.

❧

Nyla

It would be a lie if I said I wasn't disappointed.

Thanks to Amelia's mother's connections, the red carpet had been rolled out for us for this birthday party of a man I didn't know. Amelia had to attend anyway, and I was her plus one. These people with the glitterati lifestyle weren't really my speed. I'd never really understood the world Amelia came from. When I'd met her at MI5, she'd been trying to run away from her former life. But over the last three years her mother insisted on dragging her back, kicking and screaming.

I'd expected to see East Hale at this birthday party. It was the sole reason I'd come.

You wanted to see him again.

No. I wanted to talk to him about the Royal Museum of Monaco and his involvement with it.

You also wanted to take him by surprise.

Damn right I did. Somehow, he'd found the bug and what, been watching me? Spying? And why the hell did that make me flush all over instead of shiver from fear?

Because you're fucked in the head and thinking about how he tastes and not what he's capable of.

He might have my father fooled. Or worse, been able to

pull strings to get him to back off, but I had to play nice and to be honest he was the least of my problems.

But still… disappointment. He wasn't at the party. So I was going to have to go to his turf to talk to him. I exited the loo and accidentally turned left. When I turned around to head back to the party, I say the man dressed in all black easing out of an office.

The clue that he was up to no good was the balaclava on his head.

"Hey! Who the hell are you?"

He turned his head and gave me a glance over his shoulder. And there was something about the way he cocked his head that was smug and arrogant and somewhat amused, and my brain told myself that his lips quirked in just the kind of way that East Hale's did. And then I could see the full resemblance. Exact height, the frame, those ridiculously broad shoulders, tapering into a lean waist, long athletic legs.

Holy fucking shit.

It was East.

For a breath of a moment, we stood locked in place. Frozen. Neither of us breathing. Me in heels and my black mermaid-style cocktail dress, short in front and long in the back with a deep V. Him in the latest cat-burglar chic and a black balaclava.

Did I go back to the party and get security, or did I go after East and capture him myself? I knew what I needed to do. What the smart choice was. But in that split second, the decision was made for me.

East, ran.

And I chased. Because what the hell else was I supposed to do?

Oh fuck, he was fast.

Of course, I already knew how fast, but I'd run track and field back in secondary. I was quick, too. I'd even been offered scholarships to go to some unis in the States. Given enough time, I could catch him.

And I knew every exit out of this place.

I had researched the blueprints just in case something went wrong. Given my evening gown status, I could just feign that I was looking for a bathroom if I got caught, but God, why did it feel like East knew this place as well as I did?

Who the fuck is he?

A thread of something pulled at the back of my mind, but I didn't have time to examine it at the moment. We rounded a corner with him ahead of me by some twenty-five or thirty yards. But my heels slipped on the marble. When my hand caught the edge of the door to stop myself from taking a tumble, it was as if he heard me almost fall, and he slowed, turning slightly. Our gazes met, and when I saw the moss green of his eyes, I knew for certain. I *knew* it was him. "Whatever you're stealing, give it up."

This time instead of a smirk under his mask, I knew it was a full-blown grin, and that was all the confirmation I needed. I kicked off my shoes, bent down to scoop them up, and sprinted.

His eyes went wide, and he ran literally like he stole something. He exited through one of the side doors, into the gardens, and I was on his tail.

I knew this side of the property led to a massive downward slope and a maze of gardens, lush greenery, and a massive koi pond. Like something on Pemberley.

Apparently East knew it as well as I did, because instead of taking the steps that led down to the gardens, he bolted down the hillside.

I gave chase, giving up no quarter.

I was gaining on him. Closer, closer. And then from the higher vantage point, I launched myself at him. And just in that moment, he turned, his eyes wide. And he stopped running.

My heart stuttered and stopped. I was going to collide with him.

When I slammed into his body, he caught me easily, wrapping his arms around me, and we rolled together, his body taking the brunt of the impact as we rolled through the field of the flowers.

When we landed, I groaned. My bones felt like they'd been shoved into a bag and shaken around. I tried to reach for his mask, and he angled his head away from me, one arm locked around my waist, the other trying to control my two hands. "Take the mask off. I know it's you, East."

We both stilled, and he blinked at me. "Agent Kinkade, what were you doing in the hallway?"

"Says the man who is dressed like a thief?"

"For all you know, this is the latest in black tie," he groaned as he shifted.

"What did you steal?"

He shook his head and tried to stand.

"Oh no you don't." I started to pat him down. And then realized, to my chagrin, that I was sitting astride him, my hips locked over his. And to any passerby, it would look like we were... Oh, God.

I tried to shove against his chest and stand over him, but something stopped me. And it wasn't his arm around my waist. Something tugged at my dress, and there was a tearing sound.

We both glanced at where we were joined. He had some kind of hook or something, and it was latched into the knot of my dress. I tried again to free myself, and the dress tore again.

I glanced down, realizing that the knot of the dress was basically what held the whole damn thing together. If he tore it, my dress would be slit open and my tits would be flapping in the wind.

He must have realized the same thing that I did in that moment, because he grinned. "Oh, what a predicament. If you move, I see your tits." He licked his bottom lip. "And I can tell you that I have been having some very dirty fantasies about what they look like up close. Are you going to give me a show? As you know Agent Kincade, I do like to watch."

His voice was low and husky and sexy, and what the fuck was the question?

My eyes opened wide as I became even more hyper-aware of where else we were joined.

His chuckle was soft as he laid back down on the grass. "Don't mind him. He can just feel how warm you are. And I can't help but imagine you being wet and all the other ways and reasons we could be in this position."

"Shut up, you oaf. You have to unlatch me."

"I don't have to do anything. If you stand up, your dress tears open. And then, well, I'm still clothed, and you're not. So you'll have a lot of explaining to do. And I'll be out." He wiggled, and I heard more tearing sounds. I clapped a hand on his throat. "Stop fucking moving."

He chuckled. "Ooh, kinky. I think I like it. Squeeze tighter, love."

My hands were small. I would need two hands to choke him out, and it wouldn't be for fun.

"You'd like that, wouldn't you?"

"I would."

"You're a thief."

"No, not really," he mumbled.

"You're dressed in a balaclava, and you look like you've stolen the fucking crown jewels. What else could you be but a thief?"

"That answer's a little complicated, and I'm not going to tell you."

"What the fuck were you doing in Walter Jameson's office?"

"Again, princess, my lips are sealed."

"I can just take it off of you."

He rolled us over so that I was beneath him, and I gasped with the shock of the positioning. I was even more aware of that bulge.

Oh, hell.

I felt him pressed directly against my clit, and I bit back the moan.

And of course he could feel my body's response to him, and his hips hitched just so. I slammed my teeth over my bottom lip, and I turned away so he wouldn't see.

"There's no hiding your response to me, love. Pretend it's involuntary. I only rolled you over like this so maybe it'll be a little easier to detach us and you still get to stay dressed."

"I thought you wanted me naked."

He grinned down at me, his gaze slipping to my breasts and then back to my eyes. "Oh, trust me, I do. But I like my women willing. And right now, despite the fact that I can feel your heat, I want you undressing *for* me. I don't want it to be a result of me accidentally tearing your dress. If I do tear your dress, I want you to be well aware it's going to happen. And I want you to *want* it."

I swallowed hard. The way he said it, the way his voice went low and mellow, made something pool low in my belly. "Is that what you like? The ones who are like, 'Oh, yes. Sure. Go ahead. Rip this ridiculously expensive dress from my body.'"

"I like the way you say it. Does that count?"

"Just get off of me."

"I would, love, but then you'd be naked in the moonlight. And there's nothing to stop me from leaving you like that."

My eyes flared wide. "You wouldn't."

"Am I a gentleman or a thief?"

"Can't you be a gentleman *and* a thief?"

He grinned then. "I beg to differ. But again, I'm not exactly a thief."

"What did Jameson have that you needed to steal?"

"Nothing. Who said I stole anything?"

"You were leaving his office, and you're wearing a black balaclava."

"That just happened to be my outfit today. I thought it was a masquerade event."

"You're lying."

He leaned close. "I also happen to know that no one was supposed to be in that hallway, so what were you doing down there?"

I flashed my gaze to his. "None of your business." He wouldn't believe me if I said the other loo was occupied.

His lips tipped up into a smirk. "Ah, the Interpol agent. Going rogue, are we?"

"This isn't a movie. I'm not rogue. I was just looking for the loo."

He chuckled then. "Oh my God, you are a shitty liar. Everything you're feeling shows right here." His fingers indicated along my cheek. I could almost feel the heat of him brushing my face. And I wanted him to touch me.

"You don't know me at all."

He leaned close then, and I tipped my chin up. "Are you sure about that? Because right now you're in the moonlight, and I can tell that your pupils have dilated. The way you're hips are rotating just so, I can tell that you can feel my dick. And the way your teeth keep grazing over that bottom lip of yours, it's tempting me to bite it, and I know you want me to. You're just not ready to say the words yet."

My brain was foggy, and heat pulsed between my thighs.

But I wasn't going down like that. Through my teeth I asked, "What did you steal?"

He grinned. "God, Agent Kinkade, I feel like this is kind of our foreplay. And if this is the foreplay you like, it's turning me on very, very much. But I'm sure you can feel that, can't you?"

Hell fucking yeah, I felt that. He was... big.

Big? That thing's huge.

Okay, fine, he was huge. And God, was he getting harder? I could feel him twitch against me, and I bit my lip again.

"Agent Kinkade, if you keep that up, I'm going to start to think that you like this."

I narrowed my gaze even as my hips lifted. "Get off of me."

"Then stop writhing against me like you want me to fuck you."

"I am not writhing." I was totally writhing.

But then I felt him twitch against me again, and my hips rotated. Stupid hips.

"Go ahead, tell me another lie, why don't you?"

"You're rubbing against me. It's not my fault."

"Mm-hmm, sure. Now if you'd just let me..." His fingers moved between our bodies, and I held my breath. I could feel my breasts straining against the top of the dress. I was going to spill out any second.

"Fuck, the way the moonlight catches your skin, you look like shimmering gold. Do you have any idea how sexy you are?"

I swallowed hard. "Does this usually work for you as a dating tactic?"

He chuckled again. "You know, you are the most obstinate woman I've ever met. And I don't know why, but fuck, that turns me on."

I wiggled again. And he moaned this time. "Agent Kinkade, if you would like for me to get us separated, I need you to stop grinding against me and sit fucking still. And I need you to stop biting that bottom lip, because if you do it again, I will kiss you."

The thing about dares was that I'd never met one I could turn down. I wasn't impulsive, I just didn't like to be told what to do. I didn't want to be controlled. I didn't want anyone manipulating me. I could do what I wanted with my body.

And, okay, fine, it was involuntary.

I tried to keep still, I did. But it was as if my subconscious knew what I wanted or was determined to rebel against his command. Either way, I lifted my hips, and he groaned. And then his lips were on mine, his tongue sliding along the seam of my lips, and I gasped. That simple gasp gave him access, and his tongue delved into my mouth and licked against mine as his hips ground into me.

And instead of shoving him off of me, my hands, my traitorous hands went into his hair and locked him into place. And fuck, what the hell was wrong with me? He was the enemy. And he was clearly up to no good, and God, he tasted so goddamn good. He tasted like champagne and poor decisions and fun and sunshine, and God, I could kiss him forever.

There was a low mewling sound. Off in the distance. Was it in the distance? No, that was me.

His moan answered mine as he rolled me on top. I gasped. Because that was a better position, and I could move my hips just how I needed.

His hands fisted in my hair as he dragged his lips from mine. "That's it. Move how you want."

"What are we doing?"

"I have no fucking idea, but don't stop."

Not that I could. Because this man... He was everything I didn't want. He was everything dangerous. He was a criminal, and I was an Interpol agent, and I could not stay away from him if I tried. Obviously, I was mentally deficient. That was the only answer. But that did not stop me from leaning forward again at his insistence. But he stopped me just before our lips connected, and his gaze met mine. A dark ring showed around his irises now, his pupils dilated. But I knew what he was doing, he was asking my permission. He was waiting for me to pull back, to push him away, to tell him to stop, to tell him to unhook us so I could leave with whatever information he'd stolen. But instead of doing all of those things, I leaned in. I kissed him.

Because you're a fool.

And then it was teeth and tongue and lips and moaning and groaning, and his hand was on my ass, squeezing and cupping me, rocking me against his erection. And I couldn't stop. I moaned low, and he grunted. He tore his lips from mine and traced kisses against my jaw. "You're so fucking hot. Just like that. Keep moving."

And then… Splash. Ice cold on my back. And it shocked me. I blinked and turned away from him. "What the hell?"

He blinked in surprise as well. And then, his lips turned into a grin and he laughed. More splashing.

Oh God, it was raining. What the fuck? No, not rain, sprinklers.

I tried to detach from him, but again, the ripping sound of my dress stopped me.

"Fuck."

He rolled me over so that he was above me once again, protecting me from most of the splatter. And he rocked his hips again.

I should be fighting this, fighting him, but I'd been so close and…

"You worried someone's going to find you? All wet and rumpled?"

The right answer was yes. Yes, worried. Yes, concerned. Yes, couldn't go back to the party. Yes, what did you steal?

But my response was a shake of my head.

"That's my good girl. You like the idea we could get caught, don't you?"

Was that true? I'd never once cared for anything public before. Outside of simple pecks and handholding in public, I'd never been with anyone who was particularly affectionate in public. This wasn't affection though. This was raw, hungry; this was something else.

His hands still fisted in my hair, he rubbed his nose against mine, his lips barely a whisper. "You like being dirty with me, don't you?"

"I don't like you at all."

"I know. I don't like you either." And then he rocked his hips again.

"East."

"Agent Kincade."

"Why do you say my name like that?"

"Because there's something so sexy about it."

He rocked his hips again, and God, I was so close, just *right there*. And then his lips took mine once more, kissing me. As the sprinklers pelted us with ice cold water, I was soaked through. But I was so hot. My skin was burning as he rocked into me over and over, and his one hand scooped under my ass and lifted me closer. And fuck, God, the sparks, a shuddering heat exploded in my body, and I threw my head back. He tore his lips from mine and dragged them along my jaw and then my neck. And then he grunted. "Fuck. Fucking hell. You're so fucking sexy. I want to watch you come again and again. Somewhere private next time. So I can take my time and watch you. And torture you. And drag it out."

And then his body was lifting from mine. The hook on the front of his suit slipped off of the material of my dress, and he was standing. My dress was in disarray, hiked up, exposing my black silk thong. And his gaze went straight to my splayed-open thighs. Gently he pulled my dress down, and I couldn't move. I just stared up at the night sky. The mist of the sprinklers blocked out some of my view, but I could see the stars up above judging me. And then he did the one thing I didn't expect. He reached a hand down and helped me up.

"Follow me. I'll get you a jacket. But you're going to have to go to your car."

"What did you steal?"

"I can't tell you that."

He marched up the twenty meters to where I'd dropped my shoes when I jumped at him and picked them up. And then he helped me down the hill.

I winced when my feet hit the cobblestones, and he picked me up. Easily. Him dressed in all black. Balaclava on. Me dressed in black, soaking wet.

He carried me through the gardens and across the expansive grounds, to the side exit gate and an SUV. Black.

I frowned. Were the plates diplomatic? No. Government? Not exactly. He went around to one side, opened a door, and pulled out a blanket of some sort. He brought it to me and wrapped it around my shoulders. My teeth chattered. "Who are you?"

"I'm East Hale. But you know that. Or do you make out with strangers often?"

"I did not snog you. You snogged me."

He chuckled. "If you need to tell yourself that, fine, Agent Kinkade. I'm going to get in that car and drive off now. Do you have your phone?"

I frowned. My fucking phone. Did I have it? And then I glanced at my wrist and the wristlet that was attached to me. It had my phone inside. "Yes, I have it."

"Good. Call a friend or whoever you came with. I'm leaving."

"The hell you are. You are not leaving me on the side of the street in this soaking wet dress."

"You have a blanket and a phone. Hopefully it works after the waterworks."

He handed me back my shoes, and I stared at him. "If you leave me here, I will not stop coming after you."

"I expect nothing less."

And then he climbed into the driver's side of the car, and even though I couldn't see him, thanks to the tinted glass, I knew he was staring at me. And he pulled away.

I was going to murder East Hale the next time I saw him.

EIGHT

East

L ater that night I tossed in bed. What the hell had I been thinking?

You're a glutton for punishment.

Okay, yes, this was true. Absolutely. I was a glutton for punishment. And I was punishing myself big time. Snogging Nyla Kincade… again. What an idiotic fuck up. And who was I kidding? I would have shagged her right there on the lawn if I'd have let my dick have his way.

What the hell was wrong with me that I found it extremely hot fighting with her? It meant I was a sick puppy and had no business anywhere near the woman.

Every time I closed my goddamn eyes, I could hear her whimper. The way I'd swallowed it in my mouth. The way I'd coaxed her tongue into dancing with mine. The way her body felt pressed up and molded against me. I hadn't given a fuck where we were, in public at an Elite member's birthday party. Anyone could have seen me kissing a fucking Interpol agent who would happily put my mates and me in jail if she got any wind of what we'd done. But not just us; Livy, Lucas, Bryna, Sebastian, Penny, Roone, and Jessa were involved as well. And let's not forget the Chase brothers.

Either of their beautiful wives would skin me if the police came knocking on their doors. I needed to get myself together and stay the fuck away from Nyla Kincade, of that I was pretty damn sure.

The worst of it was that I couldn't even remember how the fuck I'd ended up like that. With my tongue in her mouth, her scent wrapping around me, taking full possession of my balls.

I nearly choked with need and had to adjust my dick pushing insistently against my boxers. Unable to think for myself. To breathe. To do anything. All I wanted was her. Nyla completely crowded my mind. I hadn't been able to put two and two together. I hadn't been able to think, to rev the old brain engine. Nope, she'd shorted it out.

I'd made a colossal mistake. That shit was not going to happen again. There were a million women I could fuck, but Nyla Kincade just couldn't be one of them.

With a sigh, I glared at the clock. It was three. I prayed to all hell while I texted AJ that she'd be asleep. But ever since she was a teenager, she'd had difficulty sleeping. She slept in patches. Sometimes napping through the day, sometimes not. When I texted her, she called me right away. "What are you doing up, little brother?"

"I couldn't sleep. I was thinking of you."

"Why can't you sleep?"

"Ah, don't worry about it. How's Margaux?"

I heard a mumble and whispered words.

"Shit, I'm waking Margaux up, aren't I?"

AJ whispered, "Hold on, let me get out of bed."

I could hear the rustling of sheets. The shuffling of slippers on the wood floor. I could picture her as she left her bedroom and went down the hall toward the living room. "Sorry. I thought Margaux was in a deeper sleep. But the baby is keeping her up, and she's uncomfortable."

Margaux had gotten pregnant earlier in the year. And she was six months along. Just far enough along to be uncomfortable.

"Is she having real cravings yet?"

AJ laughed. "You know, not really. I mean, she did threaten to cut me if I didn't give her a pain au chocolat the other day, specifically from Rue Grimaldi So that required some effort. But other than that, she's been mostly normal. She wants gelato a lot, so we make that a thing when we go on daily walks. But that one bakery was her only choice for the pain au chocolat."

I laughed. "Didn't you take me there once?"

She laughed. "Yes. And they have the worst pain au chocolat. They're terrible."

"They are terrible. How does a bakery that bad survive in Monaco?"

She laughed. "I don't know. But there's something that Margaux really likes about them. I'm convinced they're sprinkling crack on the chocolate, because it's the only explanation. Their croissants are hard."

"I know. Your wife has zero taste."

She snorted. "Hey."

I chuckled. "Well, I mean hey, I could criticize my big sister too."

"Screw you."

"I miss you." I murmured.

She laughed. "Well, I'm not sure I miss you now."

"Sorry, sorry. I'm just being a dick little brother."

"What's the matter? You seem tense and on edge."

"I'm fine."

"Stop it. You're not fine. Something is wrong. Why are you so on edge?"

"I don't know. Remember Garreth Jameson? Been dealing with him a lot. And I just—Christ he's a wanker." There was a beat of silence, and in that moment, I want to cut my own tongue out. "Fuck, AJ, I'm sorry."

"Would you stop it, East? Just stop. You don't have to treat me like I'm some fragile shell of a person."

"I don't think you're fragile. I think you're incredibly strong. And I shouldn't have brought him up."

"When will you stop trying to be the big brother? You're not. I'm the big sister. I protect you from things."

"Yeah, well, how about we protect each other?"

"That's a good one. Of course, East. We should do that, protect each other and shit. Now, tell me everything. You saw him and… what?"

"It doesn't matter, AJ. I just, I don't know. I wanted to talk to you and make sure you're okay."

"I'm always okay. Look, East, all of that was a lifetime ago. A million years ago. I don't think about that part of my life. Not anymore."

"Therapy, it does a lot of good, doesn't it?"

"I wish you could let it go, East. None of that matters anymore."

"I know."

"Okay, how about we not talk about him? Because he's that kind of guy that will try to get under your skin when there's nothing to get under."

"I know. But if there *was* something you needed to get off your chest, you could tell me."

"There's nothing to tell, love. Go on. Who is in your life now? What type of model or actress are you dating?"

I scowled as I rolled over. "Ah, that's the worst question."

"Oh? If it's the worst question, what's her name?" AJ teased.

"There's no one. No name."

"Oh my God, East Alexander Hale. If you think for a minute

that I believe that bullshit, you're fooling yourself. I still remember that day when I caught you kissing Elsa Holiday. You tried to act like you hadn't been up to anything, but I could see it written all over your face. You'd had your hand up her skirt. My little brother, having his first sexual experience. It was so gross. And I had a feeling you were fumbling it."

Bullshit. I was good. *No, you weren't.* "Hey, I figured it out."

"Judging by the line of women dying to date you, I'm sure you did. Or they want to date your millions. Whichever. As long as you're getting some action."

I choked a laugh. "Jesus, AJ."

"What? I'm just saying."

And because she was my sister, I told her the truth. "There is someone who's interesting. But she's bad news."

"Married?"

I shook my head, even though she couldn't see me. "No." I scratched at my abs. "No, nothing like that. She's just trouble with a capital T."

AJ laughed. "Oh, but don't you like trouble though?"

I snorted a laugh, remembering exactly what she meant. Isabelle Monroe, the Australian exchange student. My mate, Tommy Fletcher, and I had both fallen hopelessly in love with the new girl at school. Before the end of the school year, Tommy and I had been rolling around on the ground because Isabelle had promised to walk home with both of us. We never recovered our friendship.

"Fucking Tommy Fletcher. I wonder where he is right now."

"Actually, you know, I saw him when he came to Monaco."

I laughed. "He came to Monaco? When?"

"Maybe about six months ago, I think. You know how Mom is. 'Oh, you must speak to the Fletchers. They're coming,' and whatever. She gave him my phone number. So I showed them around the museum and all that. He seemed surprised to find that I hadn't somehow grown out of liking girls."

I rolled my eyes. "Twat."

"Whatever. He's an idiot. Anyway, you will be happy to know he's paunchy and looks like he's had his nose broken more than once."

That did make me feel better. "I guess there's some satisfaction in that." We both laughed thinking about stupid old Tommy Fletcher. "It's good to hear your voice, AJ."

"It's good to hear yours too. Are you sure you're okay?"

"Yeah, I think so."

There was a long pause, and then she asked me the question I knew she would ask. "Does this have anything to do with the ten-year anniversary of Toby's death?"

She didn't know all of it. She just knew that Toby had died. She didn't know how or why because I hadn't told her everything we'd found out. I hadn't wanted her to worry, because she'd have known that I would do something stupid. Which obviously, I had done. "Maybe a little. A few months ago we saw Emma, and she really needled us about, you know… about not having done anything and fought harder."

"I can't imagine how hard that is."

"Yeah. It feels like shit honestly, but it is what it is."

"I know the man that you are, East. I know that you love fiercely and protect what's yours. I know that you'll do what you need to do. But you can't do it if you're stressed out and not rested. And if it's a woman keeping you from resting, resolve that issue so you can focus on the important things at hand, yeah?"

"My big sister, forever the wise one. I love you. You know that."

"I love you too. Now, go to bed."

"You first."

I hung up with AJ and then laid back on the bed, trying to sort through the jangled mass in my brain. I could do this. I could stay the hell away from Nyla Kincade.

Or, you could see her. Deliberately direct her away from the London Lords.

Even before that thought formed, I knew it was a ridiculous plan. A recipe for disaster. A very, very bad idea. The problem was that my dick liked that idea very, very much.

❧

Nyla

The afternoon following my roll in the grass with the billionaire, I glanced up at the London Lords building and whistled under my breath. The office was connected to the hotel and had the same bold contemporary style. Glass, chrome, and elegance.

Are we really going to do this?

Looked like it. Because despite my best efforts this was the case I had, and East Hale was my best lead. So I could walk in there and deal with him. Pretend like the previous night hadn't happened. Act like I didn't know his taste or how he kissed.

Easy.

Right.

Stepping into London Lords, I got that feeling of understated yet opulent wealth. The London Lords Soho wasn't the place you went on staycation. It wasn't something the average Londoner or tourist could afford. You had to be well and truly monied to enjoy a place like this.

While the building was chrome and steel, there was a distinct elegance about it. Perhaps it was the décor and the lighting, but there was a warmth to it. Like you were instantly welcomed, and why would you ever want to leave?

Maybe it was the artwork on the walls. Maybe it was the plush carpeting under my stacked-heel boots. Everything about the place exuded the wealth of the London Lords.

"Very nice, Mr. Hale," I murmured to myself. This was my third visit to the offices, and I couldn't help but feel as if I'd missed my calling. I should have been a billionaire.

Next life maybe. I'd like to think I would do billionaire right, but knew I'd somehow still insist on keeping my job. Bad guys always had a way of leaving a bad taste in your mouth. There was no way I'd be able to rub elbows with them. The corruption would drive me mad.

The elevator dinged and slowed to a stop. When the doors opened, I stepped out into the top floor of the London Lords offices. And while I was used to going left to speak to Bennett Covington and the women who worked for him, Olivia Ashong and Jessa Ainsley, this time I went right. Because this time I was going to see a different billionaire altogether.

When I was shown into East Hale's office, I had to bite back my gasp. Two walls of his office were completely glass. It looked like we were sitting on a ledge overlooking London.

East Hale strode out of some sort of office chamber or something, perhaps a bathroom, and my breath caught. Charcoal Briony suit. Moss green tie to bring out the color in his yes. Crisp white shirt. And his hair. Lord, his hair was messily styled but so artful that it couldn't be by accident. It was pure mussed sex hair. I had to work hard at the whole in-out even breathing thing.

"Agent Kincade, what a delightful surprise. It's almost like you knew I was thinking about you." He shook my hand. His grasp was warm, firm, and completely enveloped my hand. The spark of electricity stung my palm, and I swallowed hard. I didn't jerk my hand away though. Just waited patiently for him to release me. When he did, a slow, smug smile lit that perfectly full mouth. He felt it too, and the idiot wanted to remind me about just how close we'd come to shagging alfresco.

I took a seat, but instead of doing the same, East leaned on the edge of his desk instead of sitting behind it. Was it a power play? It had to be, because he made it very difficult for me to concentrate. "Mr. Hale, why don't you take a seat?"

"I'm good here. Besides I like flirting with trouble."

"I'm not the one who's trouble."

A smirk tugged at the corner of his lips. "Aren't you? You're the entire reason I didn't sleep a wink last night. If I can unsettle you just a little, payback will be complete." His gaze searched mine and he licked his lips. "I must admit, I didn't think I'd be seeing you again so soon, but I am delighted. I have a bet with myself that you can't possibly taste as good as I'm remembering."

The way he spoke to me, Christ. I felt like I was an ice-cream he wanted to lick. My skin was prickly hot, but I refused to look away from him. I had a job to do and I needed him to answer a few questions.

He had to know he was too close. I could smell him from such close proximity, and he smelled like leather and something musky. He smelled... absolutely delicious. It swirled around me, entranced me.

His voice was a low, coaxing rumble, and I could feel myself softening, my posture changing, my lips wanting to curve into a smile. That was the danger of this man. He knew his effect on women and wielded that power expertly.

"That's interesting. I haven't really given you much thought."

His grin was quick as a flash and just as devastating as that low purr of his. "You really don't have to play hard to get with me, Agent Kincade. I assure you, I'm already quite enchanted. Matter of fact, I think we should have dinner. You know, to get to know each other better before you accompany me as my date to Ben and Livy's wedding."

"I already told you, I'm busy."

Another grin from him, and there went my panties. Eviscerated into the ether. "You don't know when it is yet."

"And I will *always* be busy. I don't date bad boys."

"Said no woman ever," he said with a laugh.

"When will you give up?"

"As soon as I can forget that that little whimper you made at the back of your throat and once I can erase your taste from my tongue. Dinner. And I promise by morning you'll be more than happy to be my date."

"Morning. My, my. So sure of yourself."

His eyes danced, and I could see he was having fun. Sadly so was I.

"Let's just call it hopeful. Besides, I said dinner. I didn't say what time zone."

"Ahh, flexing those billionaire muscles. Sorry, but it's still a no. I also don't date dodgy men with secrets. You tell me you're not a thief, but yet I caught you up to something."

"All these rules. Tell me, Agent Kincade, have those rules ever gotten you kissed like last night? My guess is no."

A pulsing heat concentrated between my thighs. *Time to bring it back, Nyla. Focus then get to safety.*

I cleared my throat. I had to right this ship, or I'd become a cliché by shagging him on his desk. "I want to ask you a couple of questions."

One side of his mouth quirked upward. "Fine. Business before pleasure. I can respect that. I do have to tell you I'm not going to answer any questions about last night. Anything other than that is on the table."

Of course he wasn't. I cleared my throat. "My understanding is that you are the London representative for the Royal Museum in Monaco. You and a Miss," I checked my notes, "Analisse Du Mont."

He blinked in what seemed like honest surprise. "You would be informed correctly."

"Might I ask your connection? I thought you were in the hotel business?"

The corner of his lips twitched and distracted me. The way he lazily leaned against his desk, I had full vantage point of his long lean body. He was every bit the rogue billionaire.

"Analisse Du Mont is my mother. She inherited a sizeable art collection upon my great-grandmother's death. My grandmother had always wanted to display the works the family had, but for several reasons never managed to, so the task eventually fell to my mother and sister. We've consigned the entire collection to the Royal Museum in Monaco. My sister is the curator."

As he spoke, I quickly jotted notes. "Your mother. That certainly makes more sense."

"Mum finds herself quite busy with charity work, so somehow I have become the London point of contact. A part of me thinks this was her evil scheme all along to bind me to her family's legacy. It might have broken her heart that I went the route of my father into business."

"But still, you don't work for your father." That had nothing to do with the case. More of a curiosity.

His lips compressed ever so slightly, his tone becoming sharp when he said, "I do not."

I wanted desperately to poke at the obvious sore spot, not to cause him pain, but because the urge to know more about him was nearly eating at me. But I kept on task. "Three years ago, your collection reported an attempted theft and forgeries of a visiting collection."

He nodded slowly. "Yes. There was a problem. I believe the thief and forger was caught."

I nodded as I took more notes. "If you don't mind, I would love to see your collection. I'm particularly interested in the authentication process the museum used. Any security from that time. A first-hand account maybe. If you could walk me through the process and how you were tipped off, that would be ideal. There are similarities between what happened at the Royal Museum and a case I'm working on."

"Interesting. Do you think it's the work of copycats? Or perhaps all the thieves weren't caught?"

"I don't know. Which is why I'd love your firsthand account. Anything you can think of, no matter how small. I would love the opportunity to examine the collection and authentication procedures."

"I can make that happen. We shared the bulk of the responsibility with the Monaco Art Trust. We were lucky the forgeries were discovered within the day."

"Who was responsible for authentication?"

"Since all of our pieces are on loan with the caveat that my sister be named curator, we are responsible. One of us is in constant oversight of the care of the collection, obviously. The challenge was with the loan of the Tillson collection. They were supposed to be showcasing a set of jewelry they had that was a sister set to something in my grandmother's collection as well as several paintings."

"Is there any possibility that the procedures were suspect in any way? No disrespect, but if the forgers were indeed caught, it would be unlikely that I'd have another piece with the same signature."

He crossed his arms then. "No, it's not possible. The Royal Museum of Monaco is one of the most well-guarded and respected institutions. There's no way."

"Is it possible to speak to your sister, just to confirm any staffing changes, background checks, anything like that?"

His brow furrowed. "You think we missed something?"

"I'm just following all avenues right now."

"Fine. I can give you her number, but it's probably better to meet her in person."

"So I would have to go to Monaco?"

He grinned. "Well, that's how it works if you want to see the paintings and jewelry up close and personal."

I closed my notebook and plastered on a polite smile. "I'm sure your family has done everything that they can, and I understand that this is an inconvenience for you, but it would be very helpful if I could look at your authentication paperwork."

"I'll make it happen."

"It's much appreciated, Mr. Hale."

The smile widened into a grin. "There is something about the way you say that. Anything for my favorite Interpol agent."

"Mr. Hale, flattery will get you nowhere."

Lies. If we play our cards right flattery will get him in our knickers.

"Well, I find flattery is useful to bring women around to the idea of having dinner with me."

I bit back my chuckle. "Never going to happen."

"If you say so. I'll be in touch to let you know about the collection."

"Thank you very much. I'll get in touch with your sister."

His wolfish grin broke free again. "Oh, perhaps you misunderstood, Agent Kincade. Not only will I arrange for you to see it, but you'll also have the pleasure of my company."

My eyes flared wide as I nearly choked on my next breath.

Speaking rapidly I said, "Well, that's highly unnecessary. I'm sure it'll go faster if I can work on my own."

He shrugged. "My family, my collections. If you want to see it, I come with you."

"Mr. Hale, I'm an Interpol agent. I have a partner. I don't need you."

"Well then, maybe you don't want to see that collection nearly as badly as you say."

I rolled my eyes. "Fantastic. It looks like we're going to be heading to Monaco together."

His grin was broad. "I knew you'd see it my way."

NINE

Nyla

When I returned to work, I went straight for Amelia's office. She had her own case. A run-of-the-mill murder. Since when had murders become run-of-the-mill? She greeted me with a, "Hey where'd you go this morning?"

I plopped into one of her chairs and then grabbed a handful of Skittles off of her desk. "Are they fresh?"

She squinted her eyes at me. "Yes, they're fresh. I put a new fresh bag in there daily. Between you and me, we eat a whole bag every day."

I frowned. "We've eaten that much sugar?"

"Yes, you have a habit, and now I have a habit."

"Okay, fair enough. I popped two Skittles in my mouth. "So, I am going to Monaco."

She lifted a brow. "What, for the weekend?"

"No, apparently tomorrow. I'm chasing a lead on the jewelry thing."

She leaned forward. "What lead?"

"Same MO on a three-year-old case. I'm trying to identify if it's a copycat or if we missed something. Don't worry about me. You have your hands full with catching a murderer. It's fine."

"But I do want to help. I don't want you feeling like I've abandoned you."

"You aren't making me feel that way. Denning has assigned you to another case. You're only assisting me. It's fine. I can do a lot of the work by myself."

"Okay. What's in Monaco?"

"That, my dear, is the rub." I popped some Skittles into my mouth. "I don't want you getting excited."

She lifted a brow. "Okay. Excitement contained."

"A couple days ago, I found this similarity between my case and a case from a few years ago featuring a couple of pieces in the Du Mont collection shown at the Royal Museum of Art in Monaco."

"Okay, why is that exciting besides, you know, Monaco? Make sure you go in and gamble in one of the casinos just for me. Do me a favor and please pack a dress."

"No, I'm not going there to gamble."

"You're always ruining my James Bond fun. How else are you supposed to meet a sexy international spy who's also hot, amazing in bed, and ridiculously wealthy if you don't walk into a casino?"

I giggled at that. "You know what? Accurate."

"Ugh, does that mean you'll be destined for losers forever?"

"Hush your mouth. We don't want the fates to hear you."

"Good point. Okay, so why is the case so exciting?"

"Well, it seems that the Du Mont family representative here in London is none other than East Hale."

Amelia's brows lifted. "As in hottie billionaire who is part of a shady secret society that we're trying to crack wide open? Dare I ask if he's the reason you left me at the party last night?"

I answered around a mouth full of Skittles. "I told you. I wasn't feeling well. Besides I didn't see him inside the party." I consoled the twinge of guilt by reminding myself I didn't actually see him *inside* the party."

"This is huge. And a lucky coincidence. Because this way, you're not actually breaking any rules. And you get to be close while you're investigating."

"Yes. Which is why I'm excited. There's something else though." It didn't feel good holding this back from Amelia. She was usually the person I told everything to.

She knew enough about me to be suspicious. "Okay... What have you done?"

I couldn't tell her about East, but I needed to tell someone about Theroux. I was going to need all the help I could get. "No, this time it's not me. I got a phone call the other night while I was at the hospital benefit bugging East Hale."

"From who?"

"Someone claiming to be Francois Theroux."

Am myriad of emotion played over her face. The most prominent being shock. "Stop shitting me."

"I shit you not. I wouldn't."

"What did your father say?"

"I winced. "You mean when I didn't tell him?"

Amelia blew out a breath as she leaned forward and pressed her fingers to her eyes. "For fuck's sake, Ny!"

"I know. I know. I walked in there to tell him and then I just couldn't. He was looking at me with all this... disappointment. And let's be honest. Even if I had told him, Denning would get to work on it not me."

"Fuck, you're right." she grunted and slammed her head back against her seat." Your father is so smart. How can he not see through Denning?"

"I don't know. Denning's probably the son he's always wanted."

It was her turn to wince because she knew I was right. "Fuck, I'm so sorry."

"It's fine. It is what it is. And after all, maybe it's nothing. I'm certainly not going to spin my wheels trying to get my father to pay attention if it's nothing."

The corner of her lip quirked up. "Abso-fucking-lutely. After all, I work under Denning. And no one told *me* to stay away from Theroux."

"Thank you." It meant a lot that she was in my corner. At least I had someone.

"Ride or die. I'll start some research, last knowns. Get a tracer on your phone. I'll be discrete."

"You're a mate, you know that?"

"Absolutely. And hey, try and have some fun in Monaco, okay? Get into some trouble."

"I'll be gone for two days max. No fun or trouble to be had. Besides, remember when we said no more shady blokes?"

She nodded. "Yup, I remember that pact."

"East Hale definitely falls in the shady-bloke category."

She rolled her eyes. "Yes, but he's so pretty. He might need a shady-bloke waiver."

I started to laugh as I stood, grabbing another handful of Skittles. "I swear it's my last fix." I liked to think that the hit of sugar made it easier for me to think.

"Fine, take the Skittles."

"Thanks, partner."

"Of course. Anytime. In the meantime, see what you can get out of East Hale. Use your feminine wiles."

I glanced down at myself, my wide-legged trousers and my plain button-down white shirt. "I don't exactly understand what feminine wiles you're talking about."

She rolled her eyes. "Nyla, how can you not see that you're a complete fucking knockout? "

"I'm an Interpol agent. I don't need to be sexy." Even as I said that, I frowned down at myself. I loved these pants.

"I'm not saying you're not sexy. Like I said, I've tried to borrow those pants off of you several times."

"And I keep telling you you're too short. You can't tailor my pants that you're borrowing to fit you."

She harrumphed. "The point is, if you wore that button down and tied the shirttails in a knot, or even better, wore it as a one shoulder, you'd be even hotter."

"You do realize I'm not trying to tempt East Hale into bed, right? You know that's not what I'm doing here."

"Of course I know that. I'm just saying. He might open up more if he thinks you're falling under his spell."

"No dice. I'll get him to tell me what I need."

"Of course you will. After all, you're Agent Nyla Kincade. But it would be easier if, you know, you embraced the thing that he loves. And from what I've seen, it's women. And you and I both know he likes you. He really, *really* likes you. You just have to feed that. Get him to trust you."

"You know what? Why haven't I realized just how diabolical you are until right now?"

"Oh, you know how diabolical I am. I'm pretty sure it's the reason we're best friends. Have fun in Monaco."

I gave her a little salute as I popped another sphere of sugar into my mouth. "Yeah, will do." As I opened the door, she called out after me. "And wear something sexy."

The last thing on earth I wanted to do was entice East Hale. The man was already dangerous to me. I didn't need to make it any worse.

Nyla

I tried to swallow the bitter burn of annoyance as I dragged my overnight bag down the stairs of my flat. I loved my flat, the high ceilings, the open space. I didn't need a modern and fancy condo, but it needed to feel light and airy. I hated the sensation of being closed in. It was probably more than I should be paying, and Lord knew, this was London. But I loved it.

But instead of having a Sunday morning lie-in, I was leaving for Monaco. With East Hale. I was frustrated after all my careful planning to bug him and his friends, and they'd never said anything incriminating. He'd found me out before I could get anything of use.

God help me. There was something about the man that just irritated me. His utter calm, that underlying arrogance, and I was going to be trapped with him for a couple of days.

There's another reason you hate him too.

But I wasn't going to think about that. No way was I going to pay any attention to that pull of awareness I had around him or the way his green eyes flashed and held mine, captivating, stopping me from movement like I was a snared rabbit. Oh, he was affable and friendly enough, but there was something underneath all that, a core of steel. A core that said he was a mountain and wasn't being moved unless he damn well wanted to be.

And I was a woman accustomed to moving mountains.

I checked my watch and frowned. I was told to be outside at bloody six o'clock in the morning, that there would be a car and—

"Nyla."

I whipped around, hand on my pepper spray. Since I was stationed in the UK, I wasn't allowed to have a gun unless I was on assignment, so my gun was locked in my briefcase along with my paperwork. But I breathed a sigh of annoyed relief when I saw it was Denning. "Oh, for Christ's sake. What are you doing lurking in the shadows?"

He rolled his big shoulders. "I was hardly lurking. I went for a run. You were on the way."

"So what, you just stood outside of my flat waiting for me? I suppose I should be happy you didn't let yourself in."

He frowned slightly. "I turned over my key."

"Did you?" That was still one of our points of contention. "Not to worry, though, I changed the locks."

His brow furrowed. "You and I both know if I wanted in, I could get in."

I shook my head. "I was always better at lock-picking than you were, Denning. I can't see why you would want in anyway because, what did you say? You were slumming it with me?"

He sighed and ran a hand through his hair. "There's been a development."

"What kind of development?"

"One that we'll discuss when you land in Monaco. Things have changed."

"Yeah, you already said that. What's wrong?"

He cursed under his breath. "You need to be watchful of Hale."

I frowned. "Correct me if I'm wrong but weren't you and my dad the ones who said to leave him alone, Denning? I don't have time for this right now. My car is arriving any moment. Just—"

A Mercedes Maybach pulled up to the curb, and a driver dressed in all black stepped out. "Miss Kincade, apologies for the delay. There was traffic on M1."

I blinked at the sight of the car and the man dressed in

black. "Right. Yeah, thanks." I handed him my rolling suitcase and turned to Denning. "You have thirty seconds to tell me what you're going on about."

"Fine. I don't trust Hale. I think it's dodgy that your father told you to let it go."

My brows popped. "What? So when I needed you to back me a week ago and you didn't, what was that about?"

He shoved his hands in his pockets. "I was sure you were off on one of your tangents. But now I'm not so sure. I have to be aware of the optics."

My heart sank just as quickly as it had risen. "Oh Jesus Christ, Denning, if you're worried about optics, what are you doing here bothering me?"

"I want you to keep us, keep *me*, informed. If you notice anything off with Hale, you must notify me immediately."

"I'm sorry, but isn't that against fucking protocol? You and Dad need to get on the same damn page."

His lips curled up into a sneer. With his light brown hair, sharp jaw and shrewd eyes, I'd always thought him handsome until his cruelty made all of his features stand out in sharp relief. "Why do you always have to be so goddamn difficult?"

And there he was. The real Denning. He wasn't worried about me. He was worried about himself. "I'm not trying to be difficult, Denning. You're just always a dick, so I respond to that."

"This is important, Nyla."

"Denning, does my father know you're here? Does your new girlfriend know you're here? What's her name? Hazel, right? Does sweet Hazel know that you are standing in front of my doorstep at six in the morning trying to whisper sweet nothings in my ear?"

His intense stare raked over me. "I'm on your side, Ny."

I suppressed an eyeroll at his intimidation attempt. "Since when? This whole thing reeks."

His brows lifted. "What the fuck do you mean?"

Stepping back, I released a silent chuckle. "This," I added, waving my hand through the air, "I'm so glad to be free of it. I want to see how it turns out for you when your fairy godfather realizes that you are a twat. Wish I could watch."

"Why are you always such a bitch, Nyla?"

I paused mid-turn and gave him a broad grin over my shoulder. "Yup. Always. I revel in it. Careful now, though. If my father hears you call me a bitch, he won't like that. And then you wouldn't be his golden boy anymore."

I pivoted on my heel and sauntered to the waiting car, leaving him standing on the stoop of my building, jackass that he was.

TEN

East

When we pulled up to the hotel in its stunning opulence, Nyla's mouth dropped open. "I expected modern and shiny, like the hotel in London."

I lifted one shoulder in an offhand shrug. "We decided what we wanted for the branding is for the London Lords logo to fit anywhere. It should be simple elegance that can blend into whatever style of architecture we find. Which also lends to our sustainability and core mission. We aim to design hotels that look like other structures near them. Monaco is known for its opulence and its glitz and glamour. So we designed this hotel to match."

"It's... wow."

Before I even approached the desk, the concierge located me in the crowd. "Mr. Hale, we're so pleased to have you with us. As we discussed, we have the suite available. I didn't realize you'd be bringing a guest."

"It's fine. Pierre, this is Agent Nyla Kincade. She works for Interpol."

Pierre, ever affable, didn't even blink when I said Interpol.

Instead he bowed low and offered to take her bags. Between him and the porter, they took all of our luggage, leaving Nyla only with her cross-body purse and me with my keys as I headed toward the garage. "Follow me."

"We're not going to the room? And PS, where am I staying?"

I laughed. "When I said suite, I meant a three thousand square foot suite with four bedrooms."

Her mouth formed a small O, and then she closed it. "Okay then."

The drive to my sister's residence was beautiful and scenic, the sun pouring in. I'd chosen to let my driver go and drive us there myself. We kept several personal vehicles at each of our hotels to use when we visited on business, and I decided the black convertible would be a great choice because of the scenery along water. When I slipped into the car and slid my jacket off, Nyla just glanced at me deviously. "You realize that this isn't some *Roman Holiday* kind of outing, right?"

I grinned. "Oh, I'm well aware. Get in."

Even though she'd been skeptical, the moment we started to drive up the coast, she extended her arms, turned her face up into the sun, and laughed. She had the kind of laugh that gripped a guy by the balls and wouldn't let go. Deep and throaty and so buoyant. When I parked at the back of AJ's building, Nyla grabbed her laptop out of the back and met my gaze, her eyes sparkling. "Oh my God, that was the most incredible drive."

"Yes, I know. I'm always stunned by it when I come here too. There's nothing quite like the Riviera, especially in summertime with all the sunshine. I'm always aware that I shouldn't take it for granted."

My inner me wanted to roll my eyes at myself.

Oh yeah, real smooth. Keep flirting with her. See how that goes. Don't forget she tried to bug you.

And that was true. She had tried to bug us, but I'd found it. Still, I couldn't look at her without feeling like I'd been hit in the sternum. She was stunning. More than that, she was smart and cunning, and she had the kind of spirit that couldn't be bought anywhere. The back door to the offices swung open, and my big sister leaned in the doorway, looking more like my father as she aged. Behind her, stood her wife, Margaux. Margaux wrapped an arm around AJ's waist and gave her a kiss on the cheek before stepping forward. "East, maybe next time you'll give us more than a two-day notice that you're coming. We would have opened the villa."

Margaux's hug was tight. AJ and Margaux had been together since I'd been at Eton. To me, Margaux was as much my sister as AJ was. But when AJ told the old man she was in love with Margaux, Dad had disowned her. Asshole. I would never forgive him for that. AJ approached Nyla first. "Agent Kincade, I assume."

"Yes. I'm Nyla." She thrust out her hand and AJ clasped it with both of hers.

"It's delightful to meet you. This is my wife, Margaux. You're going to have to forgive her. She's exuberant in her actions. Also, I'm pretty sure she's a bit in love with my little brother."

Margaux released me, checked me over like a worried mother hen, and then smiled. "If I wasn't completely in love with his sister, I would make a play for him."

AJ just rolled her eyes, and I laughed as I said, "Nyla, you'll have to forgive them. They're not used to visitors."

AJ grinned and then came over and gave me just as tight of a hug as Margaux had. "East, it's so good to see you. You didn't have to come all this way. I would have come to London next month anyway."

"I know. But Nyla here has a little problem, and I'm hoping we can help her fix that."

AJ's brow furrowed. "What's the problem?"

That was what I loved about my sister. It didn't matter what it was, or what was going on with her, or anything like that. If she heard someone was having a problem, she wanted to help fix it.

"Why don't we take this inside?"

AJ and Margaux guided us through their main quarters. Their residence was connected to the museum, just at the back of the grounds. It wasn't overly large, but they loved it and had been fixing up the nursery since Margaux found out she was pregnant. I couldn't help but notice as we walked through their house that there were about a million of pictures of myself and AJ in various stages of growing up on display. Nyla noticed too, and every now and again, she would pause at a picture and laugh. There was one where I was bare-assed, running after my sister and wailing. Our nanny had gotten that photo.

AJ liked to joke that it didn't matter what was going on, I would always follow her, even if I was bare-assed.

When we hit the living room, Margaux went to get everyone drinks, and AJ took Nyla's hand. "So, Agent Kincade, what can I do for you?"

Nyla wasted no time. "Well, I'm on the trail of some thieves. Some art, but mostly jewels. The incident you had at the museum a few years ago resembles their MO. The thieves managed to replace and pawn off forgeries in a visiting exhibit. I'd like to take a look at your collection, and maybe you can fill me in on the process of authenticating your pieces and how you detected the fraudulent reproductions. I'd love to talk to someone who's an expert on how one would even go about doing something like this."

AJ's brows popped and she turned her attention to me. "My

God, East Hale, you've finally brought home a woman that I could fall in love with."

⚉

Nyla

"Thank you so much for taking the time out to speak with me. I know you must be very busy."

A.J. waved her hand. "Oh, come on when my little brother asks for a favor, of course I have to comply."

I slid my gaze over to East. Somehow picturing him as someone's little brother was difficult. "Yes well, he must have been very annoying as a child."

The dark-haired woman laughed. "Oh, absolutely."

I settled my attention back on her. "Can you tell me about the forgery incident that occurred here?"

"Yeah. I mean it was quite odd."

"Anything you can remember from that time could be extremely useful."

A.J. rubbed at her nose. "Okay. Well, there were several pieces that had come in as part of the Tillson collection, mostly jewelry, but also two art pieces. The jewelry were these ornate, intricate brooches and necklaces, a couple of tiaras. All total, the value was about fifteen million."

I jotted notes down on my tablet. "And how did you recognize that the items weren't genuine?"

A.J sighed. "That's the thing. I didn't notice. We had hired an assistant curator to help us with the collection, and he'd been on staff for several months. We had authenticators on staff and security, obviously. But somehow the items were replaced before the exhibit opened."

"And you didn't suspect anything?"

AJ shook her head, her dark locks shifting over her shoulders. "No. We didn't notice. They'd already been authenticated and placed in our secure vault. There was no reason to think as we prepared for the collection to be shown that anything had been switched. There were no security flags."

I nodded as I took more notes. "Okay. So how did you figure it out?"

She chuffed softly. "Believe it or not, it was one of the paintings. the last one. It was discovered completely by accident because I was being a klutz. We had just gotten the painting back from the authenticators. I had just opened it up and pulled it out of its crate. We all had on our gloves and everything we needed. Security was on hand overseeing everything, and I tripped."

"Did you drop it?"

She shook her head. "I reached for the edge of the table and tried to avoid scratching the painting. But my finger caught onto the very corner edge."

"Oh shit."

"Oh shit is right. I thought I'd brought ruin to the museum until I pulled back my gloved hand and noticed the paint had rubbed off."

"Paint? But you said the piece had already been authenticated and then it came straight to you."

"That's right, but I think the switch was made either at the authenticators or in transit."

"And you figured out who was doing it?"

She nodded. "The assistant curator. He'd attended one of the best art schools in the world. Loved art and was a painter himself. But yeah, even East's extensive background check couldn't find a thing on him. It was like he was a ghost. Sure, on paper, he'd had a real life. School, great parents, the perfect life.

But his *other* life, the real one, there was no record of him. It's as if his background was manufactured just for this purpose."

"Okay, so between the authenticators and the museum, a switch was made?"

AJ nodded. "Seems that way. The authenticators certified authenticity upon handoff. When we debriefed with them, they said the painting was an authentic Thomas Ackerman, valued at about two million."

"How long between the authentication and your unboxing?"

"Probably about eight hours. That's when we noticed it. So everyone who could have come in contact with the collection and would've possibly been able to make a switch was called in by the police."

"Yeah. I remember the case. It wasn't mine. But I remember hearing about it. So, the assistant curator was part of some group of thieves?"

AJ nodded. "Yeah, the Wilsons. They're responsible for millions of dollars of artwork and jewelry going missing all over Europe. They'd never done anything this sophisticated before though. This required careful planning over a series of weeks. They could have been discovered at any time. So it was very unusual."

"And the jewels, when did you discover those had been swapped?"

AJ shrugged. "Well, as soon as we discovered that one painting was a forgery, we looked at the other painting and pulled all the jewels in the collection, and we found they were also forgeries. They were replaced with emeralds and rubies and diamonds, but lower quality ones. Gems where clarity wasn't as good., Whoever arranged for the heist paid a pretty penny for those replicas, but in the thousands, nothing in the millions range."

"And the jewels had also already been authenticated and prepared for viewing?"

"Yes. We got lucky. We would have handled them with care and shown them off to the public. Replicas."

I tried to tamp down my excitement. Maybe I could turn this into a genuine lead. "That's exactly what my jewelry forgers have been doing as well. Replacing priceless pieces with less expensive pieces. So you said it was the Wilson crew and they were caught?"

AJ nodded. "Yes. The assistant curator didn't want to give them up. But once we started looking in the right places, tracking his movements in Monaco and France and Italy, they were able to piece things together and caught most of the crew. But there was one forger who worked for them that we did not catch."

I sagged. I couldn't help tugging on that little string of hope. "And the forger, tell me the one you caught wasn't the jewelry forger? Maybe he got away?"

"Sorry, but it was. The art forger is one of the best artists I've ever seen in my life. The curator had done a few of the pieces himself, but a few of the others required a skillset even he didn't possess. To be able to replicate the Thomas Ackerman. That's just brilliant. The forger could have been an artist in their own right."

"Were most of the authentic pieces recovered??"

"Yes. If I hadn't tripped, we never would have known. We would have returned the collection, and then obviously the shit would have hit the fan. As it was, it was ugly, but we were able to recover the jewels and both paintings, thanks to the authorities. They hadn't hit the black market yet."

I sighed. "This is extremely helpful, thank you. Did you notice anything else unusual around that time?"

She shook her head. "No. And thanks to my brother, we were able to repair our relationship with the family that loaned us the pieces, and everything turned out okay. But that feeling of being duped, you don't shake it."

I slid my gaze to East. "Believe me; I know all about that."

The MO was the same as my cases. But if all of them but one had been caught and the only one who hadn't was the art forger, where were my fake jewels coming from? And where were the originals disappearing to?"

"I wish I could tell you more. I still think about it. I got lucky. It could have been a lot worse."

I frowned as I looked at my previous notes. "And nobody died? Nobody was injured, shot, anything?"

She shook her head. "No. Nothing like that. Nothing violent."

I sighed. Because the crew that had been recently forging jewelry all over Europe had no compunctions on killing.

Either my forgers were copycats, or something else was going on.

⁊

Nyla

It was easy to talk to East. Too easy. Despite myself, I liked him.

Beyond the charm and the witty comments, and that panty-melting, crawl-your-way-out-of-your-own-clothes kind of smile, he was thoughtful. And he listened. I watched him with his sister and Margaux.

I paid close attention as they talked. And as AJ walked me through the ins and outs of catching the forger, with the devil being in the details and everything from the stroke to the feeling of the painter at the time being a clue, I observed that East was a voracious learner. I would have expected him to be impatient, blasé, cynical. But there was something about him that was always eager to know more.

"You're awfully quiet. Overwhelming, is it?"

I shook my head. "No. It's good. My brain is just running through all the scenarios, the forger's signatures. It's a lot. But it's giving me a lot of avenues to investigate. I just need to piece it together."

"Glad to give you a good starting point."

We were walking along the streets of Le Rocher, Monaco's old town. The peach, vanilla and terracotta colored buildings and tight winding streets made me feel like I was transported back in time to long ago centuries.

East had driven over to this part of town and then called someone to come and get the car so we could take a walk, which seemed like a fantastic idea at the time. But now I saw it was dangerous because next to me, East was almost irresistible with his long-sleeved summer sweater sculpting the muscles at his broad shoulders, showing off the breadth of them, his casual slacks that emphasized the model-like legs, and with his hair a little windblown and smelling like ocean breezes.

But you will resist him, because you don't need that pain.

That was true. And he wasn't hitting on me.

Why isn't he hitting on me?

And then my memory, of course, helped me out. When I'd met him at the benefit, he had told me he would not lay a hand on me until I asked him to. Well, good thing I had zero intention of doing that.

"A penny for your thoughts?" he asked.

"Sorry, I'm just running the case in my head."

"I'm glad AJ was helpful."

I felt the injection of adrenaline in my blood. "Oh, she was more than helpful. I'm really impressed. The painting was flawless. I mean, at the end of the day, if something can be replicated to that level of detail, is that actually a replica, or is the creator a true artist?"

He angled his head and regarded me, eyes dancing, lips twitching in a suppressed smile. "Careful, Agent Kincade, you don't sound like an Interpol agent right now."

I shrugged. "You'd be surprised. I don't sound like an Interpol agent most of the time. Much to my father's chagrin."

His smile bloomed, and he aimed it down at me. "Let me guess, Daddy's girl wanted to make the old man proud?"

I laughed. "I've hardly made him proud. Hell, it's hard to do that when he keeps me away from most of the bigger cases. He's my father, so I know he worries about me. I just wish that I could, you know, spread my wings. I wish I could really grow. I just always feel like he's ready to clip my wings in case I do something just a little too dangerous."

He slowed his pace, taking us to the square. "Are your feet okay? Do you want to go back?"

I shook my head. "No. I like this. The weather is beautiful, and the company is okay."

He made a shocked face and clutched his chest. "Just okay? I'll have you know I've been told my company is stellar."

"You know what? I actually believe that."

"As you should." He chuckled softly and then took me back to the topic. "So why follow in his footsteps if you think he'll never let you blossom?"

I shrugged. "When Mom died, I lost my person, you know? I was eleven. And Dad tried, but he had no idea what to do for me. He just wanted to be on a chase. And we honestly didn't know much about each other. When Mom was alive, he would leave home in New York and off he would go, whether it was for the FBI or some international task force or Interpol. Then she was gone, and he had to come home and take care of me. He was going to leave his job, but I told him not to. That nothing had to change."

I frowned at myself. I never talked about that time in my life. Why was it so damn easy to talk to him? Still, I added, "I just made a choice, you know, that since he was all I had, I was going all-in with him. I was going to be exactly the kind of kid that he wanted, so that being with me was not going to be a chore or a burden."

"He's your father, Nyla. You wouldn't have been a chore or a burden." East's voice was so soft. I could hear the pity in his words.

"Well, tell that to an eleven-year-old. So I changed everything about myself to be more like him. I just wanted him to love me. And lucky for me, I love the chase too. It turns out, I'm a lot more like him than I thought."

His sharp green gaze narrowed on mine. "Then why do you seem sad?"

I brushed my hair up my face, pulling it up and tying it into a bun. It gave me something to do under his intense scrutiny. "Um, because while the drive is there for the same reasons, my approach is different. I'm impulsive, too emotional. I go with my gut, and when I can taste a mystery in the air, I cannot let go. That is where Dad and I are the same. The case he was on when my mother died is still unsolved, even today. And he's been after that case for thirty years. Thirty years of chasing a ghost. Dad has never given up looking for him, the one that got away. He's obsessed about it."

"That's a long time to chase after something you never catch."

"I know, right? I'm not sure that I could do it."

We stopped at a bridge overlooking the water, and I sucked in a sharp breath as I watched a pair of swans swim by. "Oh my God, they're beautiful."

He nodded. "Yeah, this is actually a manmade canal between a couple of the hotels. But don't get too close. Swans are assholes."

"You know, I've heard that."

I watched the stately pair swim by with several downy gray awkward-looking babies behind them. When I turned back to East with a smile, his eyes were warm as he watched me, and my belly flipped. "What are you looking at?"

"A beautiful woman."

"Pfft, how many women have you called beautiful this week alone?"

He shook his head. "Just the one. You should probably know something about me, Nyla. I only say what I mean."

Heat licked at my cheeks, and I directed my attention toward the water. "Yeah, well, I don't have a lot of experience with that."

"Not everyone is, your boss," he said softly.

"I know." I lifted my gaze, focusing on him again, and the tension between us pulled tight. Despite my brain giving the command to my feet to turn around and head back on the path they'd traveled, the idiot that I was swayed forward.

"Nyla, do you know you smell incredible?" he murmured. "I've been thinking about your scent since that first night I saw you."

"East, this is probably a bad idea," I whispered. But I didn't step away.

"I promised I wasn't going to touch you until you asked me to." That deep, velvet voice was a caress, teasing, stroking.

I laughed. "Why do you have to make this weird? There's moonlight, it's beautiful, and there are some freaking swans, so just kiss me already."

What are you doing?

I was in Monaco. It was so easy to pretend. And maybe, just maybe, for a moment, I wanted to be wanted. Was that so wrong?

Yes, you will regret this.

For once, I didn't care.

"I would like the record to show that you asked me to kiss you."

The smile made my lips twitch even as he leaned forward and pressed his lips to mine.

⚐

East

I didn't want to stop. She tasted like sunshine and Sunday mornings and bliss. Hell, I didn't think I *could* stop. She tasted so fucking good. All those nights I had lain there staring at my ceiling, swearing I imagined her smell, now I knew. I had imagined nothing. She tasted just as good as I'd remembered. I didn't want to take it too far or push too much, but I was like a starving man who had been denied the one thing he'd wanted for too long, and I was reckless. I dipped my tongue inside, searching, tasting. I might have taken the lead, but it was she who owned me. She was the one driving this. It was because of her that I felt this way.

Alarm bells made the hairs on my neck stand up at attention. My body hummed. But I was too far gone in the kiss to examine why. I just threw myself headlong into her taste and her flavor, and not giving a fuck where we were. Then I felt the hit. Nyla was being jerked away from me. For the first time since being inducted into the Elite, I was grateful for their barbarian training methods, forcing us out into the woods, in the cold and the rain, hungry and tired. Forcing us to learn to rely on our instincts, on our training, because to fight the two men who had made a grab for Nyla's bag, I needed all my wits.

But even better, as I whirled on the larger man to the left, I saw Nyla delivering several elbows. No qualms, just full lips set in grim determination.

I wanted to keep her safe. I wanted to tuck her behind me and take both of them on, but Nyla was a goddamn Interpol agent. She knew how to fight. She didn't need me in there protecting her. That was a recipe for disaster and a path that could get one or both of us killed. So I just focused on the man in front of me. I blocked his attempted hook shot to my temple.

I blocked wrist to wrist, keeping his arm far away from my body. I delivered a front kick just above his groin, doubling him over, and then sent an uppercut. He was big and meaty. Built like a fucking brick shit house, but I kept up the assault. Kept going. Strike. Strike. Jab. Kick. A knee kick and another hook brought him to his knees, and then I delivered a knee to his face. With a crack and a groan, he toppled over. I whirled on Nyla and her opponent. She had his arm behind his back. He was fighting and twisting, and Nyla grabbed him by the hair and leaned forward. "Stop fighting, or you'll hurt yourself."

"Fuck off, you bitch."

"God, you are so rude." She wrinkled her nose in distaste. "What do you want?"

"We were sent to deliver a message," her assailant snarled.

"You wanted to deliver a message?" she asked incredulously. "You came all this way and ruined a perfectly adequate kiss for a message? You couldn't have texted it?"

I threw my hands up. "What? Adequate?"

Her gaze flickered up to me, and she shrugged. "I mean, as billionaires go, you're okay."

A smirk played across my lips, but she was already leaning forward, speaking to asshole number two again. "Go on, tell me, what's the message?"

She had him in a good hold; any movement and he could break his arm. And by her pulling his hair back, he was forced to arch into a position of pain. If he wiggled, he'd hurt himself. "And I told you to fuck—" Nyla tipped his head back just a little bit more, and he howled. Grimacing, he gasped out, "Don't pursue the case, or we will kill your family."

Nyla laughed then. "Oh, you must not know who my family is. He has guns that are a lot more terrifying than you."

Then the idiot fought her hold, and sure enough, he dislocated his own shoulder. He shrieked and cried. From somewhere behind us came a crack, and a stone to the right of us splintered. I grabbed her, tugging her safely behind a car for cover. Frick then used his good arm to push himself up and ran over to Frack and dragged him toward the alley.

I started to go after them, but Nyla held me still. "Ah, hello, you idiot. Someone's shooting at us."

"They're getting away. Don't we need more answers?"

She stared at me. "They have guns. We don't fuck with guns."

I remembered then that she didn't know anything about who I really was, what I could do, just what I could get away with. To her, I was a guy who wore a suit. A billionaire with the jets, and the cars, and the fun. She didn't know me as one of the most powerful men in Britain, if not the world. She didn't know I was Elite. "Are you okay?"

She touched her jaw and cheekbone and then winced. "I'm fine. He hit like a bitch."

I bit back a chuckle. Considering I had witnessed her deliver some grade-A punches to him, I knew what this particular woman could do.

And then I saw the police lights. Someone in the building must have seen what was happening and called.

"Are you in the mood to have a conversation about this?"

She shook her head. "No. I would have to disclose this at Interpol. My father would be called, and I do not want to say a word about this just now."

I hesitated, then asked, "What did he mean?"

She frowned. "My father?"

I shook my head. "No, the guy whose arm you dislocated. What did he mean when he said stay away from the case?"

"I have no idea. I'm involved with dozens of cases."

Everything about her read insincerity. And when Nyla Kincade lied, there was nothing of the usual lightness and buoyancy in her expression. There was no enthusiasm in her look. And I could tell she was lying to me.

"Something about the painting?" I pushed.

"I told you, I don't know." She shrugged. "Besides, that would be an Interpol thing, and you're a civilian."

"Right, I'm a civilian. Come on, we can either stay here and have a long conversation with the authorities, or we can go have a soak in a tub."

I unfolded to my full height and reached for her hand. She didn't take it. Instead, she pushed herself up on her own. But when she made it to vertical, she winced. I reached for her and tucked her against my side. "You're not okay. Why are you being stubborn?"

"Yeah, see, I was trying to do that whole thing where I listen to my body and know what's going on with it, but I just got my ass kicked." She waved one hand from her head to her midsection. "All of this hurts."

"I know. Let's go. It's about time we get you cleaned up."

ELEVEN

Nyla

"**S**o, do you want to explain to me what the hell is going on?"

I stiffened at that. "There's nothing going on."

His chuckle was low as he poured antiseptic onto a cotton ball. Then he leaned forward, and the scent of the ocean assailed me. How could something smell so good and enticing as it pulled me in, tempting me to walk on its sandy shores, to dig my toes in. *Come on in, the water is fine.*

I shook my head. "I don't know what you want me to tell you, East. I don't know who they were."

"They were looking for something. What were they looking for?"

"Even if I knew, I wouldn't have the liberty to tell you that. I'm Interpol. You understand that, don't you?"

"Of course I understand that. I'm not an idiot. But I can't help you if you don't tell me something."

"Maybe it has to do with my case. Maybe it's related to the forgers," I lied smoothly. Lying was always a strength for me. It was easy. Blank face. Blank expression. Neutral. I'd been wearing a neutral expression so long that half the time I smiled and didn't recognize my face when it showed emotions. "Look, I don't know why we were attacked."

He nodded then muttered, "I'm sorry." It was so soft, I barely heard it.

"What?"

And then he applied the antiseptic.

I howled. "Jesus fucking Christ, aww that stings."

"And the lady curses like a bloody sailor. I'm thrilled. Still, I'm sorry. Look, I have to apply this on those injuries, or we could go to the hospital. You choose. I have rudimentary supplies in here, but you might need to see a doctor."

"I don't need a doctor." I tried to wiggle off the countertop, but his stupid big body blocked my way.

His green eyes went mostly dark, and his gaze bore into mine. "No. You, Nyla, will sit here. And you will let me finish taking care of you."

I tilted my chin up. "Well, you'll forgive me if I don't trust you. The last man that promised to take care of me stole my job and rubs his new girlfriend in my face every opportunity he gets. So, I'm not real keen on trusting you to take care of me, even with the simplest things like this." I didn't understand why I'd said those words to him, but something pulled them out of me.

He winced at that. "Wow, he did a number on you. You know, not everyone is untrustworthy."

"It's weird, because that's the exact opposite of what my father taught me."

He sighed. "Look, in this moment, I'm just here trying to get you cleaned up, okay? I'm trying to hurt you as little as possible. Can we agree on that?"

I shrugged. *Oh yeah, petulance, because that's the answer.* "Fine."

He nodded. Each press of antiseptic made me grit my teeth

and groan. His voice was soft. Crooning. "I'm sorry. Does anything else hurt?"

I shook my head, and all the while the scent of the ocean wrapped around me, and I could almost hear the waves as they crashed upon the shore, leaving seashells and seaweed in their wake. That's what it felt like with him. The crashing of a wave and the end of peace, but also the hint of excitement that the waves promised on a hot summer day.

Jesus Christ, I needed help.

You kissed him.

No, I did not kiss him, I allowed him to kiss me. That's different.

Uh-huh.

Fuck. I lifted my gaze to meet his, and of course, my eyes fell. His lips were so full and still slightly bruised from our kiss earlier.

God, that kiss.

The man's kisses were like the air that I breathed. Necessary for living, necessary for existing. His tongue sliding over mine had left me with this lingering feeling of awareness. And if I was being honest, the awareness had been there from the moment I'd first seen him. It was an awareness that I hadn't indulged much.

Liar.

Okay, fine. I had made some good use of my battery-operated boyfriend. Thanks to him, since our stupid fight in the park, I couldn't help having crazy longings. What was wrong with me? I knew exactly what he was, and I still found him irresistible.

You don't know exactly what he is. You have no evidence. Innocent until proven guilty.

That always irritated me about law enforcement. The presumption of innocence. Men like East Hale didn't become billionaires by playing it safe—or playing by the rules. And I would do well to remember that. Because if I kept messing with him, I was going to get burned.

But not tonight.

Press.

Hiss.

Dab.

Groan.

Swipe.

"Holy fuck."

East compressed his lips together. "Sorry. You've got a couple of scrapes here. I'm just trying to get them clean."

"You know, you don't have to do this. I am capable of minor field dressing." But I'd stopped trying to get away from his ministrations.

"I'm sure you are." Beneath his glittering eyes stretched a predatory smile. "Because, of course, you can do anything, can't you?"

"Yes, I can."

"Well, you're in luck. We're done." He tossed the used supplies in the trash, held up the gauze and bandaged up my jaw that had taken the majority of the scrapes and hits. He applied another butterfly suture to my hand, and then wrapped my right wrist. It wasn't broken. It wasn't even sprained, but it was irritated as hell. So yay, thanks to the sexy billionaire, my injuries were tended to.

"You're all set. You can go sulk in your room now."

A twinge of guilt pierced my heart. He was trying to help. "Look, I'm sorry. I just don't like being man-handled. And those assholes just now, I—" My nose stung, and my eyes started to water. What the fuck? I was not going to cry in front of this man who was basically a stranger.

Can a man be a stranger if you've gotten off to the thought of him?

Not at all relevant.

"Hey. Hey, now, it's okay."

He moved close and wrapped his arms around me, and God help me, I did feel safe. Which was my first mistake. It was so warm in his space. And wrapped there, I would start to think I was safe. I would start to think that nothing could touch me. The problem was I needed to know the truth about him before I could let myself surrender to feelings like that.

But once you knew the truth, there was no going back. There was no return to sender. Men like East Hale were not to be trusted. Handsome, rich, ambitious, and then add in a dose of his general shadiness. Absolutely not. I'd been digging for months into their little boys' club at the London Lords. The clubs they belonged to. There were whisperings of a secret society, but they were just whisperings. That big old estate out in the village of Virginia Water where I had arrested Bram Van Linsted was listed as a property of Ben Covington.

And I couldn't even fathom why the Van Linsteds seemed to have lived there or were arrested there for that matter. I'd checked into the deed of sale on the property, and it looked like it was a gift. I tried to dig up a little more, but no one would talk about it or the secret society that seemed to be connected with it, which really set my alarm bells off. Usually, there was someone willing to give up some information, but no one would talk, which only strengthened my suspicion that something was really going on there.

Worse yet, the London Lords had handed me one of the biggest cases of my career tied up in a neat little bow. Too neat. And I hadn't even been researching that case. So why hand me the Van Linsteds, the sex ring, the human trafficking, or leads on missing girls unless there was something bigger, something worse and far more insidious that they were hiding?

Or, like Denning says, you're just paranoid. And you are turning away a perfectly good dick.

Oh, Jesus Christ, speaking of dick, I could feel his body flush against mine, and between my thighs was the press of... wow. He wasn't even hard, but I felt the length of him in his trousers, and he was gifted.

Yeah, imagine if he was hard.

Stop.

I had to stop. This was ridiculous.

I wiggled and ducked my head. "Thank you. I'm not used to someone taking care of me."

He nodded slowly as his moss green eyes searched mine. "Of course." He stepped back.

The loss of his heat and his scent made me want to cry out and reach for him. Instead, I balled my hands into fists so I wouldn't make that mistake.

"Listen," he began, his tone brusque, all business. "Why don't you grab a shower, go to bed, and relax. Are you sure you don't want to call Interpol? It seems like something you should do. You're an agent. You were attacked in public."

I shook my head. "No. Not until we have evidence, because that's just me running home to my dad to cry."

He coughed at that. "Jesus, I get it. You're tough."

I lifted my brow. "Oh right, the billionaire lord, wants to laugh at me having to be tough?"

He furrowed his brow. "That's not what I meant."

"Well, it sure sounded like it. You have the privilege of never having people assume that you're weak because you're a woman, and that you can't lead because you're a woman, that you can't fight because you're a woman. And God help you if you're a woman of color. My best friend, Amelia, every day she walks in, she has to be perfect. No mistakes, because she won't get a second chance. So please, don't be flippant. I won't report this unless I have to or unless I *know* what the hell is going on. You don't turn up empty handed. That's a pussy move. Actually, no. Scratch that. That's a balls move. Pussies can handle a pounding. Balls, the slightest twitch, and they shrivel up and cry."

He just stared back at me, looking a little stunned at my outburst.

I hopped down off the counter. "I'm fine, thank you for your assistance. It's appreciated." I made sure I softened my voice then lifted my chin so he could see my eyes. "And about that kiss in the park. It was a momentary lapse of judgment. It won't happen again."

He nodded slowly as he licked his bottom lip. "That's too bad. And I want you to know, what you just said, I hear you. I was a dick just now. Never let it be said that I can't apologize and make an about face. You're right, it's not my perspective, and I am a rich ass. I do work hard for my company, but you're right. You probably have to work a hell of a lot harder. So, I fucked up, and I'm sorry. Just give a holler if you need anything." And then he turned around and walked out.

I closed the door with a soft click and leaned my forehead against it. Jesus Christ, why did he have to be so *everything* I wanted? I'd just checked him, and he took the check. He took it on the chin like a real man. Fuck. Fuck. Fuck. Fuck.

East Hale was the last kind of headache I needed.

No. Unfortunately, he's exactly the kind of headache you need.

TWELVE

East

The moment I returned to London, I knew the lads would want a status report. I just didn't expect to have to give that status report at six in the morning. And I didn't really have any answers.

I was only marginally surprised, but all the way pissed off, when at six o'clock the next morning, I woke to pounding on my fucking front door. The pounding forced me out of bed. I didn't have a housekeeper. I had a cleaning service that came every other day. I liked to cook, so I didn't have a chef. So unfortunately, I had to answer the door my goddamn self as well.

I didn't bother throwing on a shirt. I was irritated and tired. We'd taken the plane back from Monaco in the wee hours of the morning at Nyla's request. I'd crashed after arriving and making sure Nyla was settled and okay.

When I dragged the door open, I scowled. "The fucking office had better be on fire, mate."

Bridge leaned against my door and grinned. "What? You're not ready for a run?"

I glowered at him. He was wearing running gear, and my frown deepened. "What the fuck are you on about?"

He crossed his arms. "Mate, we've had this date every Monday morning for years. Get your kit on."

I scowled. "Not happening. Get out."

He laughed. "Uh-huh. No. And don't forget, I knocked as a courtesy. I have a fucking key."

I scowled at him. Maybe if I just went back to bed he would go away. It was worth a shot. So I left him standing in the doorway and headed back to the bedroom, about to climb back into bed. But then he grabbed my arm and shoved me toward my closet. "Kit, now."

"Fuck you."

"Anytime. Come on. You look like shit. That's the best time to run. That's when you need it."

"I hate you. If I put on my fucking running clothes, will you go away?"

"No. Also," he plopped onto one of the chairs I had in the corner, "I want to hear all about your getaway to Monaco. Just how close did you and Miss Kincade get on this trip?"

"Agent," I muttered under my breath.

He grinned. "That's right, *Agent* Kincade. It's funny you mentioned she's an agent, because who does she work for again?"

I rolled my eyes as I grabbed a pair of running shorts. I found an old ragged T-shirt and a clean pair of boxers, and then I shuffled into the bathroom. A change of clothes, a quick brush of my teeth, and a little ice-cold water scrubbed down my face, and I felt marginally better. When I came out, he grinned. "Still waiting to hear about Agent Kincade."

"Fuck you."

"I love when you tell me I'm right."

"I said no such thing."

I pulled on my socks and grabbed my trainers. "Are you fucking ready?"

"Jesus Christ, someone is a bit touchy, aren't you?"

"I'm not sure I like you."

"You've been saying that for years," he said with a chuckle.

"No, honestly," I said. "I'm pretty sure I'm going to get a new best mate."

Bridge shrugged. "Well, there is a replacement model downstairs waiting for us. I was the one lucky enough to be sent to come get you. Are you going to replace him too?"

I nodded mutinously. "Yeah, I think I will."

Bridge just shrugged. "Yeah, but who else would have you?"

As soon as my shoes were on, Bridge shoved me out into the kitchen, grabbed three Granola bars and a bottle of water, and he was out the door. I could only manage short grunts as he spoke, asking me many Nyla questions, which I ignored or diverted.

But once downstairs, I found a smiling, bed-tousled Ben. "Oh, he did manage to get you out of bed. Excellent, let's go."

I scowled at him. "I hate you."

Ben nodded. "I feel like you hate me every other week. Honestly, I'm not fussed."

"Christ. Where the fuck is Drew? Why isn't he the one being tortured?"

Ben shrugged. "Poor Alice is teething. Apparently, he hasn't been sleeping at all. So it's just us this morning."

Bridge practically frog-marched me out the giant glass rotating door. For once I was pleased with London's dreary weather, which meant no bright piercing sunlight to set my headache off. "Let's just get this over with."

Ben smiled. "Oh, not so fast. Before we start running, spill your guts about Nyla Kincade."

I bit into my granola bar. "I don't know anything more than I told you the other day. She's on a forgery case. I took her to see AJ, figuring she could help. That's all. But now I'm digging. Because I think she has other reasons she's not objecting to my help. She will stop at nothing when she's got a scent."

Ben and Bridge exchanged glances. "Uh-huh." Ben said. "Do we go back to her father?"

I shook my head. "No. I'm going to observe. See if she drops any clues as to what else she's investigating."

Bridge started to slow jog and I groaned. My legs felt like lead. The last thing I wanted to do was run.

Perhaps you shouldn't have had so many Irish coffees on the flight back.

That was the problem with being shoved in a sardine can with Agent Kincade. I wanted her. But I was also worried. Worried about what she was looking into and about just how much she'd heard from that bug she'd planted on me before I disabled it.

I was worried about what kind of trouble she was in, if her case was dangerous, and what that meant for her. I wasn't sure why there was some primal part of me that wanted to take care of her. Protect her. It was also the same part that wanted to club her over the head and drag her off to a very large bed. But I wasn't telling my idiot mates about that. "I'll keep an eye on her." I rushed to add. "From a distance of course."

Ben frowned. "Actually, it would be in our best interest if you kept a much closer watch."

We stopped at a light and I frowned at him. "Wait, so let me get this straight, my Director Prime is telling me to shag the Interpol agent? The agent who's been far too curious about the Elite for, I don't know, two months?"

Bridge interjected, "Your Director Prime is not saying that, because he's not an arsehole. But I am. I'm the mate who knows you well and knows that she is exactly your type, and all

I'm saying is that if you are shagging her, you might give her something else entirely to focus on."

I shook my head. "You know what? You lot have the worst love advice. Remember Camilla?"

Bridge groaned. "Oh, come on, I gave you one bad piece of advice. One time."

"I've never forgotten it. I believe you said, 'You've got to hoover the clit,' right? Because they like that."

Bridge groaned. "Look, mate, what the fuck did I know? I was seventeen. You were taking advice from an idiot."

"Yeah, I know that. I won't make that mistake again."

Ben just laughed. "Bridge, you were such a git."

Then he frowned, thinking of advice Bridge had given him. "I feel like you told me to stick my finger in Marley Adamson's bum too."

Bridge laughed. "Yeah, but didn't she like that?"

Ben snorted a laugh as he picked up his pace. "Yes, but she preferred that only when she was coming. At first she was livid."

"I still hold it was solid advice," Bridge mumbled.

I shook my head. "I feel like this just caused me to never believe a word you say, Bridge."

Bridge rolled his eyes. "You know what, you're just jealous because you know I'm better with women than the two of you."

Both Ben and I coughed. Neither one of us going anywhere near the possibility of detonating the 'him and Mina' bomb. Ben and I knew exactly what the deal was with Mina. But we'd made a promise, along with Drew, to never, not once, say a word. So, we were keeping our oath.

As the run continued, we made our way over toward Primrose Hill. Bridge pushed the pace. He was the marathoner of fucking London and loved running even more than I did. Ben could take it or leave it. But Bridge, that asshole loved to run. And I was too competitive to let him win.

When we reached Primrose Hill, Bridge called time. It was all I could do not to collapse in front of them from the heat. They never would have let me live that down. So, I pretended I was stretching while I forced air into my lungs and prayed to dear God that Ben was going to call a halt to this ridiculous pace Bridge was setting.

Instead, he kept up the inquisition. "So okay, real question. How big of a problem is Agent Kincade going to be for us?"

"Too early to tell."

Bridge scowled at that. "What do you mean, it's too early to tell? We need to figure it out. It's your job to keep her distracted."

My dick seemed to like that idea. It twitched in my shorts, and I scowled at myself. My shit was complicated enough. I did not need her to further complicate my life. But still, I wanted her, so there was that.

"Look, like I said, I have it under control. When Ben said he had Olivia under control, didn't we trust him?"

Bridge screwed up his face into the universal *are you fucking kidding me* expression.

Ben laughed. "I completely had her handled."

Bridge snorted at that. "No. No, you did not. *She* had *you* handled. Pretty much like I assume Agent Kincade has East handled."

"I'm not handled like Ben was handled. We just have to be more careful. And I'm not trying to shag her."

Liar.

"If you say so," Ben said as he stood. Bridge turned to me before he started running again. "Okay, you're not shagging her.

But, you know, if you were thinking about it, how bad do you want her?"

I frowned at that. "I don't know what you mean."

His pursed lips told me he was going to ask an actual important question, one that wasn't about giving me shit. "How much do you want her? Enough to make a mistake? Because that's the real question."

I had to think it through. I had a lot of balls in the air, especially now that I knew she might be in trouble, and I couldn't very well sit back and let her be in trouble. "I haven't thought about it."

Bridge nodded. "If you say so. But if you want her, you need to be more careful. Shag her if you want. But if you get close, just know she's not dumb. She's not like the usual sort of air-headed models that are stunningly beautiful but give no shits about anything other than their Instagram followers. She's smart. She's determined. And she can put an end to the secrecy we need to maintain. So do what you want, but fucking be careful. Everyone's future is on the line."

I stood up to my full height and met his gaze. Sometimes, even though he was Bridge and seemingly emotionless, he saw far too much. "She's not a problem for me."

It should have worried me how easily the lie chirped off of my lips, but it didn't, which was the most concerning thing of all.

THIRTEEN

East

This was a mistake. I knew it was a mistake. But still, I couldn't help myself, and I had valid reasons for being there. First, I wanted to see her and make sure she was all right. Second, my dick was still hard. No. No. That wasn't it. Second, I had someone for her to talk to. Someone AJ had recommended who'd attended Slade School of Art and had managed to make a name for herself with her raw talent and a knack for copying the greats. That knack had landed her in prison. But now that she was out, she worked for a prestigious insurance company, picking out some of the very same forgeries and helping them spot others. I'd called in a favor, and I knew she could probably be helpful to Nyla.

Third, I was still hard.

I tried to shove that thought aside. It wasn't helpful. It accomplished nothing, except to remind me what Nyla's bottom lip tasted like when I sucked on it. To make me remember how soft that patch of skin just on the inside of her elbow was and that she was completely untouchable. I liked it that way. This wasn't some woman who I was going to burn the panties off of.

Nyla Kincade had seen it all. And she was unimpressed by any of it.

The guy at the reception desk led me back to the double-pane glass doors toward the offices and down a long corridor that had names on each glass door we passed. When I finally saw Nyla's name, my heart rate kicked into full gallop.

Easy does it.

I forced myself to take a long deep inhale, just so I wouldn't have to smell her when I stepped inside. That would be for the best. I knocked on her door as I opened it, and she took a moment to lift her head. When she did, the shock was evident. But then there was a hint of something. Was that a smile maybe?

Don't get ahead of yourself. This one is tough as nails and likely to be a lot of trouble.

She waved me in, and I stepped inside. "So, this is where all the Interpol magic happens?"

She sat back and spread her arms. "Oh yes, clearly. Magic happening."

"Why do you look like you were busy engraving symbols onto a pad of paper?"

"What are you doing here, East?"

"Ah, I do love that we have graduated to my actual name, and not Mr. Hale, or that billionaire over there, or my personal favorite, jackass. I'm so glad we have progressed from jackass."

"What is it about you that won't take no for an answer?"

I shrugged. "I'm just really stubborn. That's my greatest weakness."

She shook her head. "You know what, I don't really have time for this. As you can see, I have a lot to do. But I'm not a rude person, so I guess I should say thank you for the visit, however, I really am swamped."

"This isn't actually a social call."

"Right. You could have fooled me. If you wanted a tour of the offices, all you had to do is ask."

I laughed. "The thing is, as much fun as a tour with you would be, that's not why I'm here."

She set her pen down and leaned forward. "Oh, yeah? Then why are you here?"

"I thought that maybe you would like to meet Marielle Lipton."

Her brows lifted, and her shoulders sagged briefly as though I'd knocked the wind out of her sails. "*The* Marielle Lipton?"

I nodded. "Yup. I managed to arrange an appointment with her this afternoon if you think you have time."

She gave me a look that said, oh, she would find time for this. "How do you know Marielle Lipton? She hasn't taken any interviews in, God, three years, since she was released from prison, and certainly not one with Interpol because, after all, she's free now. Free to become a valuable member of society. How in the world did you get her to agree to talk to me?"

"Let's just say I know people in high places."

"I swear to God, is one of your friends someone prominent in the government or something? I mean, just how rich are you three?"

I laughed. "Yeah, money helps. I'm not going to lie. But also I called in a favor."

The crease between her brows showed up again. "Why?"

I shrugged, keeping it cool. "Just because. So, do you want to meet her or not?"

She pushed to her feet. "Okay fine, how do you always know what to tempt me with?"

"Well…" I grinned at her. "I know what you like."

I knew I was pouring on the flirtation all the way, and she knew it too, because she just rolled her eyes and laughed.

"You cannot help yourself, can you? You literally can't. If there's a woman in the room, you just have to flirt."

"Okay, fine. I like flirting with you. That's person specific, not gender specific. Um, also, I am very good at it."

She choked a cough.

"Give me some credit. Come on, let's see if we can catch your forger. Or at least get you some help."

As we stepped out of her office, a man came striding down the hall, and I could tell from her body language that Nyla instantly tensed up. I knew he must be the ex she'd talked about on the plane. Her boss.

Glued to his side as if by surgery was a brunette with big blue eyes and clear pale skin, but she lacked that fire that Nyla had. I knew the guy was Denning Sinclair because I had just done some discreet digging on my own. And the woman with him was Hazel Frost, his new girlfriend. How he thought he could do better than Nyla was beyond me.

Nyla stiffened as she closed and locked her office door. When she turned to face the approaching duo, she murmured, "Denning," and then signaled for me to move on.

But Denning stopped, his gaze dissecting me like an insect. "Where are you two off to?"

God, what a prick.

He reached out his hand to shake mine, and I just watched him and narrowed my gaze. Ben, Bridge, and I had decided not to use the Elite's powers of influence for evil, but at this moment, I really, really wanted to. I finally accepted his handshake and said, "Ah, Denning Sinclair. Pleasure. I'm East Hale." I had the incomprehensible urge to kick his teeth in.

His brows drew down an inch. "What are you doing with Nyla here?"

I shrugged. "Well, I was lost. She was helping me find my

way. Now, if you'll excuse us, we have somewhere we need to go." And with that, I gently tugged at Nyla's elbow, guiding her toward the exit.

Once we were outside, Nyla breathed a sigh of relief. "You know what, it's good to see Denning slapped in the face like that, but he's my boss. And you can't just antagonize him." Her lips twitched as she did her level best to not smile.

I shrugged at that. "I can, and I will. He's a twat. And he's discourteous with women. So, what do you say we go and meet the forger now?"

❧

Nyla

Outside in the foggy London gray, I paused on the sidewalk on my way to the sleek black sedan that was waiting at the curb. "I'm not going anywhere with you until you tell me where we're going."

East's lips curved into a wry smile. "You never do anything the easy way, do you?"

"Nope. I don't." I folded my arms across my chest. Then I realized that it probably amplified my breasts, and I dropped them. Meeting his gaze, I said, "What are you doing here?"

"I already told you. I'm here to help you with your case."

"Yeah, but why?"

He tucked his hands into the pockets of his fitted suit. Three pieces with some kind of plaid design. There were vibrant strips in the plaid of green and blue. It brought out the color in his eyes. His shirt was crisp white, and he wore no tie. He could have easily been headed out to conquer Fleet Street, or on a date, or on a night out with the lads. He looked casual and sexy. Which was bad for me.

He was basically sex on a stick.

I was not going to be tempted. Just because I'd been weak in Monaco, that didn't mean I had no willpower. "Look, I don't need your help."

"Yes you do. You needed it before Monaco. You need it now."

I resented him being right. "Fine, I did need your help. And I appreciate it. I didn't anticipate any help beyond the introduction to your sister."

He approached me, and ever wary, I took a step back. When he was close it was harder to focus. But he wouldn't be deterred. He reached out and touched my elbow, gently trying to guide me to the car. "Nyla take the help, okay?"

"Maybe I'm wary because I don't know what strings come with it. One day in Monaco with you, and we were attacked. People are telling me to stop looking into my case. Something is up with you, and I'm caught in the crosshairs. The question is why?"

He nodded slowly. "I see someone who clearly needs help. But you know what? I'll tell you the truth. What's up is that I can't get you out of my head. You know what else is up? That despite myself, despite how bad it will be for me, I can't seem to stop thinking about you. So, instead of being smart, instead of doing what is wise and prudent, I'm here trying to help you." He emphasized that *you* by pointing at me. He did not look pleased about it.

"Tell me what's going on. Who are the London Lords?"

He gave me a brusque nod. "We are hotel magnates."

"Yeah, but who are you *really*?"

He flashed a grin. "Hotel magnates. If you think the answer's going to change just because you keep asking the question, you would be incorrect. So ask again, and again, and again. Because then I will say the words *hotel magnates* until you learn to scream them in bed. That is who we are."

"You think I don't realize you helped me with my last case because it served your purposes?"

"Or maybe it's always good to play nice with law enforcement. You never know when you'll be in a spot and need a friend."

"Is that really it?" I narrowed my gaze at him.

"My God, you are persistent, obstinate, tenacious."

"Those all mean the same thing." I barely resisted the temptation to stick my tongue out at him.

He grinned again, and my resolve nearly dissipated. Jesus Christ, he was sexy. And I could remember the slide of his tongue into my mouth. The way he coaxed it. The way he'd gripped my hips with those big hands as he rocked me over him. The low rumble in his chest when he knew that I was getting off.

I wanted *him*. I also knew he was absolutely dangerous.

So then why can't you stay away?

That was the thing about bad boys, right? They were enticing because you knew you shouldn't. And I knew I shouldn't. East Hale was going to be a problem. He was up to something. And I needed to find out what it was.

But that smaller voice deep down inside said that if he wanted to really hurt me, he would've done it by now. He'd had an opportunity in Monaco.

I could choose to trust him now. The choice was mine to make.

"One thing…" I inhaled sharply. "If you want to watch me, tell me the cameras are on. Don't be a creeper."

He lifted a brow. "You want me to watch you?" His voice was low and barely a feral growl.

Excellent. "I just want to know when I'm being watched. Who knows, you might get a show."

And then I eased past him to the car. The driver had already opened the door, waiting for me to slip in.

When East turned around, my gaze slid down that very fine form in that gorgeous suit to the very noticeable bulge in his trousers.

Yeah well, if I was feeling needy, then he should feel it too.

When he slipped into the seat behind me, he muttered instructions to the driver and settled back into his seat. "Nyla Kincade, you are trouble."

"You are *not* the first man to tell me that."

"I will be the last though."

I chuckled at that. "You wish."

He groaned and shifted in his seat. "Yeah, I do."

I had no idea what to make of that. For most of the short fifteen-minute drive, I was running over our interactions in my head. And no way was this situation with him in any way healthy. Nope. Completely unhealthy. I'd been warned off him and his friends, but I'd found a loophole. I was exploiting that loophole. But so far, I hadn't found anything on them. Nothing. Which was disconcerting because they were pulling strings. I felt like I was a dancing puppet, and I couldn't figure out where the strings were to cut them.

And then there was this other piece of him, the part that acted like he wanted me. Like I was the one woman on this planet that he wanted the most. I knew it was a game. I could see people like him playing these games with unsuspecting women. They probably got bored with their rich debutantes and socialites. Time to slum it for a while. We pulled up to a brick row home in Victoria, and I frowned. "Where are we?"

He laughed. "God, you ask a lot of questions. Just go with the flow. I promise you it won't hurt."

Go with the flow. Right. "Uh-huh."

I slipped out of the car and followed behind him to the tidy brick house. At the top of the stairs he pressed the doorbell. When the door opened, a middle-age man stood there. Tall, lean in his youth probably, but it had now given way to just being slight and slim. "East Hale. Didn't plan on seeing you again for a while."

"Ryder Stone. How's it going mate?"

"Well, it was going great until I found you on my doorstep. Will, I be needing a solicitor?"

East put up his hands. "Ah, Ryder, you wound me. As if I would bring Old Bill to your door. Honestly, what do you think of me? Besides, I've brought a friend. You're not going to make me look bad, are you?"

Ryder rolled his eyes. "Better come in then."

When we strolled in, we were led into a back room that was more office than anything. He offered to take my coat and bring us tea. Once seated, Ryder's gaze swept over me. "Miss, you are stunningly beautiful. And I would embarrass myself by tripping over what to say to you, but, and don't take this the wrong way, you have the stink of the Bill."

I grinned then. "That's because I'm Interpol."

Ryder's gaze shifted to East. "And you said you wouldn't bring Old Bill to my door."

East chuckled low. "Technically she's not Old Bill. She's Interpol. It's different."

Ryder sat back. "I don't know what he's told you. But whatever you're looking for, I don't have it, I don't know anything about it, and I can't help you."

"Now, Ryder, don't be like that. Help us out. Nyla's got a case. And you may or may not have any information about it, but you could help her at least identify a few things."

I looked between them. "I'm sorry, but who are you? What do you do?"

Ryder shrugged. "Well love, I used to be one of the best fences in London. You name it; I could move it. But I had a specialty. It was jewels. I used to have a toy store. It was my family's really. And I would smuggle jewels in and out with the toys. Until I got busted."

I frowned. "You know, I vaguely remember a case like that."

He nodded. "Yeah. And they never did find the jewels. But I got busted on a technicality. And I had two choices: Go away for a long time, or give up the money and the bigger fish in exchange for my relative freedom and a whole new gig."

"You took the deal?"

"That I did, madam. I am not cut out for prison life."

I sighed. "Well not many people are. I vaguely remember the case. You were part of the Wilson crew?"

"No, I was never part of their crew. I got drafted in their service, as they say, when I was too young to know any better. I was just the fence. But the Wilsons, they were the hardcore type. Murderers, rapists, you name it. If it was violent, they were into it. They happened to like pretty bits and bobs, too. But I wasn't down for anything violent you see. It was easy giving them up."

"Wow, so you're a grass."

Ryder stiffened then. "Yeah, I grassed them. I like to call it *surviving*."

East nodded. "Ryder was instrumental in the Monaco case. He helped us find at least part of the crew that pulled the job."

I sat forward on my seat then. "Do you know *how* they pulled it off?"

He shook his head. "Not really. My job was finding lower value gems. Ones that could be cut to look like the real deal. They were looking for the best quality for the least money, and I was able to find them. I think they already had the art forger on hand, and they had a man inside replacing the pieces after they'd been authenticated. I had a buyer set for the originals, at least for the jewelry pieces. But the buyer wanted the whole collection, not just certain pieces. So the mistake was waiting. If we would have just offloaded some of those, made out with some of the money, we'd have been golden. But that's not how it worked out. We got nicked. Not for the jewels, mind you, but for the art. Then the whole bloody thing unraveled."

I frowned. "And their man inside talked."

Ryder nodded. "Yeah. Started giving us all up, so when The Bill showed up on my doorstep, I sang like a bird. Returned the jewels and never saw a stitch of money."

"Do you know who they were using for making the fake jewels?"

He nodded. "I can get you a name. I don't know if they're still working or not. I'm out of the business."

I glanced around at the fine oak furnishings. "Dare I ask, what is your new business?"

Ryder grinned. "Well, I'm an appraiser, of course."

I blinked. And then I couldn't help it; I laughed. "You're kidding?"

"No, not kidding at all. I have the contacts, I know the industry, and obviously, I have the experience. That's legit, all above board, but I have a new name. It was part of my deal. So I keep my nose clean and stay out of trouble. I have a nice life."

I knew I had my work cut out for me. I needed to speak to what was left of the Wilson Crew. "Thank you. This is further than I've been able to get along on my own."

He nodded. "Yeah well, Mr. Hale here is responsible for my new life. So, if he comes calling, I have to deliver the favor."

I turned to East. "Why give him his new life? After all, he tried to steal from you and your family."

East shrugged. "Well, the Wilsons did. Ryder was just a

fence. And you never know when you're going to need someone like him in your life."

Ryder stood to go get us that number, and I turned my full attention to East. "So what, you're trading favors?"

East shrugged again. "Sometimes. Not everything is black and white, Agent Kincade. There are shades of gray. And, Ryder is not violent. Yes, sometimes he will take the easy way out. He's lazy. But he's also shrewd, and he's a survivalist. I like survivors. He didn't dick us about when we came calling, either. He knew exactly what we wanted, gave us what we needed, and made his deal. I can respect that."

"Wow. You really don't believe in law and order, do you?"

I had dedicated my whole life to putting the criminals away. To getting the bad guy. Things had been cut and dry my whole life. But for him? Shades of gray, like he said.

"Unfortunately the world isn't cut and dry. You lose if that's the game you play. I don't like losing. Like I said, you needed something, and I was able to provide it because I didn't cut him loose then. That's how it works. It's how most of the world works. Not many of us have the luxury of seeing the world in black and white."

"So, you're like my fairy godfather?"

He grinned. "I'm not wearing a tutu."

"No, you're wearing a bespoke suit. So I'm just supposed to trust you."

"Well, it's called surrender. You will either trust me one day or you won't. But for now, you have something that you can use. And I won't even ask for a favor in return."

FOURTEEN

Nyla

I liked him. Damn him and his stupid charm. It was hard not to like him.

Despite every instinct for self-preservation, I liked him.

He had more charm than one single man should possess. He was beautiful in that kind of way that made women stare. And he damn well knew it.

But he was also thoughtful. And smart. And considerate. And he was loyal. I could tell by the way he spoke about his mates, his sister, his mother.

The one person he did not talk about was his father. The man was good at getting information out of a stone though. We talked about my mother more, but he also rooted around my feelings toward my father. I was less than forthcoming with those feelings.

And he talked about his family... clearly leaving out his own bits. But it felt real. It felt like *connection*.

All that *and* he had taken me around to some of the best former forgers and fences in London. After Ryder we'd gone to see Marielle Lipton, the forger. Also a few other forgers and safe crackers. From the shady and dodgy to the absolutely wealthy.

Spending a day with him was like running around with Gatsby. There wasn't a single person he didn't know. Or one who didn't meet him with a grin.

And every single one of them had an East story. One where he helped them or got them out of trouble. It was like he'd taken me to everyone who could vouch for him or mark him as a stand-up bloke.

I'd expected the beautiful fancy galleries we'd toured. I'd expected the lessons on art and authentication. I hadn't expected the street artists and the students and the inspiration.

Now it had turned into… what? A date?

Sadly a day with him was the closest thing resembling a real date I'd been on since Denning and I broke up. When he'd suggested we pop up for a bite to eat, I had said yes, instead of the 'No, thank you so much for your time, Mr. Hale, but I have everything I need now' response I should have given.

I wanted to be near him. The memory of the other night, us rolling in the grass as the sprinklers rained down on us made me want to laugh more than once. And he'd caught my eye more than once to tease me and say I still had grass in my hair.

"So, are you going to tell me how you did it?"

He grinned at me then. "Oh what, you mean get a bird's eye view into your flat?"

"Yes, actually, I would very much like to know that."

He laughed. "You've been dying to ask that all day, haven't you? But then I would be revealing one of my secrets. And as it is, you've already started closing the blinds, so that's going to make it more difficult."

I narrowed my gaze. "You recognize I know how to shoot a gun, right?"

Another laugh, this one a bit deeper. "Yes, you've reminded me more than once."

"Are you going to tell me now?"

He took a sip of his scotch as we stood at the bar waiting for our table, totally ignoring my question. Then he popped off into this hidden little alcove. The lighting was definitely a mood. Not quite romantic, but the candlelight sure lent itself to clandestine affairs. He had stepped away at the far end of the bar, where the bartender, who clearly knew him on sight, called something back to the kitchen area. Next thing I'd knew, upscale bar food had appeared. Scotch eggs and sausage wraps, but these were different from the normal bar fair. They had green onions, sliced finely on top of them, and what appeared to be mango chutney, and God, all of it was so delicious.

"Just because we've broken bread together doesn't mean I'm going to tell you all my trade secrets." East said as he laughed.

"I figure if we've nearly shagged in the grass I'm deserving of your secrets."

He laughed once more, that dark rich laugh that raised my temperature and shot tingles of awareness through my system. Then, of course, it drew my attention to his Adam's apple, and then up along his jaw, and to his lips.

Stop looking at his lips. You can't look at his lips. You cannot trust him.

I snapped my gaze to his eyes then. His eyes were safer. But then he turned his attention to me and narrowed his gaze. "PS, I caught you looking."

I rolled my eyes. "You caught nothing."

He lifted one shoulder in a nonchalant shrug. "If you say so. I know I'm very nice to look at."

"My God, you are such an arsehole."

"You know, it's strange. I've been told that before."

"Again, I'm not shocked." I wiped my hand on my napkin. "Fine, if you won't tell me how you've been playing peep show with me, what were you were doing when I ran into you at the party?"

His grin was sly, and he asked, "How are your appetizers?"

"No you don't. Don't you dare change the subject."

He chuckled. "Okay. I'll tell you. But you tell me first."

"Not a chance."

"I guess we'll both have to live with the curiosity."

"Just tell me. You know you want to."

"Go ahead and admit it, Nyla… I'm not so bad."

He's not. "Yes, you are. You know what? I'll tell you something you want to know if you'll admit the secret society really exists."

More laughter. God, he was just full of laughs, wasn't he? "Why are you so obsessed with the *secret society?*" He used air quotes when he said the last two words.

"Call it a hunch, but I know something is not right. This would all go faster if you tell me what it is."

"I'm telling you the London Lords are three businessmen running hotels. That's all."

"Uh-huh. And I'm an Amish virgin."

His gaze flicked over my body as if to call out the lie with an unspoken 'the hell you are.' But instead, his voice was low when he said, "Well now, that would be a damn shame."

I shrugged. "I had a case when I was in the US. Nasty stuff. Crazy international crime ring. It was quite exciting actually. An Amish gang had paired themselves with an Irish gang to sell guns and other weapons."

He whistled low. "You know, it's no wonder you have no faith in humanity. The kind of things you see, I can only imagine."

"That would be accurate. My faith right now is a little derailed."

"Well hopefully, I'll restore some of your faith in my abilities by finding you delicious restaurants."

"Yeah, what is this place exactly?"

"I call it 'The Hiding Spot.'"

"Is that its real name?"

Another flash of his grin and I was pretty sure my panties were in that melted category. "The restaurants and the decor in the hotels are my purview. So whenever we come across some new and fresh chef that we want to try out, I put them back in the kitchens here."

"So this is a restaurant?"

"Yes. Actually, it's more of a proving ground. He does this British comfort thing. You should eat his chocolate pie. It's honestly complete insanity. It made me want to slap my nanny."

I choked a laugh then. "Of course, you had a nanny."

He winked at me. "Didn't everyone?"

I laughed. "No. The rest of us are mere mortals."

His phone rang, and he glanced down at it. "Um, would you be all right if I just step in one of the back rooms and take this call?"

I nodded. "Actually, can I get another plate of this?"

He signaled to our bartender/waiter who gave a nod and winked at me. And then he was gone around the corner. And for the first time all day, I felt like I could take a deep breath. God, that nervous energy being around him felt like first-date jitters. Butterflies in the tummy. Anticipation dancing and skipping and jumping all over my skin and my nerve endings.

See? You do like him.

No, I did not.

All of a sudden, someone slid into the seat across from me as the bartender brought me another plate. "Here you go, miss."

He nodded to the man sitting across from me then. "Mate,

I'm not serving you anymore. Three drinks, maximum. It's how the boss likes it."

"Just give me my fucking drink."

I slid my gaze over. "That seat is taken."

The man that turned his gaze back on me was handsome in that sort of overly polished sort of bland way. Neatly trimmed hair, pale blue eyes, decent jaw. But something about the roundness of it suggested that there would be softness there in the future.

"Well aren't you a pretty thing? Been left all alone, have you?"

He smelled like gin and poor decisions.

"Listen, I just want to enjoy my food and drink. That's all."

"Well, in that case, you're going to enjoy my company too."

"No, I'm really not. That seat is taken, and I advise that you vacate it before my companion realizes you've plopped yourself in it."

"Now, now, I'm just being friendly. Why is it you can't accept a friendly chat?" He leaned forward over the table. "What is wrong with women these days? Either you chat to a woman and she thinks you're ready for fucking marriage and kids, or you chat to a woman and she's a complete cunt that thinks she's God's gift." The sour liquor smell hit me in the face as he wagged a finger back and forth. "You're not God's gift. You're not even pretty. I'm merely bored and trying to get the fucking bartender to serve me another drink."

"Fabulous. In that case, you won't mind me telling you to go fuck off out of my friend's seat." I met his gaze levelly and did not waver once.

And maybe that was my mistake, because that classic mask of irritation and annoyance mixed with drinking bravado was a recipe for disaster.

"Look, you stay, and I'll move." I stood and picked up my purse, but then he grabbed my elbow hard. I glanced down at his hand. "You'll want to remove that."

"Oh yeah? Make me."

I placed my free hand on top of his and easily used my index and middle fingers to turn his wrist. He yowled, and then I added pressure to his joint for good measure.

"I already told you once, so don't make me repeat myself. Do not touch me."

"You're a cunt."

"Well, I mean, I do have one. I think you're misunderstanding the grammar here."

"You—" He didn't get to finish because somehow, he was being thrown back. It happened so quickly. He was wrenched out of my hold and his back was against the wall, and then someone in a suit was choking him out.

"Holy shit, East. East, stop. Stop. Stop. Stop. I'm fine. Honestly, I am fine. You can let him go."

"Jameson, you fucking touch her again, and I *will* kill you."

"Already been there, mate."

East squeezed harder, and the guy's eyes started to bulge out. "Hey, look at me. We don't want to do this. Not publicly, not here, not anywhere. Let him go. I'm fine."

When that still didn't work, I stepped between them, wedging myself between East's hands as he asked, "What the fuck are you doing? Get out of the way."

"Look at me, I'm fine. Let him go."

His gaze met mine, and he blinked several times and then released the hold.

From some shadowy corner to my left, a nondescript bouncer appeared. "Easy boss. I have him."

East released the other man then. His gaze met mine and

dropped before I could get an answer. Then he turned and strode out, leaving me standing there at the bar wondering what the fuck had just happened.

&

Nyla

Thanks to the bartender, I found him on the roof, the wind slightly rustling his dark hair. "Are you okay?"

He didn't turn around. "Yup, fine."

I sighed. Great. Taciturn. I was used to taciturn. "I'm just saying, if you're not fine, I might make a half-decent listener."

"I'm fine, Nyla."

"East, you're not fine. You almost took that idiot's head off. I mean, I don't know him, but based on what he did earlier, he seems like kind of a twat." I raised a brow in query. "So I assume he deserved it?"

"That's a safe assumption to make."

"Great, he deserved it. But then, why did he deserve it? And are you okay, or are you going to leave here, break into his place, and kill him?" I held up a hand. "If you are, I advise that you don't tell me because I feel like I'll need to report that."

I heard that chuckle, the small exhalation that was part laugh, part irritation. "I wish I could. But I can't let my personal feelings about him get in the way."

"Personal feelings. Okay." I gestured toward the rooftop door. "I handle men like him every day."

"I know."

"Okay, so as long as you know that."

As I spoke, I moved closer and closer. "So, do you want to tell me what's going on?"

"Sorry, I scared you. I just—" His voice broke off.

"You just what?"

His voice lowered to a growl. "I hated seeing his hands on you."

"I—" What was I supposed to do with that? "I'm just saying how you handled it was not ideal. I think you owe me some kind of an explanation."

"Do I?" He turned his gaze on me. "You said it yourself, we're barely even friends."

I winced at that. "I was being facetious. I appreciate you stepping in. I do. But honestly, I thought you were going to stab him in the eye. So I'd really like an explanation. I don't know anything about you, East Hale. So, tell me something about you so that I don't have to disappoint you and tell you that you are never going to see me again. Unless, of course, if I'm going to put you in jail."

He laughed then. "You don't want me in jail. I'm too pretty to go to jail."

I rolled my eyes as I approached the railing and placed my elbow on it. "So talk to me."

"I went to school with him. I've known him forever. I am pretty certain he assaulted my sister."

My mind spun. Of all the things I'd expected him to say, that wasn't even on my list. Anything but that. I thought back on how that guy had been too handsy, a little bit drunk, and not listening to my more-than-firm no. And the look on East's face as he safely extricated me and then rounded on the other guy like he could have put a hole in that bloke's face and not thought about it twice. Which was not the picture of elegance that East presented.

East Hale was old money. His family were gentry. His mother was an heiress of a vast art fortune. So where had that bottled up anger been hiding?

"It's fine," he insisted. "I'm fine. You don't have to do this, check on me. You're the one who should be checked on. Are you okay?"

I crossed my arms and nodded. Because somehow, up here, with nothing but the city lights of London below us, I could tell the truth. I *had* been a little scared. Not that I didn't know what to do or how to handle somebody like that, but that flare of fear that women are told to swallow, that we're told to never feel, that moment when someone wanted to use a woman's body against her will, it was very real. It was something male agents never had to contend with. But every single female agent did. "The point is, I'm fine now. I'm okay. You were there, thankfully. Though we both know I can handle men like that. Everything turned out exactly like it was supposed to."

"Yeah, I suppose."

"Tell me about your sister?"

He shrugged. "I don't know. AJ was like every other big sister, I suppose. Annoying. As a kid I desperately wanted her to see me, you know? She was always off at some tennis tournament or something. And there are some moments where I had to miss football matches and things because she was so damn good at tennis, and I really had to be there and see it. There were moments I was jealous of her. I always thought I was never going to be some wildly famous football player. But she—she could have gone all the way. But, you know, other than the annoying brother-sister stuff, we were close."

"You two seem so close now."

He nodded. "We are. I don't know, though. Something changed that night. There was a party at our house. Mom and Dad... We'll just say they were noticeably absent for a lot of our teenage years. God only knows where they were at the time. I still remember the look on AJ's face after Jameson left her bedroom. She looked shell-shocked. I didn't know what to do or what to say, how to offer her comfort." He released a ragged sigh. "So I just placed a hand on her back and rubbed. It was a gesture I remembered Mom used to do for me when I was little. As it was, I didn't get much myself in the way of comfort. I didn't realize how much I really missed it. Not that I needed much, but that easy knowledge that somebody was there and cared for me would have been nice."

The deep timbre of his voice sent a lull through me, even though I was the one comforting him.

"AJ was never really the same after that."

"Did you try talking to her?"

"I did. All the time. I can understand Mom and Dad not knowing, but me, I was her brother. I saw it. I had to always take it upon myself to protect her. From what I didn't know. I'd never thought I'd have to protect her from a mate. Someone I knew well from school. She tried to tell me he'd just called her names. That he just made her feel uncomfortable, but the way Jameson looked at her that night, the way he looked at me with derision, I knew something had happened. *I knew.* But I couldn't do anything about it. Not then, and now I could, but I'm an adult, and beating a man within an inch of his life, well, that's not how things are done."

I frowned. "Do you want me to look into him? If he did hurt your sister, he's done it to someone else. Maybe someone wants to come forward and speak up."

His brows furrowed as he turned his attention to me. "What?"

"I mean, since I've seen firsthand for myself how handsy he gets, if he's taken it further, I'm sure someone somewhere has reported it."

He blinked at me. "So you'd look it up, just like that?"

I nodded. What didn't he understand? "I mean, if you want me to. Because how many girls were just like your sister? Too scared to say anything, to even talk about it. I'm sure he's done it before." I spread my hands in front of me. "I can look."

He studied me for a moment, his eyes warm and going darker. "You're an interesting woman, Nyla Kincade."

I shrugged. "You know, I'll take interesting over beautiful any day."

His lips twisted into a smirk. "The thing is, you're interesting in a way that your beauty isn't worn around you like an armor or shield. Sure, your face is stunning, and your body is, wow, and even though you've got a tough shell, you feel deeply. I can see it."

"Don't get excited. I can't guarantee anything, but I can certainly look."

He shook his head slowly. "I really appreciate the gesture, but I've already looked."

"Oh, come on. I have access to databases you've never even heard of."

He chuckled low. "Trust me, I understand, and I appreciate it, but when I say I've looked, I have *really* looked. I've had a poke at SIS and MI5 and anything anyone might have on him. There's nothing that will stick."

I blinked. "You expect me to believe that you have access to the agencies? Hell, I can't even get into the SIS."

"It's amazing what money will buy you access to."

"You really will use your money for anything, won't you?"

He shrugged. "For my sister, yes. But I couldn't find evidence to put him away. Nothing that's not circumstantial anyway. And I know good agents like you demand things like proof."

"Well, what he just tried to do to me was proof enough." I released a sigh. "But tangible and usable in court, I'm not sure."

"Isn't that the kicker."

"So what, you're just going to give up?" How could he not want to kill Jameson? Hell the idiot had barely touched me, and I felt like I could take a blow torch to his feet.

"No." He shook his head. "But I need to tread lightly. Vengeance is on the horizon, but it needs to be done carefully."

"I don't understand. He's done this horrible thing. He should pay."

He ran his hands through his hair. "Fuck, he will, but my hands are tied. I have to follow a code."

My brows snapped down. "What do you mean?"

"Nyla, I can't talk about it. The more you know, the more dangerous it is for you."

My brain whirred, and I staggered back from him. "What do you mean? What are you planning?"

He shook his head. "Nyla, once you know, you can't unknow. And there are people who would hurt you for that knowledge."

I'd been right. From the beginning, I'd been right. "You are hiding something. You and your mates. There is a reason you seem untouchable. It's because you are."

He sighed then licked his lips. "We call ourselves the Elite."

My mind whirred. "The corruption. The underground dealings." My stomach pitched. I'd wanted him to be different, so I'd fed myself the lie.

He shook his head. "It's not like that. At least not anymore. With Ben at the helm, we're cleaning up. For years we've watched our fathers use us as pawns. We're not playing by those rules. But there is a code. You aren't supposed to know anything about it for starters."

I tried to follow along as he told me how they'd been recruited, the training they had to go through. The lengths that some would go to in order to hold onto power. And the most interesting tidbit of them all... that Ben Covington was now at the helm.

"So two months ago when you handed me the sex trafficking case, that was what, to get me off your scent? Van Linsted was a way to keep me busy?"

East scowled. "No. Bram Van Linsted is a liar. His family held onto their power and position for thirty years, and to move against them meant unpleasant, even dangerous, consequences. And that corruption you talk about. The filth of power. That was everything they stood for. And it was vile. We couldn't let it continue once we knew. But we couldn't very well tell you directly."

My brain tried desperately to fit the jigsaw pieces together. "The trafficking ring. Was that part of the cleanup?"

He nodded. "The men involved. They went after Liv."

The knot in my stomach tightened. "Christ. Because of Covington?"

His voice was soft when he spoke. "No. She stumbled into it because of a book she was writing. So we had to protect her."

"Jesus."

He voice was low. "Nyla. I don't trust anyone. But I'm trusting you with this."

I could see it in his eyes. I didn't want to see it. I wanted him to be lying. But no. He was telling the truth about all of it.

The real question was, what was I going to do with the truth?

FIFTEEN

Nyla

I was still reeling from East's confession when I shoved my keys into my lock. The hairs on the back of my neck stood at attention when the knob turned easily.

I pulled out my phone, set it to dial 999, and then eased myself into my flat, turning on the lights as I went, checking and clearing the tiny powder room off to the right and then the hallway. It was when I rounded the corner that I saw the actual reason for my alarm.

Denning, on the couch with a glass of scotch in his hand, watching my bloody TV. "Jesus fucking Christ, I could have killed you."

"But you won't." His voice was surly and gruff.

"What are you doing here, Denning?"

As I asked him, I kept my phone in my hand, with the panic button at the ready as I turned on the lights.

He winced as light flooded the room. "Do you mind turning off the lights?"

I shook my head. "Yes, I mind. There's a strange man in my flat. So I'm not going to turn off the lights so you can get along with murdering me."

"You know full well I'm not going to hurt you."

"Do I? And look, for the record, you are trespassing. I'm an Interpol officer."

"And so am I."

The inherent threat had my hackles up. "This place is littered with cameras, live recording and sent to an offsite feed. So just think about that."

He sighed and sat back as he cradled his glass. "You think I would actually hurt you?"

"Well, considering you've done actual harm to me, then, yes. My answer is yes."

He sighed again and then shook his head. "You don't know anything at all, do you?"

"Nope, I guess I don't. What do you want? And please, just cut the bullshit and tell me why you're here so you can get the fuck out."

"Are you fucking East Hale?"

My jaw dropped and I sputtered. "What the fuck?"

"It's a simple question."

"First of all, as you're my ex, it's none of your business. Second of all, as my boss, you have no right to ask me who the hell I'm fucking. That's an HR violation."

"Don't evade, Nyla."

"You really don't have any right to an answer. Especially not after what you did to me."

He cursed under his breath and then sat forward. "Fine. I don't have the right to ask. But you know as well as I do that we couldn't continue the way we were."

"Ah, you know what?" Still holding my phone, I folded my arms across my chest. "I don't even know what this is about. All I know is that you are in my flat uninvited, asking questions that are none of your business, and it's time for you to go."

He sighed and ran his hand through his hair. "I know how things ended up hurt you, and I went about it the wrong way. I should have told you before I took the job."

"You think this is about the job?" I stared him down. "No, this is about you being creepy as fuck right now."

"Look, I saw an opportunity and I took it. Unfortunately, I had to give you and our relationship up in the process. You think that doesn't haunt me every day?"

"Oh my God, yeah, you look so haunted with your young grad student plastered against your side."

"Look, just seeing you with him today and him putting his hands on you like he owns you—"

I held up my hand to cut him off. "Well, there's your first problem. Assuming that someone could own me. Your second problem is being an overall douche. I know you can't help it. It's just part of who you are. Since we're doing this right now, I'm going to point out your shortcomings. First of all, you broke in here like some kind of creeper. You are my boss. What the hell are you doing here?"

"I didn't like how Hale was looking at you. Like he owned you. I hated it. You have to be careful with him." He shrugged. "I came to warn you."

I barked out a laugh. "What? You're insane. And Hale has actually been helping me on this case today. He took me to meet Marielle Lipton."

He frowned. "The forger?"

"Yes, the forger. She got out of prison a few years ago, and now she works for an insurance company."

"Have you heard of the Elite?" he suddenly blurted out.

I frowned at him. "What?" The hairs on my arms stood at attention. I knew I was being paranoid, but I'd only just found out myself that they existed.

"Yeah, it's a bloody secret society they're part of. Hale and his mates. I asked some contacts of mine. It's one of those organizations shrouded in secrecy." He stood and began to pace. "That secret society stuff. No one can get any information on it. And I have asked all over Interpol. It's a hush-hush group, which means, of course, there are probably several special agents at the highest level who are part of it. I know Hale is part of it. All I've been able to piece together is that Ben Covington is the head."

"You've already come here once to warn me, and I told you it wasn't necessary. And now I find you in my flat, in the dark, drinking my scotch, and you're talking about how I need to be careful of East Hale and some secret society?"

"Technically, it's my scotch. I know you don't like scotch. I left it behind."

So like him to twist the subject. "Well, for your information, I bought some for a party. And you would never buy this kind of stuff because you're a cheap bastard."

He winced. "I'm just frugal."

"And that's good. So am I. I just don't like my every decision to spend money frowned upon, especially when it's my money."

He sighed. "Same old argument, damn it. Why can't you just let it go? Why are you so fucking compulsive and irritating and bossy and—"

I glared at him. "The best part of everything you just said is you no longer have to deal with it because you dumped my ass, remember?"

He sighed. "This man, East Hale, he's dangerous. His mates are dangerous. Why can't you see that?"

"You're a hypocrite."

He stopped pacing and crossed his arms. "I'm trying to do the right thing. Hale shouldn't have come anywhere near Interpol. I'm going to make a task force. Take them all down."

"You know full well you need cause for that, and without it, you won't get anywhere. Besides this is bullshit. You could have backed me at the briefing, but you didn't. And now you're in here with the same bullshit trying to act like you believe my theories? Please don't. This is plain old-fashioned jealousy. And maybe East Hale and his mates *are* part of some secret organization. I don't know," I lied. "Right now, Mr. Hale is someone assisting me with an investigation. If you can't handle that, have me yanked from the case. But if you do that, I'm going to ask a whole lot of fucking questions." I held up my phone. "And I'm going to send my Dad this little video here of you in my flat, drinking my alcohol, acting like a weirdo. Even you can't explain this away."

He stared at me. "Are you that vindictive?" He watched me warily. "Nyla, I'm just trying to keep you safe."

"No!" I made a slashing movement with my free hand. "That's some bullshit men use to excuse their behavior. And guess what, I'm no longer in the mood to excuse any of your bullshit behavior. You used me. You dumped me. Now you're feeling jealous. I have no time, and I am in no kind of mood to be good to you. If you come near me again, you'll find out just how far you have pushed me."

"You need to understand. Men like East Hale are dangerous. You think I chewed you up and spat you out? All that money, all that power, imagine what he's going to do to you."

A laugh slipped out. "The joy of that is that even if I were dumb enough to get involved with anybody again, whether it was a man like East Hale or a bum off the street or the next Jack the Ripper, that would be for *me* to determine. Not you in your ivory tower, making your decisions and condemning me to them. No, I'm not here for that today. Or any other day for that matter. So I will be filing a harassment charge with HR, asking that they keep this matter private, but it will be on your permanent record. Come near me again, and it will be the end of your career." I narrowed my eyes and glared. "Do I make myself clear?"

His brow furrowed, and he stared at me. "You're making a mistake."

I tilted my chin to stare up directly into his eyes. "No. We are done. Your jealousy is your problem, not mine."

"Nyla—"

I marched to the door and yanked it open. "Out."

For a long, horrid moment, I didn't think he would comply. But the moment he did, I engaged all the locks and leaned back against the door, tears pricking at my eyes.

Make the call.

I didn't want to make it, because I was scared about what was going to happen, but I made it anyway.

Before he could even mutter a greeting, I blurted out, "I need help. Can you please come?"

East

The git really was going to force my hand.

Belinda's husband tumbled out of the bar with his arm wrapped around a woman who was not his wife. They both swayed on their feet. When the woman tried to shimmy out of his grip, he grabbed her wrist hard and tugged her back to him. I almost stepped out of the shadows then. Luckily, some other drunk outside had a sense of right and wrong and called out, "Oi. That's no way to handle a lady."

Jack Lloyd was no gentleman though. "Mind your fucking business."

The woman tried to get free of his grip again. The other guy wasn't letting up. "Oi, I said that's no way to treat a lady. Let her go."

Lloyd, assessing the other bloke, shrugged and shoved the woman away from him. She stumbled, almost falling over, but the drunk caught her.

"It's not fucking worth it, mate."

I followed him. Knowing exactly where I needed to apply pressure to make him rethink his ways. Leave town for bit even. I knew exactly what needed to be done. Normally I watched from afar. It was easier. I'd threatened someone's money, their bank accounts. And they would ease up, level off. It was called leverage. But this guy? No. What he cared about was his "freedom." His ability to roam and drink and gamble. So I was going to have to restrict his movements. Or let him know that those gambling debts he'd racked up... that I was going to buy the debt and the debt had come due.

I had several options, depending on what he said. But alas, tonight wasn't going to be the night. Instead I got a phone call.

Nyla's voice was still as husky as always, but there was a noted tremble in it. Then she said the words that I never thought I'd hear Nyla Kincade say to me of all people. "I need your help."

I abandoned Jack Lloyd right then as if I'd never even thought to stop him. Oh, I'd see him later. But at the moment, Nyla was my worry.

I knew where she lived, of course, but she gave me the address anyway. When I turned up to the block of row houses in Camberwell, I glanced around. This area of Vauxhall was established, quiet. Close enough to the tube and directly across from a parking garage where I'd placed my cameras in order to surveil her townhouse.

London Lords owned the development. There was a

security gate with a doorman and a pretty courtyard with a community fountain. There was also a gym on the property.

Sooner or later she'd figure out how I watched her and cut off my access to her, but for now, she was letting the wolf inside the henhouse. I could've let myself into her flat, but considering how frightened she sounded, I wasn't going to do that. I knocked when I arrived, and she opened immediately. She leaned against the door. "Is now a good time to tell you I feel dumb having called you?"

I needed to get in her flat to make sure she was okay. I didn't have my laptop. Breaking into the CCTV feed from my phone was going to be more difficult and take more time for me to confirm whether someone was in her flat or not. "Are you alone?"

She nodded. "Yeah. I sent him packing."

I frowned. If she didn't need me to physically do something, what did she need? I wasn't used to being unsure. "Are you okay?"

It was only then that I realized she carried a glass of something amber because she brought it to her lips and took a long sip. "Um, okay is not the right term. Not the one I'd use anyway."

"Let me in, Nyla."

She stepped aside. "In." Even though she said she was alone, I did a sweep. Kitchen was easy enough, and the whole dining room area was open. I checked the closet, the bathroom, and then turned down the hall toward the bedroom. My breath caught. It smelled like her. Something fresh with just a fair scent of sweetness. Like clothes drying on a line. With maybe a vanilla candle. It smelled like her. And God help me, I was hard. But I tamped that down because she'd called me for a reason. She had called me because she was... what, scared? I strolled back out into the living room. "What's the matter?"

"I don't know." She put her glass down on her coffee table and sat on the edge of her couch, pulling her knees up. "I... It was just... I don't know why I called you."

I lifted a brow. "Last I checked, Agent Nyla Kincade was a tough cookie. If you called me, it was for a real reason. Just stop beating yourself up and tell me what happened."

"I got home. Took the tube like always. Came to my flat. And Denning was here."

I frowned. What the fuck had that git been doing in her place?

"My ex. Well my boss." She started blabbering as if I had no idea who he was.

"I know who he is."

"Right, because you know things."

I shrugged. "I do know things, but why was he in your flat? Was there some pressing work thing?"

She shook her head. "No. He just let himself in like he owned the place."

"Does he still have a key?"

She frowned at me and shook her head. "No. I changed the locks, but that wouldn't stop him."

"Is it standard protocol that your superiors have access to where you live?"

"No. But he's Interpol. We all know how to pick a lock. And we know how to disengage a deadbolt."

"But you didn't engage the deadbolt when you left, did you?"

She shook her head. "No. I have two locks. Honestly, I shouldn't have to engage a deadbolt too."

She had a point there. She had a doorman, but bypassing him was easy enough. All I did was flash my ID, and lookie there, easy access. But I wasn't going to tell her that. "Okay. What did he want?"

Nyla slid her feet back down to the floor and then ran her hands through her thick mane of dark brown hair. "Uh, he wanted to tell me to stay away from you. That you were dangerous. That I was going to get hurt if I continued down this path with you." She licked her lips in what I now recognized as a nervous gesture. "He also knows about the Elite. I swear I didn't tell him. He already knew."

My gut twisted. I shouldn't trust her. But there was something in her eyes that told me she hadn't divulged that to him. More than likely it was her father.

"I don't know what's happening. A little over a week ago, my father sat me down and told me to back off the London Lords, back off the stupid secret society angle, back off everything."

"Okay. And you did, right?"

She laughed. "Well mostly. Until I got call from Francois Theroux. He said he'd turn himself into me if I looked something up for him."

I dragged in a breath. "Jesus Christ, Nyla."

"Theroux is my father's case. The case I told you about that he's been chasing for more than thirty years. But Denning doesn't know about that phone call, yet now all of a sudden, he's interested in pursuing the secret society angle and taking down the Elite.

"What?" I frowned at her. "I don't get it. You didn't share what I told you about the Elite with him, did you?"

Her gaze lifted to mine. "No. I wouldn't do that. And I believe you. What you said about you and Covington changing everything, I believe you."

I studied her face and saw her sincerity. She wasn't being dishonest. She hadn't confirmed anything for Denning. "Okay. So let me ask you this. Did he exhibit any of this behavior when you broke up with him?"

She shifted then. Her nose wrinkling. "Well, no actually. Because I didn't break up with him. He broke up with me. He decided since he was going to be my superior it was not appropriate for us to continue to see each other, and I was blindsided by it, like a moron. I know, some Interpol agent I am."

I couldn't help it. The pull to comfort her was too strong. "You're a great agent. You follow your instincts." I stood in front of her and then pulled her to her feet and wrapped my arms around her. "I'm sorry. He's a wanker. Full-on, grade-A wanker. So what we're going to do is circulate his photo to the doormen. And then we're going to change your locks again. I don't trust him not to have made an imprint and a cast. And then you're going to start engaging your deadbolt every time you leave. Do you understand?"

She sighed and nodded. "Yeah, I understand."

"Do you have a gun?"

She furrowed her brow. "It's in the gun safe. I'm authorized because I was with MI5 before Interpol, but I've never had occasion to use it."

"Do me a favor. Just take it out and put it by your bedside when you sleep at night."

"Why?"

"Because I don't trust him. Not with you."

"This doesn't make any sense."

She spoke into my chest, her warm breath heating me, and I had to beat back the immediate wash of desire. Because that was not what she needed from me right now. What she needed was comfort.

"He was clear that he didn't want me anymore so why? Why is he doing this?"

"Do you think he's rattled because of something you're working on? Maybe it's the jewelry case."

She shook her head. "No. He's my boss. If I solve it, he still gets credit, so that's not it."

The fact that Theroux had contacted her had my brain spinning. What did Theroux want with her? Why had he offered her his capture? That didn't make any sense. And why go to Interpol instead of just pressing us to get him whatever information he wanted? I needed to meet with the lads and let them know that there was another player in the game.

Every instinct in my body told me to lie. To hide. To not share myself with her. But I couldn't do that. I was compelled to bare my soul to her. "You should know that Theroux contacted us too. That night at the hospital gala."

Her jaw fell open as her eyes rounded. "W-what the hell? What in the world is going on?"

"I don't know."

"What did he want from you?"

"He hasn't told us yet. Just like with you, he wanted blind compliance. We are not inclined to give it." I left out that we might not have any choice.

Nyla's hands shook as they clenched my shirt. "I'm scared."

"You're going to be okay. I'm not going to let anything hurt you."

Nyla wrapped her arms around me tighter and burrowed in, her bones melting and relaxing as her body sank into mine. And if that wasn't the ultimate show of trust for her, I didn't know what was.

She tipped her head up, eyes wide, lashes still damp with tears. "I shouldn't have called you, should I?"

"Hey, if you're scared, call me. If you're tired, call me. If you just want to drink a whole bottle of whiskey because you're pissed off, call me. I want to hear your voice."

"Why are you like this? I can't seem to stay away from you. And believe me, I've tried."

"Then stop trying."

"I know I shouldn't believe you. I know I shouldn't trust you. But I do. And it terrifies me."

My heart jumped. Because she trusted me. And I trusted her. The thing I never gave to anybody. Suddenly my sphere of loyalty and protection expanded to include just one more person. Nyla was in the bubble now. And I knew I would give my life to protect her.

"East?"

I was so busy trying to beat back the pulse of attraction, it took me a moment to respond. "Yeah, Nyla?"

"Thank you for coming."

"Always. Even if we're on opposing sides of something, I will always come for you."

"I believe you."

SIXTEEN

East

My skin was humming.

She was so damn close, and the scent of honeysuckle wrapped around me, infusing itself into my skin, into my veins, intoxicating me, making me sway on my feet.

Then, she tipped her head up. The gentle angling of her head made me groan. Because I knew. I knew I was going to get to taste her again.

From this angle, my gaze flickered down to her lips, the bottom one just a little bit fuller than the top one. The cupid's bow of her upper lip forming the perfect kiss shape, and I knew how she would taste. Everything low in my belly went tight and clenched. My balls already aching just for a taste. The chills crawling up my neck as anticipation spiked my blood, making it roar. Her tongue peeked out to lick her bottom lip and I fought back a groan, but still one escaped me. There was no fighting it. There was no holding anything back. My cock twitched in my trousers, and I knew. I knew that there was no stopping this train. I was so fucked.

I closed the gap between us, slid my lips over hers, and kissed her. God she was sweet, so goddamn sweet. When she parted her lips on a gasp, I knew what she was asking me for. She was asking me to take. And what do you know, I was a taker. I was also a giver, but she'd find that out soon enough.

God so sweet, but the spice chaser on her was unbelievable. Like every stroke of my tongue was met with a surprise. I licked into her mouth, desperate to know every secret she had, wanting to leave no corner unexplored, wanting to make her just as crazy as she was making me. Wanting to make her beg for it. There was so much I wanted to do with her. Wanted to do *to* her. But the way my balls were aching just from a kiss, I was not going to be able to hold out. I needed to get some control, slow this train down. Or it was going to be embarrassing for me and disappointing for her.

But there was no slowing down the train because Nyla wrapped her arms around my neck, slid her hands into my hair, and tugged gently. And she moaned.

Fuck. Me. Fucking hell. I wasn't going to make it. My cock twitched against her, and that groan. It just ripped out of me as I dipped my knees slightly so I could capture her mouth better. She was tall, but still much smaller than I was.

Our tongues stroked together, and I slid mine over hers as we parried for control. I thought I was driving, but I wasn't sure I was. Because when I tried to make her play, she teased and darted, making me chase after her. Jesus fucking Christ. Nyla Kincade knew how to kiss. I was the one weak in the knees; I was the one whose head was spinning; I was the one who was losing my shit.

That part of me that screamed *danger*, the self-preservation part of my brain, didn't even come online because the part of my brain that was now in full control of my body wanted inside her. I wanted to bust open those locks with explosives, lock us both in under all that rubble and never leave. Because I was going to consume her. And she was going to *own* me.

When she whimpered, it was like that last thread of control I had on myself snapped. And then we were clashing teeth and tongues and hands, tugging at clothes, trying to claw to get closer to each other.

We were desperate. I tugged at the silk blouse that she'd worn on the plane. And she pulled at my shirt. I didn't give a shit about mine. I tore my lips from hers, and I ripped it off in that impatient way that blokes do. With hers, I tried to be gentler. I really did. But still, I heard a rip, and I couldn't find a fuck to give about it. We were just a flurry of need, and finally, I couldn't take it anymore. I picked her up. My hands over her ass, gripping her soft flesh.

And Christ. She was so tight. Firm in all the right places but still soft. I peeled one eye open to find the nearest surface and found the counter easy enough. When I settled her on it, we were in perfect alignment. My cock to her heat. But God, I needed to get her naked. Now.

I dragged my lips from hers and kissed along her jawline, inhaling her skin. Trying to drag in more of her. Make her part of me. My lips nibbled at her ear, mixed with chaser licks. I finally managed to get the stupid blouse off with some maneuvering and a little help from her. My hand slid up her bare back, up and down her spine over and over. Her skin, Jesus Christ, she was so soft everywhere. Every damn where. God.

Impatiently her hands worked my belt, tugging jerkily. I felt like there was a part of me that should do this gently.

Take her to the bed, easy. Slow.

I wanted to take my time. But the time for slow and easy was long past.

She tore her lips from mine. "Oh my God, East. I just... My hands are shaking."

I had no brain cells. If I was being honest, nothing was working. All I could do was nod mutely and try and help her. Clumsily we worked my belt and yanked it free. Nyla took it and threw it somewhere. And all I heard was a clattering somewhere in her living room. Neither one of us cared though. As my trousers fell down, I made stupid stomping motions to try to get them off and still meld my lips with hers. She was working the button on her trousers. Finally I gave up the fight. One simple flick of the wrist, and there went her bra. I should've had finesse. I should've been gentle. But God, I think I ripped it. I also didn't give a fuck. I stepped back and dragged her trousers down. She lifted her hips, helping me to work them off her ass. When I glanced up, I choked. Jesus Christ she was stunning. Her skin was all warm honey tan, and her breasts were perky. More than a handful. She would fit my palms well. Her nipples were high and a dusky tan color and made my mouth water.

"You see something you like?"

I licked my lips. "Yeah. I think I do."

Her smile tipped at one corner first before spreading over her whole face. And Jesus Christ, she was a stunner. My gaze drank her in as I tried to figure out what part of her I wanted to devour first. And I kept going back to her nipples.

I wanted her more than I'd probably wanted anything in my life. And I wanted to take her raw and dirty and fuck, I wanted to do things to her I had probably never done to anybody in my life. What was it about Nyla Kincade?

Nyla leaned back on the countertop. "East, I'm waiting."

Her impudent words shook me out of my stupor. "Are you now?"

She smiled at me then. And then parted her legs. "Fuck." I should've known she wasn't going to play fair. She was wearing these champagne colored knickers that were mostly lace. And if I looked hard enough, I could see a small thatch of hair. Oh fuck, I wanted to lick her.

She was not in control here.

Are you sure about that?

My dick also chimed in. *Look, mate. We just want inside. Now is not the time to wrestle for control. March forward, lick something. Stick me inside. Easy.*

I knew what my dick wanted. I knew what my mouth wanted. Hell, my hands were itching to touch her. But if I let her be in control now, I was going to end up completely whipped.

Oh, you mean there's a chance you're not already?

Shut up. I wasn't sure who I was mentally berating. Probably my dick.

"Oh, so you mean to tease?"

She flashed a grin, and she looked so innocent and so dirty. "Oh, I'm not teasing now. I'm not teasing yet. You'll know when I am."

"Oh, really?"

I hooked my thumbs into my boxer briefs and slowly walked them down, freeing the full length of my cock. I knew what I looked like. Thick and long. I knew I was big. I was rewarded by her eyes going wide and her lips parting and a small, "Oh."

"Ah, that's the perfect way I want your mouth. You're going to suck this."

All she did was nod slowly and lick her lips.

Again, she was in control because now, because all I could think about was her mouth on me, her tongue swirling over my head.

What happened to you being in control?

Shut up.

"Bring it on over here, and I might suck it."

"Might?" I coughed a laugh. God, she was so sexy.

I gripped the base, slowly sliding up the shaft and rubbing over the tip. I was so sensitive I hissed. And then smoothing back down, the precum making it so much easier to glide.

Nyla bit her bottom lip. "Okay, enough teasing. Come here."

No. I don't think I will just yet. "Panties. Knickers. Gone. Now."

She lifted a brow. But then she hooked her thumb into the delicate straps of lace and satin, lifted her hips, and did away with her knickers. But then her knees were together, which wasn't what I wanted.

"Open your legs."

She lifted a brow. But then complied.

"Like this?"

Fuck. Fuck. Fuck. She was teasing me. She was going to kill me. She was doing it on purpose, and she liked it.

"Wider."

She assumed a wider stance. Propping herself up and bracing herself.

God, her lips were mouthwatering.

And then Nyla did the one thing I didn't expect. She slipped a hand down her tummy and over the thin strip of hair leading to my promised land. "East. I don't know if I can wait. I need you so much."

And then the tip of her middle finger slid over her clit, and I fucking lost it.

Still working my cock, I stalked over to her. "Oh, someone's a little tease, are you?"

"Well, I mean you do like to watch, don't you? I'm just helping."

I kissed her harshly. My tongue taking full control. Letting her know that I was in charge and I was not fucking around.

She gave me a muffled groan and kissed me back. I could tell she was still touching herself.

I let go of my cock. Her hand brushed over him, and I shook.

She paused. And then instead of playing with herself, she wrapped her hand around me and stroked.

I would love to say that I had some witty repartee, that there was something I could say that was going to make any kind of sense. But fuck, when she notched the tip of me against her clit, I'm not embarrassed to say I saw stars. Okay? I got a little dizzy.

My knees might have buckled. Shoot me. But it would've happened to anyone.

More precum.

She moaned my name then.

"East. Wow. You are so hot and hard and soft at the same time, and I don't think I'm going to make it."

"Fuck, Nyla."

"East, God. Feels so good."

And then she did something else unexpected. She released me. Whether it was to loop her arms back around my neck and bring me closer so we could kiss or whether it was deliberate, I didn't know. But when she released me the tip of my cock nudged her cleft. And God, she was wet. So wet. Dripping. Soaking. I held perfectly still. There was something I needed to do. I just needed to remember what the fuck it was.

She held perfectly still too, but I could feel her pussy clenching around the tip of my head. And I couldn't do anything. I couldn't move, I couldn't think, couldn't breathe.

"East, oh my God."

"I know. I feel it too. I… We… I can't."

"No. Of course you can't. We're not teenagers."

"No, of course not."

But her pussy did that thing again, trying to draw me inside. And fuck it, my hips notched up just a little.

"Fuck."

Her eyes went wide. "Oh my God. You're not going to fit."

I notched my hips back. No. We weren't going to do this. Not like this. Not like a couple of horny teenagers. We were going to be safe and get a condom. But the condoms were in my pants. God, where were my pants?

She squeezed around the tip again, and I dragged my lips from hers, planting my nose at the inside of her neck. I panted. "Nyla, we have to stop."

"I know."

"Okay. So, stop doing that."

She did it again. "It's not like I can help it. I want you inside. But Jesus, you are so big."

My hips notched forward again, and I slid in even further.

She moaned. "If it helps. I'm clean and I haven't had sex in over nine months."

"I'm clean too, but this is still a bad idea for so many reasons."

"I'm on the pill."

"Even if you are, I need to protect you."

Her pussy clenched around me again, and I fucking lost my mind.

Come on, condom.

I shifted backwards, but she followed me.

And God help me, I nudged forward, about a third of the way in.

My eyes rolled back into the back of my head.

"Oh my God, is this what this feels like?"

She whimpered at my intrusion. "You've never had sex without a condom before?"

Somehow, I found the strength to shake my head. Even though all my concentration was in trying to pull out. "No.

She planted both hands on my cheeks and lifted my head. "It's okay. We're okay. I have an IUD. Practically foolproof. We're fine."

I forced my gaze open and tried to clear my vision. Because all I was seeing were stars and bliss and heaven. "Nyla."

"Okay, let's stop. I'll go to the bedroom. I think there are condoms in my nightstand."

"You think?"

"I don't know. Like I said, it's been over nine months."

I held still and tried to release a slow steady breath. "There are condoms in my wallet."

"Okay, let's get your wallet."

But then she clenched around me again. "Nyla."

She met my gaze and lifted a brow. "East."

I saw it. She was trying to make me lose control. We were in a battle of wills. We both knew what we should do, but we were both too far gone now. And then I notched my hips back, and slammed all the way home.

She cried out and planted her hands back behind her on the counter. "Oh my God. Oh my God. Holy fuck. Holy fucking shit."

I dragged my head up. "Are you okay? I'm sorry. I didn't... fuck."

"Just start moving. God. Do not stop."

Oh. She liked it. So I did it again. And again. And again. Then I dug my hands into the flesh of her hips and held her still. And I fucked her. When I raised my head, she arched her back, giving me free access to her tits, and I tucked one of the turgent tips into my mouth and moaned. Because all I could taste was honeysuckle and her, and she was taking over. I slid a hand over her hip and traced a thumb over her clit. The moisture between was slick and hot and so slippery. Nyla kept lifting her hips, notching herself closer to me. With every thrust she met mine. And fuck, I was going to die like this. And I didn't even care.

With my other hand, the one that wasn't occupied with her clit, I reached around her ass and cupped her better. Bringing her flush against me with every stroke. Her eyes rolled into the back of her head, and my name was a litany on her tongue. My grip slipped, and my middle finger slipped over the pucker of her ass, and she gasped.

"That's it. Relax for me. You like that, don't you, dirty girl?"

Her lips parted on a gasp, and I knew what she needed. I knew what was going to make her fly apart.

Keeping my finger right where it was, I gently pressed and circled as I leaned forward and teased her nipple in my teeth, circling, licking, biting. Leaving little love bites all over her. Like I was marking her as mine. She slipped a hand into my hair, tugged, and held me at her breast. Her hips were going wild. Forcing me to speed up. And God, I was lost. I knew that I couldn't hold back, not with her. Not anymore. And so I pressed my thumb hard over her clit and rubbed in furious strokes. I dragged my head from her breast. She whimpered a complaint, but her eyes were rolled back in her head. And then the shaking started in time with the clenching around my dick, like she was trying to yank my orgasm from me by hook or by crook, and God, I was going to let her. She wrapped her legs around me tight, forced her hips up, and then she was screaming. "Oh my God. Oh my God. Oh my God, oh my God, oh my God, oh my God. East."

"That's it, you dirty girl. God, I'm going to do all kinds of dirty things to you and you are going to love every minute of it."

She drew in a shuddering breath. "Yes. Yes. Everything. Oh my God."

I would love to say that I held on through her orgasm. I would love to say that I made it, and didn't die, and didn't completely lose my shit. I would love to say that I could've given her another one. But I couldn't. Because when she went off. Squeezing, pumping, sheathing her slick wet heat over me bare, I lost my shit. I came so hard, if I hadn't been holding on to her to steady me, I would've passed out. I would've just collapsed onto the floor. I really would've, but somehow bracing her to me stopped my imminent fall and my whole body jerked and seized as I released into her. Jet after jet after jet. My body locking into hers, and hers snapping around mine like we never intended to let each other go. Ever.

Her head snapped up to meet mine as I managed three more short strokes, and then her fingers joined mine over her clit and she pressed again. And then one more time, she flew.

SEVENTEEN

East

I watched in consternation as Bridge sank the five into the corner pocket just like he said he would. It was always annoying when Bridge and I played pool because whoever went first was going to win. So I started keeping score of who went first the last time. Ben was good at billiards but not as good as Bridge or me.

I loved the way it made sense and had order. And Bridge, he was a shark. Growing up in the East End, Bridge didn't exactly have the upbringing of the rest of us. His was grittier.

At eleven his father plucked him out of the poverty he and his mother had been living in and dropped him off at Eton. He'd had a rough go when he first arrived. All sharp edges. And now he resembled a diamond, but his edges were still there. He might sound as refined as the rest of us, but he'd had a far different start to life. And once he had something set in his mind, he wasn't going to lose. And, neither was I. Hence, whoever shot first always won.

"Where's Drew?" Bridge asked.

I shook my head. "I don't know. I don't spy on you lot, so

I've been waiting him out. He's been making himself unavailable. I tried for lunch, dinner, a drink. He's *busy*. And he's avoiding us."

Bridge laughed. "I know. The question is, why are we letting him?"

"He has to give me permission to break the no-watching rule."

Bridge laughed. "When have you needed permission to curb your voyeuristic tendencies?"

"Hey, we have a pact. I don't watch *you*."

Bridge coughed then, and it sounded an awful lot like *bullshit*.

"I don't," I muttered incredulously.

"Are you sure?"

"Are you kidding? Between you and Mina and Ben and Liv, I'd have to wash my eyes out with bleach."

Bridge flashed a grin then. And as always, I wished he'd smile more. He looked younger, carefree. I knew different, but God, he was always so serious.

Bridge eyed me as he bent over the table trying to get the perfect angle to sink the four ball. "And how's it going with Agent Kincade?"

I sighed. "It's fine."

Bridge grinned at me. Without looking at the ball, he tapped it with the pool cue, and it sailed easily into its spot. "Uh-huh. You know you get this look on your face when you lie. You're not very good at it."

"I'm not trying for subterfuge." That was true. For those I counted worthy of my trust, I didn't lie. What was the point? But, as Bridge knew, when it came to *other* people, I was a very, very good liar. I would do anything to protect the team.

Oh yeah? Is that why you told Nyla everything?

I swallowed hard. "She's different, Bridge." She sure was. I'd stayed over last night. Again...mostly by accident. I kept meaning to leave... Then she'd nuzzle me and somehow I'd end up inside her again. At least we'd made promises to provide our doctor's notes. Because now that I'd been inside her bare, I didn't think I could stop. And fuck, I liked making her messy with my cum.

I liked knowing I was leaving a part of myself behind. Which was just... Yeah, yeah, I had problems.

He grinned. "I know she is. She's got you all twisted up. I can tell. You look somehow satisfied and constipated all at the same time. What are you going to do about that feeling you have?"

"I want her. But it's probably not the best idea I've ever had."

"Do you trust her not to betray you? That's what you're really worried about, right?"

I scrubbed a hand over my face. "Well, I mean, we did steal a massive diamond. And she's on the trail of some jewelry thieves."

Bridge grinned. "Yeah, we sure did. But, in our defense, we returned it to its rightful owner."

"I still can't believe we got away with it."

But if you keep fucking Nyla, she's going to trip you up.

Maybe she wouldn't. Maybe she did actually trust me now. Fuck knows I already trusted her more than I trusted anybody.

"As it turns out, Prince Lucas is a very good thief. It would have been terrifying knowing him as a kid. Can you imagine him cleaning you out every time you saw him? Light fingers that one."

"I'm sure you knew many like him."

"You would be correct, mate, but they were small time in comparison. He is something else."

"Yeah, and we were his accomplices. So you can see how Interpol and me mixing might not be a good idea."

"Yeah, but you feel how you feel. How much do you want her? Can you walk away?"

That was easy enough to answer. My whole body jerked at that idea. The idea of walking away from Nyla, leaving her alone, never touching her again, never holding her again... That one hurt. "No, I don't think I can walk away."

Bridge watched me carefully, and then a slow smile spread over his lips. "Well, well. Looks like you've finally fallen. I wondered when it would happen with you. Because on the surface, you're the most affable of all of us. The good guy. I mean you're a bit of a perv with the watching all the time, but hey we all have our kinks."

"I like to observe."

"On the surface, you're the welcoming one, the one women gravitate to because you're easy to be near. But you're the one who trusts even less than I do, though you're also the most loyal. You would lay down your life for the three of us. For Liv, for Mina."

Yeah, not so much for Mina. I would lay my life down for her if it meant Bridge's happiness. But on her own? Nope. I wasn't sure I'd even put her out if she was on fire. But I kept that to myself.

"Yeah, yeah, I'm a good guy. Don't we finish last?"

Bridge laughed. "Well you're not *that* nice."

I grinned at that. "No. No, I'm not."

"If you actually trust her enough to share anything about yourself, then she's worth it. Your instincts are never off."

"Yeah, but what if they are this time? We have a lot at stake"

"You think we all don't worry about that? We do. But sometimes a woman comes along and, no matter what your mind tells you about what's good for you, you can't stay the fuck away."

"Isn't that the truth."

"In that case I'm happy for you. Couldn't have happened to

a better bloke. And now you'll spend your life trying to protect her. Good luck with that. She's Interpol. She's forever going to dive headfirst into danger. And there's not a damn thing you can do about it."

My stomach cramped at that idea. *Fuck.*

"Fantastic. Bloody fantastic."

Bridge laughed. He moved around to the seven ball and sank it easily, then he stood. "Well, there's the eight. Corner pocket."

I groaned. "Of course. You know if you're going to invite me to play pool, then at least have the decency to let me play."

Bridge grinned. "What fun would that be?"

"Next time it's my turn."

He chuckled. "Okay, I hear you."

And then I asked him the question that I knew he wouldn't want asked, but if we were poking at my inner workings, I was going to poke at his. "So, are we going to talk about Emma?"

His smile fell, and he flattened his lips, forming tight lines around his mouth. His brow furrowed. "What about Emma?"

"Well, the thing about Emma is that every time she's around or anyone asks you anything about her, you make that face."

"She's a pain in the ass, and she's trying to get herself killed. I mean, I understand her vendetta for Toby. I get it. But she should leave it to us."

I watched him, forcing myself to suppress a smile. He had no idea he wanted her. This was going to be entertaining. "Sure, if you say so."

"What? You don't agree?"

"I believe that Emma is extremely capable. I also agree that we should look out for her. And Toby's death, that's on us to avenge. I don't want her hurt. But she's his sister, so I think she has a say. I think we probably need to bring her in on the team, but I know you don't want to." I put up my hand before he could start shouting at me. "Bridge, she's his sister. Without her, we wouldn't have gotten the video of Van Linsted, Jameson, and Middleton and what they did that night. We wouldn't know who to go after. We wouldn't have any proof."

"I know. I appreciate it and I'm grateful she did that, but she needs to stay the fuck away from this. We lost Toby. Can you imagine if something happened to her? Do you understand what that would do to me, to you, to all of us?"

I watched him. "Bridge. She's not yours to protect."

I'd never seen him look more murderous. The furrow in his forehead deepened, and he looked like he was baring his teeth at me. "What?"

"You're acting like Emma's yours to control. That she's yours to protect. And yes, we owe it to Toby to take care of her. But she's not *yours*." The way I said it must have finally gotten through to him, because he took a step back and sucked in a short breath.

"I know that."

"Do you? Because you're acting like she is."

"I'm not. I just get angry every time I think about her putting herself in danger. I remember that we weren't able to protect Toby, and we won't be able to protect her if we don't keep her out of this."

"Uh-huh."

And there went the brows again. "The fuck is that supposed to mean?"

I put my hands up and slid my cue stick back into its holder. "What that's supposed to mean is your level of anger right now, this whole macho, me-Tarzan-she-Jane situation you've got going on for Emma, you know, *not* your fiancée, tells me a lot about your feelings for Emma."

He coughed a harsh chuckle. "I don't have *feelings* for Emma."

"Okay. But you might want to figure out what the hell this is before you get married."

"East, I love Mina. You know that."

"I know. I've always known. Which is why I allow her to stay."

Bridge lifted a brow. "You couldn't do anything about it even if you didn't want her to stay."

I smiled. He and I both knew different. If I wanted to vanish her, I could. Mina Tomlinson would no longer exist. But I wouldn't do that because he loved her. At least that's what he said. But now I could see Emma lingering on the edges of his consciousness. Maybe she was a better choice for him.

It's not for you to decide.

No it wasn't. Bridge was going to have to do that all on his own. "I hear you. You love Mina. So we'll drop it."

"Good. Also, you lost."

I glanced down at the table. No more balls. I sighed. "Fuck you."

And then he was back. My Bridge. But I had already seen it. He had feelings for Emma Varma, and he had no idea.

EIGHTEEN

Nyla

My hands were sweating. My mouth was dry. The last place I wanted to be was inside the tidy row house in Richmond upon Thames. Was this where Denning had moved?

The house looked like everything that he would want. Crisp and clean, pristine garden. Nothing out of place. Nothing too wild or too bright. Staid.

"Wow, this is boring."

East's voice was low and rumbly and made me smile. "It is isn't it? So, this is where the twat that broke into your house lives?"

"Please, East, can you behave?" I still couldn't believe he'd agreed to come as things between us were so new. I wasn't even sure what the hell this was. I just knew I couldn't turn up at dinner alone. Even I didn't have that much self-confidence.

He put his hand over his heart. "Of course, just for you. I'm absolutely going to behave. Whatever you want. And then later tonight, I'll misbehave in those other ways."

A warm flush spread over my entire body. I ignored the little voice in the back of my head that screamed *this is dangerous*.

Because God, I knew this was dangerous, but I felt myself completely falling. And I was still on that precipice where it might be safe enough that if I torqued my body just so, I would be able to grip the ledge and not fall over, and I would be safe. But I was in that breath between thinking I could recover and feeling myself falling, and if anyone didn't say that was the scariest part of any ride, just at that point where you knew you were going to make the tumble away from safety, they'd be lying.

"Hey." He stopped me, holding my hand and then wrapping his arms around me, cocooning me in his heat and his scent, and my knees felt like a puddle. But it was instant relaxation, and I felt safe. When I inhaled deeply, he laughed. "Are you sniffing me, Agent Kinkade?"

"Yes, I am. You smell amazing. What is that? It's like pine and something."

"Honestly, I don't know. It's some fancy French shit Jessa got me for my birthday."

"You're telling me you don't even know what you're wearing?"

"I have a lot of cologne."

I took another whiff. "I don't think that's the cologne. I think that's you."

His chuckle was low, and it sort of felt like he was vibrating. It felt amazing.

Stop it. Stop it, stop it. You will fall over. Fall deep, no climbing back out of this one.

But even though I was fighting, I knew it was too late. I knew because I wanted him more than I had ever wanted anyone in my life. "Right. All right, firing squad."

"You know, you don't have to do this."

I sighed. "Well, yes, I do, actually. Because if I don't do this, it says I'm afraid. And while I *am* afraid, I'm not going to let *him* know that. I'm not going to sit in my flat too cowed to do anything. He stepped over the line, and I'm going to face him. I love my job. I need my job. But I don't need this. I won't hide. I won't be afraid. I haven't done anything wrong."

He kissed my forehead. "That's right. And don't forget I'm here for you."

"Yes, you are. You recognize that when we walk in there, it'll be like I'm waving a red cape in front of him, right?"

East grinned then. "Oh, I know. I'm counting on it."

He rang the doorbell, and Hazel answered with a bright smile. Honestly, there was no reason to hate her except that she was just so damned exuberant and seemingly warm. And even I recognized that I should tell her *run, girl, run. Run as far and as fast as you can.* Not that she would listen, because I hadn't listened to that voice, and she looked like she was in love. Even though I knew that she was not to blame, there was a part of me that just couldn't like her. But still, I plastered a smile on my face. "Hazel, hi. Thanks for having us."

"Oh, I'm so glad you could come."

She pulled me in and gave me two kisses on my cheek, and I stiffened. I didn't like being touched by people I didn't really know. But East was there, smoothing the edges of my discomfort. With his charm and his smile, he introduced himself. Hazel just blinked up at him, jaw slightly agape. Would I get used to that? Women staring at him like he was a giant, lickable ice cream cone on a hot summer day? I wasn't generally jealous. But the way she looked at him made me want to scream, *go get your own man.* I felt East's fingers press into my lower back, and Hazel led the way into the house.

Past the foyer, the living room was to the left. It was dark, but warm. Fireplace, neat and tidy. Books stacked evenly on the bookshelf. I knew Denning well enough to know that they would be categorized by author last name and each shelf would be different. My bookshelves were haphazard, disorganized, tossed together. But I liked reading to be an adventure. I liked not knowing what I was going to pull off the shelf. At any rate, past the living room, further to the right, was a staircase leading to the second floor, and then down the hall, I could hear chattering voices from the dining room. When we entered, my father stood. "Nyla. You're here."

"Yep. Guess I am."

Dad frowned when he saw East. "You brought a guest."

I sighed. "Yes, dad. This is East Hale."

East was completely at ease. He shook my father's hand. "We've met before."

My father coughed then. "Yes, sorry. Guess I'd forgotten our interaction."

East grinned. "I'm sure you did. It's all right though. Nice to see you again."

Something in the set of my father's jaw made me frown. Why was he being an ass? East kept his hand around my waist, but it didn't feel like a brand; it felt like support. What the hell was going on with my father? Amelia came over and gave me a kiss on the cheek. "Holy hell. He's even more gorgeous up close."

I smiled at her. "I know."

"I'm going to need details."

I flushed then. "Um, not all the details."

"Well, some of them. Because, wow."

We were whispering, but I could knew East could hear us because his fingers trailed just past my waist over my hip, and was that... Did he just grab my ass?

The two other members of our team, Kyle and Jacinda, came over, and introductions were made. Tony and Ayalla were on assignment, so they weren't joining. Denning hadn't bothered to greet East. He stayed seated. Not that it bothered East one bit. When we took our seats at the dinner table, East made a point to sit right next to him. Denning was at one head of the table, and my father was at the other. Next to Denning were East and Hazel. For the most part, Hazel kept the conversation to innocuous topics, sports, vacations, things like that. Although during the sports discussion, my father and East got into a heated debate about the future of Manchester United. But about halfway through dinner, I started to relax. I felt Denning scowl, but it didn't bother me because East was my barrier.

He was my shield. He was keeping me safe.

But when Hazel turned her attention to East, eyeing him again, she smiled. "How long has this been going on? You two seem awfully cozy."

Amelia leaned forward, traitor that she was. "Yes, you do seem very cozy."

"I, um—"

East jumped in. "Well, it's new. Trying to convince this one to go out with me was shockingly difficult."

Denning muttered, "I'm sure you usually flash money. Makes it easier when the women are hookers."

I heard, Hazel heard, and of course East heard, but my father, Amelia, Kyle and Jacinda hadn't. Hazel turned a shocked expression on Denning and gave him a disapproving shake of her head. "What was that about?"

East grinned. "Well, as everyone here knows, Nyla is a tough cookie, smart, intuitive. Keeps me on my toes. That's why I like her."

My father, on the opposite end of the table, heard that particular comment. "And just how many relationships have you had, Mr. Hale?"

"East, please. Not many. That's what makes Nyla special."

Denning was an outright ass then. "Yeah, well, you don't call the ones that you shag and leave behind relationships, do you now?"

I hissed with an intake of breath. Hazel piped up then. "I am so sorry. I don't know what's gotten into him. Denning, that was rude. Apologize to our guest."

Denning frowned at her. "What? It's Nyla who should apologize for bringing the likes of him in here." He glanced around the table. "Has everyone forgotten that not two weeks ago Nyla had a hard-on for the London Lords? She was convinced that they were up to their eyeballs in corruption."

I winced. "Well, clearly I was wrong. And now, I actually know them." East took my hand.

Hazel shook her head. "I'm so sorry. Denning, stop."

My father cleared his throat. "Denning, that's enough."

Denning shook his head. "No. It's not enough. We're all going to sit here and pretend that two weeks ago Nyla didn't ask your permission to get taps on them?"

All I could do was shrink into my seat. But East took my hand and held it on top of the table for everyone to see. "Two weeks ago she didn't know me. Now that we've been getting to know each other, things are different."

My father didn't seem to like that very much, but he said nothing.

Denning stood. "No. I'm not accepting this."

Hazel stood. "What has gotten into you?"

I sighed and forced myself to sit up straight. "Is this a good time to mention that Denning broke into my flat a couple nights ago to tell me to stay away from East?"

I turned to my father. "I was going to file a report, but I didn't out of respect for you. If you want to deal with him yourself, feel free."

Denning sputtered. "What? That's a lie."

"Oh, really?" East challenged.

I sighed. "East, just let it go."

East shook his head. "If it's a lie, then if we check security cameras, we wouldn't see you in her hallway that night breaking in, right?"

Denning's face went red. "You'd have to get a warrant for that."

East grinned then, and there was a slightly evil edge to it. Part smirk, part maniacal smile. "I should probably mention that I own the building Nyla lives in."

I whipped my head around to him. "Seriously?"

He shrugged. "Well, you never asked."

My father went ashen. "Denning?"

Denning sputtered. "She's making a mistake."

Hazel started to cry then.

There wasn't much more to be said. "I think we'll be leaving now."

Amelia's eyes ping-ponged like a tennis match between all of us. East squeezed my hand and mouthed, *Are you okay?* I shook my head. No, I was not okay.

"Dad, I'll see you at work. We can talk about this tomorrow."

East still said his goodbyes. Unfailingly polite. Charming. He even managed to get Hazel to stop crying. Amelia leaned into me. "Um, I am so all about this new situation. Because he is sexy. And you deserve someone taking care of you."

"Yeah. Or did I just implode my life?"

"No. Denning's that asshole, remember?"

"Yeah. I remember."

I said goodbye to my coworkers, who were now gawking at me, and to my father. I apologized to Hazel for ruining her evening. She was gracious though and pointed out that it was

Denning who was being the ass. East and I headed to the door, leaving before we'd even gotten to our dessert course.

Once outside the house, I breathed a sigh of relief. "Oh my God. I never want to do that again."

"You don't have to. I'm sorry."

I shook my head. "No, don't be. You didn't do anything wrong. Denning did. I don't know what the hell's wrong with him. Or why he even cares, honestly."

"You're serious?"

I frowned. "What?"

"Love, he's jealous."

"Well, of you."

"Yes, but he doesn't like that someone else is playing with his toys."

"Um, he has like a nineteen-year-old girlfriend."

"Hazel's not nineteen. She just looks young. And, he's doing that to get your attention. He's annoyed that you don't seem to care."

"Why is he annoyed? He dumped me. Took my job."

He shrugged. "It doesn't make sense. But the moment someone else is touching something he thinks is his, he doesn't like it."

"I'm not his."

"Yes, well, I know that because you're mine. I mean, you're your own person, and also you're mine."

I turned to smile at him. "Are you sure about that?"

"Yep. Absolutely sure. Now come on. Let's get you home."

"Oh. Someone's eager."

He pulled me into his body, and I felt warm and safe again. Happy. I also felt the outline of his erection as I pressed my body into his. "I'm always eager for you, but you just had a long night, so I'm going to let you get some rest. The next time we're together, I don't want anyone else to be on your mind. You understand?"

I swallowed hard. "Yeah. I understand."

He kissed me on the forehead. "Good, now let me take you home." And just like that, I fell right over the edge of that precipice I'd been clinging to. Because he knew what I needed and was willing to give it to me, no strings attached. When was the last time someone had done that for me?

NINETEEN

East

That was not how I'd planned the evening to end. Denning Sinclair was a problem. One I could deal with easily. A couple of quick taps on the computer and he'd no longer be a problem for Nyla.

But she won't thank you for it.

No. She wouldn't. She'd want a legitimate way to be rid of him. One that was completely aboveboard. But the urge was almost too strong to resist. I could burn him. In the Elite you were allowed one burn. One complete annihilation of someone's life where no member could step in to rescue them.

Ben would let me. I could use my burn on him. Hell, if I was inventive, I could do my own version of a burn. But he might have powerful friends to bail him out. And once I buried him in a deep dark hole, I didn't want him able to crawl out again.

And, Nyla won't like it.

Fuck. Things were a hell of a lot easier when they didn't require caring about someone.

I took the left bank of elevators that led to the door nearest to the bedroom suite in the penthouse. As I rode up to the top floor, I pulled my phone from my pocket and frowned down at the thing. It was unlike me to let my battery run so low. But I'd been distracted by Nyla's taste and scent and the press of her body against mine. That constant hum of electricity that ran over my skin and reached my dick. She was all the way under my skin, and I knew there would be no excavating her now.

Not that you want to.

I didn't want to. I wanted to keep her. But the question was, would she stay?

When the elevator doors opened, the hairs at the back of my neck stood at attention, and I frowned. There was a whiff of something—*was that cologne?*—in the air. And it wasn't familiar. It didn't smell like Ben, or Bridge, or Drew. It was something that smelled cheap. Heavy. Thick. I wrinkled my nose and instead of letting myself into my bedroom space, I walked the length of the wing over to the main door. Following the scent. It was thicker by the door. I frowned. I had no fucking weapons on me. How was I supposed to know I was going to need weapons?

Using the keypad, I typed in my code. And to my chagrin, I didn't hear the deadbolt disengaging. It was unlocked. *Motherfucker.* My brain did a quick mental calculation of whether my housekeeper had come today. It was Thursday. She didn't come on Thursdays. She came Monday, Wednesday, and Friday. Was it possible I'd gotten the schedule wrong this week?

No, dumbass. Someone has been here. Someone other than you.

Sometimes Ben or Bridge would stop by when they were just downstairs. But either of them would have texted me.

Your phone is dead.

Okay then. So it might not be cause for alarm. Still though, I eased the door open, and treading lightly, I stepped into the darkened kitchen, grateful that the evening shades hadn't been pulled down and the streetlights of Soho gave me some light and created shadows where I might hide at the same time.

A quick glance through kitchen told me nothing was amiss. But there was that scent again.

I could see most of the living space from the kitchen because of the expansive open floor plan. I could see the full living room and dining area, and both appeared wide and open and untouched.

But still, every instinct I had said something was not right here. Something was wrong. Very, very wrong.

I inched forward farther into the hallway and checked the guest room, double bath, and the closets quickly and efficiently. At the guest room, on the carpet, I removed my shoes and my socks. It would make me quieter. And also gave me more grip. With my shoes on, I'd slide all over the place and that wasn't going to work if I had to fight.

I felt ridiculous. This was insane. There was probably no one here. And if I could have just checked my goddamn phone, I would know that. When I stepped into my bedroom, it was just as dark as the living room. I flicked the lights on and sighed with relief before I felt it.

There was just the briefest shift of movement behind me, and I whirled. Before I could fully turn my body, I had a hand up protecting my face somewhat, but that left my side exposed and I took a hit to the rib.

"Son of a bitch."

I quickly did a mental catalog of the intruder. Close to my height. Decently muscled. Maybe beefier than I was, which meant I was likely quicker.

I blocked the next blow with both my arms and threw an elbow. Then I wrapped my left arm up and around, trapping his arm as he swung and tugging him closer to me. With my right arm, I gripped between his shoulder and his neck, digging my fingers in deep as I was pulling him close and delivered two knee strikes, making him grunt and double over. On the third one, I shifted my stance back just a little, and gripped his hair instead before delivering my knee to his face. The sickening crunch sent a sizzle of satisfaction through my body.

But I made a mistake. A fucking rookie mistake as he collapsed in front me, groaning. Instead of delivering a final knock-out punch, I quickly continued to survey the room and leaned down, getting a glimpse of his face. "Who the fuck sent you? Was it Jameson?"

But the piece of shit's eyes just rolled back in his head. He didn't answer. I shook him. "I said, who the fuck—" The swift movement in the room behind me was a surprise. Then a hit to my kidney sent a spasm of pain racking through my entire body. It hurt so bad all I wanted to do was curl into the fetal position and lay there bleeding and pleading for my life. Another shot to my kidney. I was able to tuck and roll, deflecting some of the impact, but God, it hurt.

I rolled onto my back. Another assailant. This one heavier. Beefier. Bigger.

I kicked out, making a direct hit to his knee.

"Get the fuck out. Get the fuck out."

When he winced and groaned, I managed to roll myself over into a semi-seated position and slid my right leg under my raised left knee, planted both hands on the floor next to my right knee and pushed up. Once I was on my feet, I staggered and swayed. Jesus Christ, kidney shots hurt. I'd forgotten how much.

And then it was basic hand-to-hand, and all I could do for several moments was block his shots.

But he was whip fast, like a pit fighter. As big as he was, he should not have moved so quickly.

You have the advantage. This is your flat. You know where things are.

I groaned, blocking another side kick.

With both hands up in L-formations, covering my face, I bent my body slightly to block the kick, and then I delivered an elbow. I got him on the throat, which staggered him back. Then I made the dive. At the foot of my bed, taped under the frame, was a gun.

I reached for it quickly, raised it, and shot.

It dinged him, but he was moving quickly, dragging his friend, who had started to get up, behind him. And they were running.

I squeezed off another round. I didn't know if I hit anything besides drywall, but once again, I pushed to my feet, gun in hand, running after them.

I'd been taught from the beginning, if you can get up, stay up. If you can neutralize your target, do so. Only kill them if you must.

I ran. But they weren't there. The door was wide open, and I heaved and breathed a deep sigh.

I slammed the door shut and quickly went about clearing the east wing of the flat. Bedroom. Bathroom, inside closets. When I was done, I wheezed and went back to my security alarm to check. Sure enough, there had been several silent pings.

But they'd only been here a few minutes before I arrived. The cameras had caught them. But they'd had my goddamn code. How did they get my code?

I winced and wheezed, just wanting to crumple into a pit of pain. For some reason my goddamn face hurt too. Had one of the assholes gotten me in the face?

Jesus Christ. Before collapsing on my couch, I plugged my cell phone into the charger and sent a text to the lads. "We have problems." And then I sent them the link to the security feed.

Bridge: *On my way.*

Ben: *Motherfucker. Stay put.*

Before I could collapse back into the cushions, the phone on the side table rang. I answered with a groan. "Hale."

"Uh, sorry to disturb you at this hour, Mr. Hale, but there is a Miss Kincade down here to see you, and she said that you'd want to see her."

Fuck. Fuck. Fuck.

If Nyla saw me like this, it would only serve as fuel to the fire that we were up to something. But she was already here and there would be no stopping her, because she would hang out in that lobby until she saw something she didn't needed to see, which would be Ben and Bridge coming for me.

"Send her up."

My worlds were about to collide. But it was already happening, and I was too goddamned tired to stop it.

❧

Nyla

Honestly, I'd come to get lucky. Don't judge me.

My pussy replied. *I'm totally judging you. But also, I need him...*

I'd tried to get some rest after East had brought be home. He'd been the perfect gentleman. He hadn't followed me in, even though I'd wanted him to. I'd wanted him to chase the shadows away. But he'd given me the sweetest goodnight kiss and left.

I'd done the whole bedtime routine. Brushed my teeth, braided up my hair. Slathered on much too expensive cream on my face. But I'd been restless. Unsettled. I'd spent a good thirty minutes trying to sleep before I gave up and got dressed. I knew what I wanted. I wanted East.

I arrived at the hotel and they allowed me up after confirming it was okay with East. When I arrived at his penthouse, I stopped short when I saw a smudge of blood on the door, and East swung it open before I could knock.

"Come on in."

I could see the traces of blood and broken glass everywhere. What the hell?

I reached into my purse and palmed my baton, because honestly, it was the only weapon I had. I'd left my damn knife at home. But I was ready.

I pushed in, ready to do battle with someone. But East just flopped onto the couch, bleeding and seemingly unable to move. "Oh my God. What the hell happened?"

"Somebody broke in here. That happened."

"How could the penthouse in this hotel have someone break-in?"

"You know what? That is an excellent question for later. For now, if you don't mind, I'm just going to go back to dying. What are you doing here?"

I held up the bottle of rosé and shrugged. "I came to ply you with alcohol so you might shag me."

His brows lifted as he met my gaze. One slightly bruised eye looked me up and down, making heat lick over my skin. "Oh, Agent Kincade, I might just let you steal my virtue. But newsflash, you don't need the alcohol. If you'd been in any kind of mind space earlier, I would have shagged you against your door in full view of your neighbors. But now, do you mind terribly if I just lie here and you can, you know, hop on? I can definitely get it up. I just can't move the rest of my body."

My jaw dropped, but no words emerged.

"I can still make it good for you, but maybe if just this time you'd rip my trousers down and, you know, we'll figure it out."

I thought he was kidding. I honest to God thought he was joking by making a lewd suggestion like that, but then my gaze traveled down to... Well, there was the thick length of him pressing insistently against his trousers. "East Hale, you look like death. Like someone literally tried to beat all your breath out of you, and you think you're getting lucky now?"

"Well, a beautiful woman just walked into my flat and told me she had big plans for shagging. Trust me, I can make it work."

"You're an idiot." I placed the rosé on the table. "Where are your washcloths?"

He feebly pointed in the direction of the hallway. "In the closet, it's the second set of doors on the right. You'll find towels and washcloths and the like. And the ice, obviously, is in the freezer."

"First aid kit?"

"In the linen closet with the towels. You can't miss it."

I slipped off my shoes, not wanting to possibly dent the gorgeous acacia hardwood. Then I quickly shuffled off to get the supplies. I found the first aid kit and washcloths where he said they were. In the kitchen, I dragged open some drawers until I found a plastic bag and hit the crush setting on the ice dispenser and filled the bag. And then I found a bigger bowl and filled it with warm water. It was a major balancing act, but I managed to carry everything to the living room.

Was it possible he looked even worse than he had three minutes earlier? "Jesus Christ, who did this to you?"

First, I cleaned up his eye, removing the blood as he hissed when I pressed a bit on his bruise. In the first aid kit, I found bandages and butterfly sutures, those tiny ones that can be used in place of stitches. Something told me East was not going to the hospital.

"You don't have to do this. I can take care of myself."

"Yeah, right. Someone broke into your flat. Have you called the police?"

"Nope. Besides, you're here."

"You know that's not how it works. I'm Interpol. I work on large task forces. This isn't my purview. We need to report this."

"Nope. Please don't."

"Why not?" I sat on the coffee table across from him and stared. "What are you into that you're so afraid someone would find out?"

His moss green eyes met mine. There was so much turmoil and emotion swirling in them. But I couldn't read them clearly. Was there deception in their depths? I wasn't sure. Was there fear? No.

"There's nothing you need to worry about, I swear," he said.

I sighed and then leaned forward and wrapped my arms around him. Our lips were ever so close, and he sniffed me. "God, you smell amazing."

"Yeah, I know. I put perfume on for you. I was taking no chances with my orgasms."

He coughed a laugh. "You're just as cocky as I am."

"Yeah, well, just so you know, my pussy is also magic."

"Oh, I know." He coughed. Then he kept coughing as I gently rubbed his back.

"I need you to sit forward a little bit so I can get your suit jacket off."

"It hurts to move. Help me, please."

I pulled him forward, and that motion somehow had him planting his face right on my chest. He sniffed deep. "God, can

I fuck your tits? You don't have to hop on. You could just bend down, bare them, and I will figure out how to rub my cock between them. Just, please…"

"Oh my God. Really?'

"I will point out you are the one who has my face in your tits."

And that was how Bennett James Covington and Bridge Edgerton found us. Bridge paused in the doorway, met my eyes, slid his gaze down to East's face, laughed, and then made himself at home. Covington was next. He didn't even register any surprise. "Mate, if you're trying to tell us that you're shagging Nyla, we pretty much figured that out already."

East groaned. "She was trying to smother me with her tits. You came just in time to save me."

I scowled down at him. "No, he's an idiot. He won't sit forward so I can take off his jacket and see how bad the wounds are."

Ben's brows snapped down, and I caught that movement. He started shouting orders about first aid kits and ice. But I shook my head. "You idiots are late. I've already done that."

Both of them lifted their brows. "Oh, right."

Bridge chuckled low. "What part of the first aid are you on now? I'm sure I could point out where East has the most pain…"

I narrowed my gaze, and he laughed. I was struck dumb for a moment. Because I'd never seen so much as a photo of Bridge Edgerton smiling. We hadn't interacted much, honestly. But his smile, it was like sunshine. Wasn't it a shame that he didn't smile more?

"Idiots. You're all idiots. Grade-A idiot number one right here," I said, pointing at East.

And then East did the thing that made my pussy clench; he planted a kiss right in the center of my cleavage, and I gasped. "What the—?"

He mumbled against my skin. "I'm sorry. It's just, I don't know if I'm ever going to get the chance again, and you smell so good."

To be fair, I had just told him I'd come there to shag him.

I glanced up at his friends. "You lot, come help me."

They were both huge. Just as big as East was. And they eased him forward, helping him out of the suit jacket. Then I unbuttoned his shirt and winced when I saw the ugly purple bruises already rising up. "Jesus Christ, I'm going to need more ice." I nodded at Bridge. "Please."

Luckily, he didn't argue. Ben eased himself next to his mate. "So, what happened to the fancy alarm system?"

"The alarm system wasn't functioning because my fucking phone is dead."

Ben cursed under his breath. "That's a low-tech situation."

East grumbled. "You think I don't fucking know that? The real question is, how the fuck did they get in?"

Ben's brows drew together. "We need to go ask the staff. Is it possible that it was Todd? His key card has been revoked, but what if he had someone else's?"

Todd Spivey had been Ben's sometime driver and security for Livy, but then he'd attacked her in Ben's flat. Since we'd opted to deal with him legally, he was out on bail. There was something to be said for dealing with things the not so legal way.

East shrugged. "I don't know. I'll look into it." He winced as I did finger palpations. I asked, "Do you think he needs a doctor? I'm worried."

Ben's brow furrowed. "How bad is it?"

"I mean, from what I'm seeing here, he's taken a couple of kidney shots. The stuff on his pecs, that's superficial. He might have a broken rib. I'm worried about internal bleeding."

Ben pulled out his phone, and before I knew it, he was

mumbling something at someone and then turning his phone off. "Doctor is coming."

I blinked. "What, just like that?"

He nodded. "Yes, just like that."

I shook my head. "Who are you people?"

East shrugged and then groaned. "Long story."

Bridge came back with the ice, and we strategically placed the packs around him, using an ace bandage to wrap them in place.

Ben gave me a nod. "Thank you for looking after him, but Bridge and I have it now."

I laughed. "Ah, I think not. I'm not leaving. So you three better get used to me being here. I'll wait for the police too."

East groaned. "Jesus Christ, Nyla. I am in no mood to argue with you right now. I'll have the security work with them on the break-in in the morning, okay?"

I opened my mouth to argue, but I could see he was in pain. I popped two Paracetamol out of their silvery packets, put them into his palms and handed him a glass of water.

He sipped and swallowed. "You know, you make a half decent nurse. I do love a woman in uniform."

I lifted a brow. "You know, I might take back what I said earlier."

He flashed a grin. And even though he was battered, bruised, and injured... God, he was still so sexy. I looked between him, Ben, and Bridge, and the other two stood.

"Okay, Bridge and I are going to go deal with security," announced Ben. "We'll also deal with the cops and let them know that you will file a statement with them in the morning. In the meantime, are you all right, mate?"

East nodded. "Yeah, if someone would bring my iPad over here, I'll change the security protocols now. So this place will be secured for the rest of the night. And then when all is said and done, we'll try to find out who broke in."

Bridge brought it over, and East nodded a thanks.

Ben was already headed to the door, and Bridge turned to glower at me. "The doctor will be by to check on him later. Make sure that tomorrow we find him in better condition than he is now, yeah?"

I met his dark gaze but didn't back down. "I'm going to make sure he gets in bed and that he gets to rest."

Bridge gave me a nod. It looked something akin to a thank you. They weren't just business partners. They were mates. Actual mates. The London Lords were a family.

When his two friends were gone, I studied East closely. "You ruined my perfectly good evening plans. So let's get you to bed so you can rest, and I'll take a rain check."

"Woman, I see you. Always trying to get me naked. You should buy me dinner first."

"You should buy *me* dinner."

"What, I'm injured and an invalid, and you just want me for my body."

I couldn't help but giggle. "Come on, off to bed with you. I'll stay until the doctor comes and leaves."

I slid down next to him and helped him lift his arm over my shoulders as I helped him onto his feet.

"Stay, please. Please don't leave." His voice was so soft, so pleading, and I got the impression that he wasn't used to asking for anything.

I also was worried that he would need much more than the two Paracetamol. I nodded at him. "Yeah, okay, I'll stay."

He groaned as we shuffled toward his bedroom. "If I had known all it took for you to come spend the night was to get my ass kicked, I would have hired somebody to do it ages ago."

༄

East

It was dark in the initiation room. Everyone wore their robes and their masks. The dark red silk hanging off of our frames, obscuring our bodies, making us all the same. The masks obscured our faces, and the only thing visible were our lips and jawlines. If I looked closely, I could make out my mates. I knew their faces as well as mine. The only lights were the lanterns built into the walls from initiations long ago.

I climbed out and was made a brother. It was the one thing my father wanted. The one thing I willingly gave him. But I only gave it because of the lads. Ben was here, Bridge was here, Toby, Drew. We were all together. So I could acquiesce on this. Because if it had been just solely for my father, I wouldn't have done it. I would have fought it tooth and nail. But it was too dark. Something was wrong with the lantern. And suddenly everyone's robes were black, no longer the dark red I was used to. Why were they black?

The images in my mind changed and everyone stood around a coffin. Masks came off. Drew, Ben, Bridge all standing, surrounding me. My mask was still on. But there was one coffin still shut. It was Toby's coffin. I glanced around at my mates. "Open the coffin. Open it. What are you doing?"

None of them answered me. None of them looked at me. And they were hoisting the coffin onto their shoulders. No. Not Toby. Please, God, not Toby.

I screamed. No. Not Toby.

I tripped awake, thrashing, and the hiss of pain hit me on the left side. "Fuck."

There was a female voice. Soft. Quiet. "Shh. You're going to hurt yourself."

"Nyla?"

"Who else?"

"Sorry. What are you—" Had I come home with her? The sheets smelled like my sheets. And the smell of fresh linen and vanilla or flowers. Had I brought her home? Smart on me. But why did I feel like I was blissed out?

I tugged her closer to me, and she was soft and naked. I frowned. No, not naked. She had knickers on. No way in hell would I have taken her to bed with me with knickers on. I slid my hands up her smooth, flat belly and palmed one of her breasts. She moaned. "East. You're supposed to be taking it easy."

"Who said?"

Despite the throbbing pain in my left rib, my dick was ready to go, happy to go, more than ready to say good morning to Nyla.

She shifted in my arms, onto her back from her side. And her gaze met mine. She blinked. It took me a moment to see the whiskey in her beautiful hazel eyes. "There you are. Good morning."

She shook her head. "It's not morning. It's about four o'clock."

I winced. "Four o'clock? What an ungodly hour."

"I know. I've been checking on you every hour or so. I didn't mean to wake you when I got back in the bed."

"Um, thank you."

"You were having a nightmare."

I sighed, wanting to go back to that moment where I was fondling her and she was filling my big palm. Overflowing even. Could I make love to her without pain?

What's a little pleasure without pain, right?

My cock twitched again, and I groaned. "Maybe we can talk about it later. Right now, I really want to suck on your tits."

She stroked a hand down my face, and I kissed the inside of her palm. "Welcome to my bed. Why don't I remember you coming in here?"

"Because the doctor gave you a massive pain pill. You should feel better."

I frowned. "Pain pill?" And then it came rushing back. The god-awful dinner. Leaving her at home because I knew that emotionally she was wrecked. I should have stayed. I should have picked her up and shagged her against the door, making her forget everything. But instead, I had come home and been jumped in my own flat. Bloody fantastic. And then she'd come to play my nursemaid. And fucking hell. I remembered the doctor, the poking and prodding. The assessment that I did not in fact have any broken ribs. They were just bruised and would hurt. And no internal bleeding. I would recover. I would be significantly less pretty for a while, though.

And then he'd given me something for the pain and left. He told Nyla to check on me every hour or two, to make sure I hadn't hit my head and gotten a concussion. Fabulous. That's why I felt so groggy. "I had hoped that you were in my bed naked for another reason."

"I have underwear on. And I had a T-shirt. I just got up to get some water and then spilled all over it. So I came back in without it."

"I am not complaining, I promise."

She rolled onto her other side so that she faced me. My eyes had adjusted to the darkness. And I could see the outline of her face better. Those gorgeous cheekbones. The curtains were open, so I could see the hints of dawn in the sky over a slumbering London. "Tell me what happened in your dream."

I didn't want to do this. But I'd been dreaming of Toby a lot lately. "You know how we talked about the Elite?"

Her voice was quiet and soft when she nodded and said, "Yes."

"We had a friend. Me, Ben, Bridge, Drew. You haven't met Drew yet, but you will. His name was Toby. Tobias."

"Okay. Is he in London?"

I shook my head. "He died on our initiation night."

She didn't move a muscle. No wilted brow, no sitting up, no nothing. But I could feel the tension slam into her shoulders. "What happened?"

"The official story ten years ago was that he had a massive heart attack. Which none of us believed. But it was so quick. We all emerged from our coffins, reborn so to speak. Except he did not. Ben clawed the damn thing open. And he was lying in there so still."

"Do you know what happened?"

"Not then. We were all so shell-shocked. The senior members who were doctors tried to revive him with CPR, and he was taken to a hospital, but they pronounced him dead on arrival, and then the ceremony had to go on. At least that's what they told us. They shuffled us through, and we went through the routines for our initiation. I was so dazed. Numb. I couldn't feel anything. For a long time I was convinced I would never feel anything again. And it was slow to come back, the sensation, any emotion. I was just completely clicked off, I guess."

"Makes sense. You lost a friend."

"And the thing is we all swallowed the lie. We didn't stop to think about why Toby would have had a heart attack. The guy was a runner. Had done several half marathons. There was no reason for him to have a heart attack. He was perfectly healthy."

"I'm so sorry, East. People have heart attacks all the time. Even young people. Athletes. It happens."

"I know." I nodded. "It does happen. And so we believed

it. But about six months ago, at the ten-year anniversary of our initiation when we all joined the Elite, we were leaving and ran into Emma Varma."

She frowned. "Who's that?"

"She's Toby's sister. When we were at school together, our group of friends was so tight. We'd spend holidays with the Varmas. Summers. When we didn't go to their house, Toby came home with one of us, and sometimes she came along."

"Okay. What does she have to do with this?"

"She was there to confront the Elite. She was there to confront them about what they'd done to Toby."

Nyla's brows furrowed. "But you said he had a heart attack."

"I said we *thought* he had a heart attack. Emma insisted she was certain that there'd been no heart attack. We found out that Toby's death had been no accident."

She moved then and shifted back just half an inch. Her gaze roamed over mine. "What do you mean not an accident?"

"No one killed him or anything, but there were three who contributed to his death. Bram Van Linstead, Garreth Jameson, and Francis Middleton. Van Linstead was supposed to be on watch. All the coffins were fitted with cameras inside. So we were all watched and monitored. We all had heart monitors on as well. He was supposed to be making sure everything was fine. Jameson was the ears. He listened in to the auditory feeds. Was checking to see who was losing their shit. They could hear everything. And then there was Francis Middleton. His part came after the initiation. We insisted that something wasn't right. We didn't believe he'd had a heart attack. So we begged them to look into what had happened in the autopsy. But everything came back normal. There was whole campaign about the unfortunate situation, and money was donated to the Varmas for the tragic loss of their son. Everything was neat and tidy, and the Elite wasn't mentioned in any of it. That was courtesy of the Middletons. They are crisis managers. The whole family. For generations. They are the ones who tell the lies. They speak no evil."

She gasped. "They covered it up?"

I nodded slowly. "Yeah, they covered it up. Toby hollering. Screaming. Begging to be let out. He couldn't breathe in there."

"Oh my God, I am so sorry."

"Deep down, we knew, but we swallowed the lies."

She frowned. "Bram Van Linstead, his sudden rash of misfortunes... That was you?"

I didn't know how much to tell her. I'd already said way too much. "Yes."

"You found the corruption. And you fed it to me."

"Yes. But you were already on the path. You were just looking at the wrong Elite members."

"Oh my God."

I didn't know how mad she was. "I'm sorry. We didn't know you then. We had to protect Ben."

Her brows snapped down. "I'm not mad about that. I'm horrified that you had to go through that."

"Someone left Emma a video showing that if they had just opened the coffin, just let him out, he would still be alive."

"There was video evidence?"

I nodded. "Yeah. And they left it for his sister if you can imagine that."

"That's horrible."

"Yeah. So anyway, we essentially pulled an illegal burn on Bram. But it took some time. We wanted to prevent him from being Director Prime."

"What's Director Prime?"

"It's our leader. Each Director Prime holds the seat for ten years. They can be reelected by consensus of the membership. Or they can be challenged. And a Van Linstead had sat in the Director Prime spot for thirty years, and Bram thought he'd be next."

She whistled low. "His father, his cronies, the things that they did."

"They used the Elite under cover of propriety. They used us all."

"So that's what it was. That underlying, I don't know, but I could sense it... hate."

"I didn't want to be in the Elite. I didn't want to be in any organization with my father. But I did it for my mates, and it turned us all into something else."

"So why won't you let me take them down?"

"Because we already have a plan for that."

"Oh no, no, no, you're not vigilantes. You're going to get yourselves hurt."

"We took down Van Linsted."

She shifted but not out of reach. "How? What did you do?"

"Doesn't matter. The point is that a Van Linsted no longer sits on the proverbial throne. Ben does. And when we deal with Jameson and Middleton, then we're going to dismantle the Elite."

"You're serious?"

I nodded. "Yeah, I am. We've rooted out the Van Linsteds and anyone doing dirty deals with them, but there's so much more corruption we probably don't know about."

"Let me help."

Oh hell. "No, Nyla. There's a way that this is done."

"Vengeance for your friend."

I searched her gaze and said simply, "Yes."

"East, this is a recipe for disaster."

"I'm going to do it whether you want me to or not." Someone had come for me, but they'd made the fatal error of leaving me alive.

"And get hurt? What if this is what they want?"

"Well, then they should have killed me."

"Stop saying that. What am I going to do if you die?" Her bottom lip quivered. She was serious.

"Nyla, I'm sorry. I was being facetious. I'm not going to die."

"You could. They could have killed you last night." She tugged at the sheet she held to her breast. "God, I don't want to feel this, but now that I am, you want to rip it out of my hands?"

I wrapped an arm around her and pulled her close despite the pain. "You feel something? Do tell."

"Stop it. I'm serious. You could have been seriously hurt."

"I'm serious too. They should have killed me, because now I know they're gunning for us. Someone has secrets they don't want us to know. So we're going to unearth them. And we're going to expose them. And then we're going to bury them alive."

"East. I want to help."

"You don't need to do anything."

"I want to be there for you."

It was my turn to lift my brows then. "Nyla, you're Interpol. You can't help. You can't be involved in this."

"Yes, I can. I can do something. Your friend died. And someone hurt you. So if someone hurt you, that means that they hurt me. I have a stake in this."

That was not what I'd expected her to say. "No you don't. I want you far away from this."

"In that case, I'm getting out of bed now."

I held her still. "No, you're not. You and me, we're doing this."

"Yes, but that means together. You don't put me in a corner. Don't call me Baby. Don't put me on a pedestal. Let me help."

I could tell she was serious. "Are you sure you want to do this?"

"Yes. I'm sure. Because I don't know why, but I trust you. And I don't trust anybody."

"Well, welcome to the party."

"So what, this means that I'm yours?"

"Hey, let's just be clear, you didn't kick my ass. I let you win."

Her mouth opened and she was about to scoff, but I leaned down and covered her lips with a kiss. When I pulled back, I whispered against her softness. "Hush, woman. I understand last night you came in here to get shagged. If you can be careful with my side, I can definitely take care of that for you."

"You're injured."

"Oh, let me show you just how injured I'm not."

TWENTY

Nyla

I felt like a teenager sneaking home. Instead of getting up on time, I'd let East convince me to stay in bed. What was I supposed to do? The man was a miracle with his tongue.

And so there I was, sneaking into my own damn office. It wasn't like I could claim to have been researching a case, following a lead. For all anyone knew, I'd gone to ask East more questions.

Sure you did. Like, how big is your dick, East? How many times can you make me come? Or like, just how good are you at eating pussy?

I knew that answer now.

"There you are."

I whirled around and plastered a giant smile on my face. "Amelia. Heyyyyy, I was just going to come and find you."

"You bet your arse you were. I want to hear every single detail about East Hale. The man looks like he was made to kiss."

A flush crept up my neck.

"I... Um..."

"Oh. My. God. You're *sneaking* into the office. That is bed head. That is your *I shagged last night and have to wear a bun because my hair is too unruly to tame* look."

Fuck. She knew me too well. "For the record, I did go home to shower and change."

"Yes. Tell me everything. Deets! Friends don't tease friends like this."

"Okay, but can we do it one night after work? Wine and curry at mine? After last night, I don't want to risk Denning lurking and overhearing."

"Deal."

"So what's up? You look like you want to tell me something."

"Actually, I have excellent news."

"Okay, tell me your excellent news."

"Look, I know that we've been looking at the London Lords really as an entity. As these sort of power brokers, right? But what if it's more than that, and what if it's not just them?"

Oh shit. I knew where this was going.

"Not just them?" I hedged.

"Yeah, what if they're part of a network. Think of it like a club. We all know that London has a long history with secret societies, right?"

My stomach pitched. "Uh-huh."

"Well, think about it, something elite like at Eton or Oxford. The sons of the richest and the wealthiest. What if it's like that and it's more than just the London Lords? It's all of the richest men in England? Denning actually gave me the idea last night. He was on and on about his favorite secret society movies."

I hated to lie. Hell I was bad at it. But East had trusted me. *And Amelia is your partner.* "I mean it's entirely possible. Secret societies aren't an uncommon thing. But again, no one ever admits to being in one, and we can't prove that a whole secret society is bad. What have you found that supports your theory?"

"Well, let's pretend that the London Lords are in one. And Bram Van Linsted claims to know all about them. So, assume he's part of it, right? And remember when you went to pick him up and arrest him? They were having some kind of party. Everybody was black tie, that sort of thing. But what if that's their headquarters? What if it's real?"

"Okay. Say it's real. How do we prove that they're up to something?"

"Well, we can question them about the sex trafficking ring, their involvement. I mean because what if it's like *Eyes Wide Shut*?"

I coughed out a laugh. "You think they're having crazy sex parties in London?"

"Maybe. Maybe that's how the trafficking began?"

"Remember, we found not a hint of evidence that linked the London Lords to sex trafficking or anything illegal. And as far as we can tell, if they are part of any organization, they did things the hard way. Except for the financing for their first boutique hotel, they begged, borrowed, and stole what they had to in order to get started."

She worked her bottom lip. "Right. But there is one link in there between all of our sex trafficking arrests and the London Lords. Drew Wilcox of The Wilcox Financial Firm. He handles financing for all of the people arrested for sex trafficking as well as many of London's best and brightest."

"Did the Wilcox Financial Firm handle any of the black-market money?"

She shook her head. "No. But in case I missed anything, I have the forensic accounting experts going through it. We can go over it at the safe house I have set up. When Denning broke into your place, I figured it was a good idea to move any evidence we have on this case out of your townhouse. I didn't trust Denning not to mess with it."

My eyes went wide. "You put it in a safe house?"

She grinned. "Yes. Ingenious right? It's a small studio space we never use."

I never anticipated that Amelia would go so far down the rabbit hole. "Well, here's the thing; if we find evidence of a secret society, what exactly are we going to charge them with?"

"Well, we can't charge them with anything specific because obviously having a group with membership is not a big deal. But if we could expose corruption, collusion, prove they're like the underworld... Wouldn't that be enough?"

I could see where she was going. And the question was, did I trust Amelia's instincts, or did I trust East?

East. You trust East.

Shit. I trusted Amelia hands-down. But about this, I did trust East too. I believed what'd he told me about the Elite. So how could I let Amelia go down this path?

"Okay look, I hate to say it, but I feel like my dad was right."

Her eyes went wide. "Oh my God, did you just say your father was right about something?"

"Okay, okay, I get where you're going. But I mean, honestly, we've got nothing on them. Sure, maybe a secret society. And maybe collusion for the sex trafficking, but that would mean that they would *all* have to have known about it and deliberately turned a blind eye. And I don't think that's the case because *they're* the ones who gave us the evidence."

She sighed. "Well, if we do find evidence of a secret society, there's still corruption."

"Yeah. I agree, but that's not under our purview is it? That's the Yard."

"I know." She sighed. "I just want to know if we're right. I'm pissed at your dad because he just dismissed us outright."

"Yeah, me too actually." I was pissed about that. Especially since I *was* right. And so was Amelia. But she was barking up a tree that wouldn't yield any fruit. I didn't want to, but the next time I saw East I was going to have to let him know that Amelia had started piecing together the puzzle. Sooner or later, she was going to learn about the Elite, and some of those men didn't want to be outed.

She sighed. "Okay, I'm going to put a pin in this, but I'm still checking the financials. Maybe I'll get lucky and get a hit. It's not like you to give up so easily."

"I'm not giving up."

"Or you just have a crush on one of the London Lords, and you're hoping he's a good guy."

I was hoping. And more than that, I believed he was a good guy. Even though I didn't want to believe, I really did.

I just hoped that, once again, my instincts were right.

East

As I tugged Nyla toward the palatial house in Belgravia Square, she dug her heels in. "Would you relax. They'll love you."

She swallowed hard. "I know you say that, and you probably believe it, but I don't know."

"Look, I'm the one who doesn't trust anybody. If they see me trust you, they will too."

"But, East, I'm nervous."

I squeezed her hand. "I get it. It can be hard."

"And I *was* investigating your friends. Come on."

"Yeah, there's that. Ben might give you shit for it. But I got you."

She dragged in a deep breath, the motion making her breasts lift in her light sweater. She'd picked an off-the-shoulder cream sweater dress, knee-high boots, and a thin strip of gold dangled from each ear. Her hair was thick and slightly curling in the breeze. She looked stunning. "Look, these people are my family. And since you and I are on the same team now, they need to be too."

"Okay. I just… I don't even know what we're doing."

I turned to face her slowly. "Well," I said as I tugged her closer to me, even as she tried to dig in. "You are the woman that I'm obsessed with. Which doesn't happen ever. So if I wanted to lock it down, I'd say I'm going to go ahead and just give myself the boyfriend stamp."

She shook her head almost as if she was having a seizure. "What? What are we, fifteen?"

"If you want, I can snog you in the bushes like we are."

She snorted a laugh. "We've already been there."

"Yes, we have. This time there'd be no sprinklers. So maybe I'd lift up your dress, slide your thong over, push into you just a little. You know, just the tip."

A flush crept up her neck and into her cheeks, giving her a pretty pink glow.

"Jesus, maybe I *should* throw you into the bushes."

"No. Everyone will see."

"That my darling, is part of the fun."

"You really are an exhibitionist."

"Depends on the day. But seemingly with you it's just hotter."

She swallowed hard. "Okay, well we better get inside before my knickers are drenched."

"You know, it's funny hearing you say knickers with that slight American accent of yours."

"It's *not* American. I'm just as British as you are."

"Yeah, but you've lived in the States half your life."

"So?" she huffed

"Just saying. Come on." Her hand was soft and warm in mine. I marched up to the door and didn't even bother ringing before I opened it. But Ben had been paying pretty close attention to security ever since Livy's stalker situation, so Livy almost met us at the door. "East, there you are." But she didn't hug me like usual. She went straight to my left. Her smile was warm and sweet, and her arms stretched out as she wrapped them around Nyla. "Agent Kincade, thank you for coming to our home."

When Livy pulled back, Nyla blinked at her. "Um, Call me Nyla. And thank you. Especially considering that I was such a thorn in your side."

Livy shook her head. "You were doing your job. And well, too. We just happened to get caught up in the crosshairs."

"Yeah. I'm sorry, I guess."

Livy shook her head. Ben's booming voice came from around the corner of the stairs. "I hear awkward apologies."

He ran up, shoved his fiancée out of the way, and also hugged Nyla. But he lingered a little long for my liking. "That's enough, Ben," I muttered.

With a cheeky grin, he winked at me. "Now you know how it feels."

He slapped me on the shoulder and then turned his stupid dazzling grin on Nyla. "Welcome. Don't sweat the whole investigating us. You wouldn't even be the most awkward introduction into the group."

Nyla's smile wavered. "Thank you."

I tugged her inside, and she made the rounds. Bridge and Jessa she already knew, but she had only a passing acquaintance with Lucas and Bryna. And Roone hadn't joined them on the trip this time. He was back in the Winston Isles taking care of some things for Sebastian.

"Well, it's nice to see everyone."

Telly came from the kitchen then. "Oh, the new kid." Telly's smile was wide as she went and shook Nyla's hand. "I'm Telly, the former new kid. So now they get to give you shit. I'm no longer the rookie." She gave a fist pump. "Yes."

Nyla's brows rose. "You're Telly Brinx."

Telly placed a hand on her hip and grinned. "That would be me. I am the best hacker on the squad."

I coughed. "It's so sad that you think that."

Telly looked me over and returned her gaze to Nyla. "Ah. Yes, East likes to think he's my competition, but he's not."

"Listen, Telly, I can still kick you out of here. That's how we roll. Ben's house, my house."

She laughed at that. "Yeah. Good luck getting that idea past Liv."

Liv hip checked me as she darted around to grab a handful of some nuts off the charcuterie board. "Nyla, I'm sorry. Have a seat. Don't mind East. He and Telly are still jockeying for position. Wait till you find out that Telly has a bigger dick than he does."

Nyla coughed. "Not likely."

I grinned at that. Ben and Bridge looked like they wanted to vomit.

Telly dramatically flopped into one of the massive overstuffed couches as she man-spread with a wink. "What do you say, East? Want to pull them out? See who's bigger? I think your girlfriend is biased."

I just shook my head. "Oh, Telly. I know for a fact you looked into me, so you've seen that photo from Ibiza. You know exactly who's bigger." Telly flushed then, which I didn't expect. Well then. Fantastic. If that wasn't just awkward for all of us.

Bridge scrunched up his face. "Ew. Must we remember Ibiza? I thought we all made a vow to never, ever talk about it again."

Jessa just laughed. "Nyla, it's good to see you again. You have to overlook them. They're always like this."

We got to our seats, and I tucked Nyla practically on my lap. She tried to shift her weight, but I held her steady and then nuzzled her neck, which made her do this soft purring thing. I could tell she was uncomfortable until she saw Livy practically fall on Ben, who then started to slide his hand up her thigh. God, couples are so disgusting. But suddenly I understood the need.

Telly shoved popcorn in her mouth and spoke around it. "So, we going to talk about the whole *Nyla Kincade is part of the crew now* thing? And how did that all come about?"

Nyla shifted. I held her steady. "Well, I was helping her on her case, and she found me irresistible. That's how that happened. But the big thing is that Francois Theroux contacted her too."

Bridge and Ben sat forward, and Ben nearly unseated Liv. Liv just smacked him. Bryna's eyes went wide, and Lucas frowned. "How do you know Theroux?"

Nyla shrugged. "He's my father's white whale. Dad's been trying to catch him for over a thirty years."

Ben frowned. "But why is Theroux contacting you?"

"I don't know honestly. A couple weeks ago I got a phone call asking how if I would like to catch him, followed by a text message with a photo and proof of the date."

Ben sat back then. Livy just whacked him again and then jumped up to sit next to him instead of on top of him.

Nyla followed suit.

I missed her already.

"All right," Bridge said as he rubbed his jaw. "So, Theroux contacts Nyla, and he contacts us. But who else do you think he has invited to play his game?"

Ben pushed to his feet and poured himself a drink. "Well,

it makes sense that he would contact Agent, sorry, Nyla." He gave her a smile. "Using your first name is going to take a bit of getting used to. If he's looking for some kind of information, it makes sense that he contacted Nyla because she's Interpol. She has access to databases that even East or Telly can't get into legally."

Telly shrugged. "Speak for East. I can get in anywhere."

I scowled at her. "You wish."

Nyla laughed. "I think I like you, Telly."

Telly grinned back. "I think I like you too."

I snorted. "Telly, shouldn't you be at home with Carmen? You guys leave for your wedding in three weeks."

"Yes, and everyone is invited except for you, East. Nyla, you can come without him though."

I just grinned at Telly. "A chance to ruin your wedding? Of course I'll be there."

I was teasing of course. I wouldn't ruin Telly's wedding. She was a pain in the ass, but I sort of liked her. Or at the very least, I'd gotten used to her.

Telly rolled her eyes. "Okay, so Nyla is Interpol."

Nyla added, "I was also MI5 before moving to Interpol. But just as an analyst, nothing fancy."

Bridge whistled low. "Okay, that makes sense then. So why us?"

Nyla frowned. "Yeah, why'd he reach out to you?"

I left that question to Ben. "We're not sure yet, but he claimed to have something that would incriminate Garreth Jameson."

Nyla scowled at me then. "Yeah, so what were you stealing at the Jameson's that night?"

I shrugged.

Bridge laughed. "She caught you?"

I shrugged again. "Maybe."

Ben guffawed. "I knew you'd been busted. Your comms went out, and then... nothing. Next thing I knew, you turned up at the SUV soaking wet."

I just glared at him.

Nyla laughed. "You didn't tell them?"

"What I told them was that I'd found you snooping around so I got out of there."

"That is not what happened. I caught him and I chased him. Would've taken him out too if there hadn't been... an incident."

Lucas leaned forward. "Oh, do tell."

Bryna whacked him. "It looks like it's probably their business."

Bridge shook his head. "No, we want the details."

Ben nodded. "Oh please, do."

But Liv came to my rescue, beautiful, awesome, fantastic Liv. "Shut up, boys."

Nyla laughed so hard. "Oh my God, no. It was an accident. We got attached somehow, and then there were sprinklers. Anyway. He walked away with whatever he stole, and he still won't tell me what he took."

I grinned at her and gave her my best wink.

She pinched me.

"Ow."

"I'd like to know."

Ben just shook his head. "East just stole information off of Jameson's computer. That's it."

"So, is this how it goes, just like a team meeting? Am I in the lair now?"

Bridge guffawed. "Nicest lair I've ever seen."

"Then you haven't been paying attention to Bruce Wayne," I retorted.

Bryna and Livy howled. "Amen. Christian Bale's Bruce Wayne? Yes. I'd be in that lair."

Ben looked wounded as Liv enthusiastically high-fived her girls. "This is much better than Bruce Wayne's."

"Yes, it is baby. It is." She placated him and patted him on the knee.

He inched away. "I see what you're doing."

Nyla smiled, and I could tell she was relaxing and enjoying herself. And I relaxed too. Because having her here next to me, I didn't feel like the outsider looking in. I felt complete.

TWENTY-ONE

Nyla

I was exhausted. When my alarm had gone off, I grumbled about it. Look, these things happen. I didn't want to leave bed. I didn't want to leave East's side. I was in the twilight zone now.

I'd gone and fallen for him, even though there was so much I didn't know about him. My gut was telling me all the things that I needed to know.

You mean all the things that you want to know, not need to know.

I shoved my hair off my face and tried to decide if I was going to wash or not. Brunch with my father was a standing tradition. I knew better than to be late.

Maybe I'd forgo the washing and just spritz a little water to clean it a bit.

Last night had been a revelation. The people that I had seen as the bad guys, the criminals, I hadn't known them. Now they were like real people. And they wanted to help me. It felt like they were pawns in a bigger game too.

Or are you just making excuses?

God, I probably just wanted this to be true. But I knew it in my gut that East was not the bad guy here. So what the hell was going on? If I didn't figure it out quickly, my career would be up in flames. And unfortunately, he might get caught in the crossfire. So I needed to figure it out.

"So, you were just going to get into the shower without me?"

Despite my rambling thoughts, I smiled as a warm male stepped into the shower behind me.

The shower was enormous. It could have fit six people comfortably. There was no need for him to be so close. "You're a little close there, aren't you?"

"Well, I think you need my help washing your back."

I giggled. "My back huh?" His hand slipped over my belly and down between my legs, seeking his favorite plaything. "You know, that's not going to happen."

"What?" He nipped my shoulder and then trailed kisses along my neck. "Are you sure that's not your back?"

"Yep, mm-hmm, yeah, totally sure."

My knees wobbled. He had my number. I was complete jelly for him.

Hell. We'd barely made it out of Ben's house last night. Strictly speaking, we *hadn't* really made it out the first time. He dragged me into a closet, pulled down my dress, and sucked on my tits and played with my clit until I'd come all over his fingers.

He was very naughty.

And the thing about that house was that it was so enormous I don't even think anybody noticed we'd been gone or suspected what we were up to. It was weird.

Well, okay, Telly seemed to know. Because she'd looked at him and winked and gave me a big old thumbs-up sign.

Oh, what was I doing?

His fingers stopped, and he nudged the side of my hair. "Hey, I can feel your brain spinning. Just enjoy what's happening, okay?"

"I'm trying, sorry."

"No, don't be sorry. I know this is probably a lot."

"It's hard to have a conversation with you when your fingers are…"

He slid his finger over my clit again. "When my fingers are what?"

"Ah, being naughty. So naughty."

"Well, naughty is my middle name."

"I know. East Naughty Hale."

"Well, I like it. I'm going to change my birth certificate now."

"Are we going to talk about this?"

He nipped my ear. "Yeah, we can talk about this. But how about we make love in the shower first. You go see your dad. And then we can talk about what's happening with us, okay?"

I gasped when he slid a finger inside me. "Oh God." I cleared my throat. "So there's an us."

"Oh yeah, there is absolutely an us. You're in my snare now, Agent Kincade, and I'm not letting you go."

"Jesus, East." My breath caught.

"Yes, Nyla?"

His voice was a whispered chuckle against my skin.

"You're killing me."

"Oh, what a way to go though, right?"

The heel of his palm rubbed against my clit as he fucked me with one finger.

"You know, I was having the best dream about you last night."

"How does it feel?"

"Amazing. Slow. I want more."

"Ah, more of that?" He slid his other hand up over my belly and cupped my breast, gently touching the tip. They felt full.

Too full. Achy. And I moaned at the contact. "God, Nyla. How did I not even know it could be like this with you?"

"Oh, I think you knew."

He chuckled. "Oh, you're right. I did know. Which is probably why you've been under my skin since the moment I saw you."

Then another finger joined the previous one, and I gasped. "Oh, boy."

"No, love. I'm a man. You can feel how much."

And I certainly could. The length of him was slapping against the small of my back. "Oh yeah, I can feel that. He wants some attention?"

"Yeah, I think he does."

"Well, you have to let me go so I can turn around and maybe talk to him."

"Nyla, I'm busy."

"You are in fact busy."

I was too close, and I wanted this to last as long as it could. Because once I saw my father and the day got away from me, I might not be able to see him for a bit. "But I think you want to watch, don't you?"

His fingers stilled. "Fuck. You do know what I like, don't you?"

"Yep. I sure do. So what's it going to be? Making me crazy like this, or watching *me* make *you* crazy?"

It wasn't even a question. He eased his fingers out of me. But East being East, he slid them over my clit, pressing firmly, making my breath catch. At the same time, he pinched my nipple hard, and a shudder ran through my whole body. When I turned around, the water now on my back, I glowered up at him. "You did that on purpose."

He backed up several steps until his back was against the hard tile wall. "You bet."

On the wall there were button controls for the shower. He softened the spray and turned on the other showerhead so that the water would angle just on my back and not into my eyes.

I stalked toward my prey. Because that is, in fact, what he felt like. When I reached him, I stood on tiptoes and angled my lips to his, kissing him gently.

That kiss alone was enough to make his body shudder, and the length of his erection bobbed against my belly. "Fuck. Even a kiss from you is enough to make me crazy."

"Well then, prepare to be out of your mind."

He laughed then. "Oh my God, that was cheesy."

"You know what, you think of something flirty to say when you're really turned on. I dare you."

"All right, we'll make it a competition."

I rolled my eyes. And then with my hands on his hips, I lowered myself gently.

Before I did anything, he started to shake. "Oh my God. I don't know if I can take this."

"Well, you're going to have to."

With one hand I reached for him, wrapping my hand around the base of his erection, and he went stock-still. When I glanced up, he was staring down at me, his brows furrowed in concentration. "Are you okay?"

"Oh my God, I might die. I might honestly die."

"I'm pretty sure you're not going to die. Hang on."

When I stroked him, another shudder racked through his body, and his hands went in my hair. "Oh my God, I'm not sure if this was a good idea."

"Shut up. I'm in charge now."

And I was. When I angled him down to meet my lips and rolled my tongue over the tip of him, he cursed, fisting my hair tightly, and his body jerked. "Oh my God. I'm going to die."

"Yep. What was that you said? What a way to go?"

Then I wrapped my lips around the full head and eased my mouth down over him. I pulled back slowly, making sure he could feel every bit of my tongue. With my free hand, I cupped his balls, gently squeezing and tugging them. His hands tightened in my hair. He wasn't moving me, but it was as if I was his anchor. My name was a choked cry on his lips over and over and over again, and I could feel his balls tighten. I was ready. Prepared to take him down my throat. I slid my head down as far as it would go and then relaxed, forcing every part of me to not clench, and I took him even further. East's hands dug in my hair, and then I wasn't in control anymore. He held my head still and eased me back gently. I eased back down again, but then his hands tightened, pulling me off.

"Now. I need to be inside you."

When I refused to comply and even used my teeth a little, he barked an order. "Hands on the wall now."

I eased off, making a popping sound as I released his cock. "Well, there's no need to yell."

I stood easily and complied, turning my body around and planting my hands on the wall. In a flash, he was kneeling behind me, and then his lips and tongue were on my lips. Licking, licking, licking. His tongue sliding in and out of me. Owning me. And then his tongue left my pussy. Slipping up. "Oh, my God."

"Yeah. Bend over more."

I did as I was told, and East went to town, leaving no part of me unlicked, untouched. I was completely open to him, and all I could do was hold on for dear life. When he stood, his lips traced over my spine, and his cock notched against my pussy. He growled in my ear. "You've been naughty. Filthy. Bad, bad girl." With his foot, he kicked at one of mine and said, "Wider." I adjusted my stance.

He kicked my other foot. When I didn't comply fast enough, he canted my hips so that my breasts were pressed into the tiles, and then he stroked home.

His pace. This was not the East I was used to, the one who tried for control, but there was no control in him now. He was completely gone. He slid one hand up to my breasts, pinching, testing, weighing. The other was on my clit as he set a punishing pace. His lips were at my ear. "Do you know how fucking much I love being inside you? Coming inside you is like a revelation. I could do it all day. I never want to fucking leave."

The water sprayed down on us, and just when I thought I couldn't take it anymore, he stopped, pulled out, and I cried, "Ah no, I was so close."

He shook his head. "No. We're not done. Wrap your arms around me." He turned me around slowly and nuzzled into my throat.

Then he picked me up, braced me up against the wall, and without preamble, he slid home again. "This time, when you come, I want to watch you."

And I knew in that moment that there was no walking away from East Hale. He would break me in a way that I'd never been broken before. Leaving him might actually kill me. I was lost. I was falling. That crash landing was going to hurt like a bitch.

But there was a part of me that just didn't care because this felt much too good.

He held me up by my ass. He drove into me. Muttering dirty things and love things. "God, you feel so good... I love being inside you... I cannot stop fucking you... Never letting you leave... That's it, baby... This cock belongs to you..."

With him murmuring against the hollow of my throat, I came apart. Shattering. Giving every piece of myself to East. Knowing I might never be whole again.

With a roar, he came inside me. Holding me in place, biting down on the skin at my collarbone. Jesus Christ, he was going to leave a mark. And I wanted him to. What did that say about me that I wanted to be claimed by someone? In particular, this someone. Someone that had more secrets than I could ever hold. But I was his. And he was mine.

❧

Nyla

For once I was not late for brunch. Dad hated it when anyone was late.

I figured after the disaster of dinner at Denning's just the two of us would be a better idea. Problem was, when I turned up at his house in South Bank, he didn't answer. Nor did he answer my first three texts.

I tried his office phone, same result. I eventually just let myself in, only to find the place empty and quiet. Sort of a mausoleum atmosphere. Even though I could tell the flat was empty, I still called out. "Dad? Dad?"

The photo on the bookcase caught my attention almost immediately. In it, I was eight. We'd been on holiday in Santorini. Mom was gaily planting a big sloppy wet kiss on the side of my face. I was laughing at the wind. Dad was watching us indulgently. And in the background, just in the corner, there was a man. He was in silhouette. And he was watching us as if observing. I didn't know why, but I sort of got a melancholy feeling. I'd never thought to look at him before. But now I felt like he'd been watching us, sort of feeling like an outsider.

I was probably giving far too much credit to my thoughts about a random man in a photo, but for some reason, he'd caught my attention.

"Dad?" I called again.

No answer, as I'd suspected. I checked the calendar in his office, and it indicated that he had planned to be in the office for an early meeting. Had he forgotten brunch? Maybe he was still there.

I locked up behind myself and quickly jogged down the stairs back to my car. I couldn't shake the idea that I was being watched, though. Someone had eyes on me. Was that East? Was he watching me right now?

I should be annoyed or concerned or irritated, but I let it go, and fifteen minutes later, after I haphazardly parked my car in the parking lot, I took the stairs two at a time to the glass doors and yanked. Amelia was blowing up my phone.

"Amelia, yeah."

"Oh, there you are. I have something I want to show you. I'll shoot you an address."

"Oh, okay. Is it urgent?"

"Nope. It'll keep, but text me when you have a second."

"Okay, will do."

I impatiently swiped my ID. I didn't bother with the elevator because it was notoriously slow and instead just jogged up the stairs. I found my father in the conference room staring at his computer as I burst in. "Dad, I've been calling you half the morning."

He lifted his head briefly before turning his attention back to the screen. "Dad, are you listening?"

"Sit down, Nyla."

I frowned at him. "Okay... Everything all right? You missed brunch and I—"

"Nyla, I'm sorry, love, but I need your badge."

"Excuse me?" I frowned, unable to compute the words he was saying. "For what?"

"That dinner with Denning."

"I didn't do anything. I didn't even want to go to that dinner. I was forced. And furthermore, he was the one who acted inappropriately."

My father did that silent thing he always did when I was a child, signaling he wanted me to shut up and listen, so I did.

"He did act inappropriately. He is also on administrative leave for two weeks."

"So why are you punishing me then?"

He sighed. "I wish you wouldn't look at it that way. But Denning has filed reports on you, every insubordination, every break of protocol. I had to do something, Nyla."

"So what, you're just rolling over?"

"You have been given a long lead. Too long. And then you turn up at dinner with a..."

"Were you going to say suspect? Do I need to remind you that *you* warned me off looking into them? You did that."

"I know. And I was right. There is nothing illegal that I can find on Mr. Hale. But you knew that was going to set Denning off. It's a pattern with you, Nyla. You can't let anything go. You can't leave well enough alone."

"It's what makes me a good agent."

He folded his arms. "It's what keeps you from being a great agent. You need to learn to play the game better."

I stared at him, tears pricking my yes. "All I've ever wanted is to be like you. It's funny, because it was the last thing on earth you wanted."

"You're not like me, Nyla. You're like—" He cut himself off and sighed. "I'm cut out for the politics. You're not."

"I'm your daughter. How can you do this?"

"I know it doesn't seem like it, but this is for the best."

"For who? Me or you?"

"Nyla—"

I stood and reached into my back pocket for my badge. "Here you go. Are you happy?"

"Of course not, Nyla. You'll receive your salary while your suspension is pending final review."

"Whatever. Are we done?"

"Nyla—" I didn't wait for him to finish. I just turned and strode out, my vision going fuzzy from the tears.

TWENTY-TWO

East

When I knocked at Nyla's door and she answered it, I knew something was wrong. Instead of her usually sleek waves, or any kind of style, her hair hung in a scraggly mess, though it looked quite a bit more full than normal, and she spent a lot of time running her hand through it. Her eyes were red rimmed and puffy. Her skin was blotchy, and she was holding a half empty bottle of Rosé. She was also wearing a T-shirt that read *I cannot quit, as I am currently too legit* and a pair of gray joggers.

"Well, I guess we won't be needing this." I held up the bottle of wine I'd brought.

"Oh, we will. Because this one is for me, and I'll finish it, and then I'll help you finish that one."

Her words were slightly slurred, and I followed her into her townhouse. I'd seen it numerous times from a different angle. But somehow, from the inside, it was cozier, warmer. I closed the door behind me and locked it. Then I set the wine on the counter, sliding off my jumper and hanging it on the back of one of the stools at her island in the kitchen.

She shrugged. "I will probably have to vacate this place, as I was suspended today."

My brows popped upward. "What?"

"You see, dear old Dad suspended me indefinitely. Apparently, Denning has been busy writing me up. Meanwhile Denning only got a two-week paid administrative leave."

I blinked rapidly as I joined her in the living room. "We can fight it. We *will* fight it." And I was serious. I planned to show a history of stalking. If I only got one burn in life, I was more than happy to use it for Nyla.

"Denning says I've been in subordinate. And basically this is happening because they can't control me. I'm a damn good agent."

"I know, darling. I know." I sighed and then slid down onto the floor next to her. She dropped her head onto her knees and started sobbing. Fuck. Tears. I was never good with tears. I didn't really know what to do with them. All I knew to do was offer physical comfort, and I wasn't sure she was going to want that. But still, I wrapped my arm around her shoulders and tucked her into my side, because all I wanted to do was protect her and make everything better for her.

"Your instincts led you exactly where you were supposed to be."

"Yeah, that's just it. He says I'm too temperamental. I follow my feelings too much. Oh, and I'm too cocky. But here's the funny thing; he would never say that to a man."

It was my automatic response to frown. And I wanted to say, 'No, Nyla. He's your father. He would never say that.' But I realized that was at the base of the misogyny that permeated so much. "You think that's what's going on here?"

"Patriarchy. Misogyny, yup. Absolutely. I knew Denning stole my job. I just didn't know that he hated me that much or that Dad would believe him so blindly."

Fury boiled under my skin. Roger Kincade and I had come to an agreement. He, of course, knew about the Elite. He knew what was required of him. And he knew enough to back off from the London Lords. But that was never supposed to touch Nyla. Not once. And I hadn't known about fucking Denning. I had fucked up. "Listen to me, we can fix this, all right? I'm sure that after giving your father some time to cool off, he will come to his senses and realize that you are an asset—"

She didn't let me finish. "But it's such bullshit."

I couldn't help it, a chuckle burst out. "Ah, my sweet Nyla. Your mouth really does run away with you."

"I know, but God, I'm just so furious. Denning broke into my goddamn flat. And my father did nothing, said nothing. What am I supposed to do now?"

"Right now, you finish your wine. You deserve it. But look, the Nyla Kincade I know wouldn't just give up." I shot her a smile.

She nodded and then swiped a hand under her nose.

I reached around the coffee table and grabbed a tissue box, pulling two free and handing them over.

She took them from me and blew her nose. "Sorry I'm such a mess."

"I get it, you're upset."

She shook her head. "I'm not upset. I'm incensed. I'm not sad and simpering and whimpering because my daddy took away my toy. I want to do murder."

I blinked. Jesus Christ, she was a warrior. That was so goddamn hot. "Look, I want to help. Anything you need. This isn't the end."

"Oh, sorry, you thought me sitting here and drowning my sorrows in Rosé meant I was giving up? No. This is just the tears before the rage. Denning is getting what's coming to him. I believe in justice, and I will not let it go until it's mine. And my father, well, my father has something going on with Denning. And I love him, but what he's done is wrong." She gave a slow shake of her head. "And it's not just me. Amelia should have been promoted years ago. Given access to different task forces. I love him, but he has to change. So, I'm going to take my night, drink my wine, and cry. And then tomorrow, I fight."

The corner of my lips turned up. "You're fucking gorgeous, you know that?"

"Yeah, I bet you say that to all the girls."

I shook my head slowly. "No. I don't. I only say what I mean. I have a long history of not being able to trust people. So I don't offer bullshit platitudes."

"Good. I don't like bullshit platitudes either."

I leaned over and kissed her forehead. "Good thing we're a team then."

She nodded. "And I'm really sorry."

I frowned at that. "For what?"

"I don't know what I was thinking investigating you and your friends. I just—Something in my gut was telling me to hunt down Ben. Like I just knew there were secrets around him, and I needed to unearth them all. But people deserve their secrets, I guess. I'm sorry."

I blinked at her. What was I supposed to say? Her instincts were right. We did have secrets. So many fucking secrets.

"I had zero business bugging you, and God, you could have had me sacked. And you didn't. I don't know why."

"Because I was curious about you. I was curious about the woman who was willing to put everything on the line. You intrigued me. There is so much more than meets the eye with you. And I can't get you out of my head. What can I say?"

"How about you don't say anything and kiss me instead?"

She lifted her face toward me, and I brushed her lips softly with mine. Everything in my body tightened at her nearness, her taste, her scent. But I forced myself to pull back. "How about we drink this one, put on a terrible action movie, and we have a cuddle, yeah? And then, when you're sober, I want to pet that pretty pussy and make her purr. Does that sound good to you?"

"I'm sober right now."

I chuckled. "My love, you are far from sober. So come on, finish the wine. The sooner you finish the wine, the sooner we get to—"

She smiled sloppily up at me. "Make my pussy purr."

I laughed. "Yeah. But God, please stop looking at me like that, because right now, I really am desperate to make it purr."

"So maybe I should just, you know, take off these joggers. In case I should sober up really quick, giving easy access."

I swallowed hard and glanced down at her long, shapely legs. "Nope, keep them on. Sorry, Agent Kincade, you aren't stealing my virtue tonight. Not again."

She sighed then started to get up. I frowned up at her. "Just where are you going?"

"I'm going to put on the coffee and drink loads of water. I'd rather have a purring pussy than wine any day."

I laughed. "That can be arranged."

And I did arrange it… several times. Right there on the living room floor.

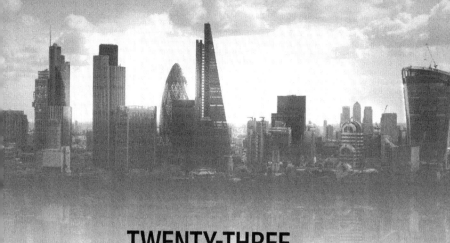

TWENTY-THREE

Nyla

I woke to a heavy arm wrapped around my waist, pulling me into a hot, hard body. I blinked my eyes awake, recognizing the drapes in my bedroom, which we'd forgotten to draw last night.

Oh yeah, you were busy shagging East.

I smiled to myself as we snuggled closer. His voice was a low purr. "You want to go again? I thought you'd be tired."

I giggled. Honest to God giggled. When did I become *that* girl? But there was something about the way he made me feel. Alive and a little bit naughty and like I belonged to someone. I loved that feeling. I rolled over in his arms, and he smiled sleepily at me. The stubble on his cheek was dark. And God, that was so sexy. I could stay in bed with him forever. But if I was really going to do this, really going to take a step and start something new, something brand-spanking new, then I needed to go take care of something first. "I have to go do something."

"What? Now?"

I pulled myself up slightly to glance at my clock. It was 6:30. "Well, I know for a fact Dad likes to get in by 7:30, so if I want to go into the office, clean up my stuff, get all my important case files, things that I want to keep to myself, now is the time to do it." It should have worried me how easily the lie tripped over my tongue, but I didn't want to be the one to tell him that I'd ignored my father's direct order. Yes, I completely recognized that was the wrong move now, because I—surprise, surprise—could be wrong. And I was wrong. I'd been completely wrong about him and the London Lords. The enemy was in my own backyard. I'd been looking outward, not inward. And that was my bad. I was going to clean up the stuff that I needed to, give Amelia what she needed, and I was also going to clean up the wires that I had set up.

East wasn't my enemy. Sure, he and his friends were powerful, and I probably should pay attention to what they were doing, but they weren't doing anything criminal. And for once, I felt good with someone. Not like I was having to constantly validate my reason for existing. I liked this feeling. I didn't want to chase someone down anymore, at least not when it came to relationships. In terms of the job, I'd have to figure something else out. But for now, if I wanted East, if I wanted to be with him and enjoy this thing between us, I needed to let all that other shit go.

"Hey, what's going on in that beautiful head of yours?"

"Just thinking. I've really got to get into the office."

"Will you stick around a little bit? Maybe we could have breakfast?"

I groaned. "I like the idea of coming back to you in my bed. But maybe we can arrange that some other time."

"Okay, party pooper."

As it turned out, he made it worth my while when I rolled out of bed and he rolled with me, scooping me up quickly.

I giggled and squealed. "Put me down. I'm heavy."

"Please. You weigh barely anything."

"Ugh, I'm tall. I'm not one of those petite little things you can toss around."

He set me down gently, and then his thumb and forefinger tenderly gripped my chin. "Hey, you are a badass. Anyone who ever told you differently was a complete and total arsehole. Do you understand?"

I nodded. "Yeah. I understand."

"Good, now you have a three-second head start before I chase you into the loo."

I knew he was serious. All he had to do was say one, and I took off running. But he didn't even give me till three before he was already charging after me.

And what ensued was lots of kissing. Soapy, delicious snuggling, and then, well, he had a satisfying breakfast after all. Of me. In the shower. And as I gripped the towels and closed my eyes, I couldn't believe just how lucky I'd gotten, because how was this my life?

I could have this. All the time. I just had to let that other part of me go.

As East kissed my neck and lifted me gently off my feet, placing me against the wall, my brain was unable to think clearly except for one tangible thought; no one had ever made me feel like this before. And I was never going to let that feeling go.

Thirty minutes later, after I tossed on some joggers, a T-shirt, and a hoodie, and then East had gotten dressed in the same clothes he had worn the night before, we left my flat together. He had to go to the guest parking lot to grab his car, and I just indicated I was going to take the tube. It was faster. Then he gave me a long kiss as he left me at the tube. "I'll text you later."

"Send me nudes."

He chuckled and gave me another soft kiss on the nose before heading to his car.

I jogged down the stairs, but instead of heading left, I turned right. It was time I let the London Lords go. I was going to focus on my future and what was going to make me happy instead of listening to that niggling part of my gut. My gut was wrong. My gut sucked. Two stops later, and I was at the address Amelia had texted me the day before.

Giving up, are you?

I'm turning my focus to something else.

When I unlocked the flat, I found Amelia with a stack of papers, cleaning something up. She turned to me and said, "Jesus Christ, there you are."

I wrinkled my brow. "What? Have I been missing?"

"I've been calling you since last night."

I winced. "Ah, I might have turned off my phone." And then I winced again when I realized I hadn't charged it either. I'd mindlessly grabbed it this morning without even looking at it. "Sorry, I hope it wasn't urgent."

"I just wanted to make sure you still wanted to pack all of this up. I can't believe you're just abandoning this investigation after all the work you've put into it."

"Shit, Amelia, I'm sorry. That was my bad. I should have texted you right away. I went to see Dad yesterday, and he benched me. He suspended me."

Her brows popped. "Wh-wh-what?"'

"I know. Indefinite suspension for insubordination."

She sputtered. "That son of a bitch. That is some serious bullshit. All this shit Denning pulls, and what he's done to you, and he tags you on insubordination?"

"Yeah, that's basically what I said."

Amelia started pacing. "Oh my God, I am going to write a complaint so big."

"To who? He's section chief."

"We can get a lawyer, you know?"

"What? I'm going to sue my dad? I'm just—I'm so tired of the bullshit. And I told him to take his suspension and shove it, so I'm probably pretty fired."

Amelia shook her head in disbelief. "No. Don't you dare. There's a lot of work to do."

"Look I know this is going to feel like I'm abandoning you, but honestly, I just—I'm really tired. Things are changing with East, and I sort of just want to enjoy that for a minute."

She blinked at me. "East. No, no, no, no, Nyla. Don't tell me. No."

"Yes." I shrugged and gave her a wink. "Yes. Maybe. A little. Don't judge me."

Vehemently, she shook her head. "No, Nyla, no."

"What is wrong with you? Look, I like him, okay? You were right, I have feelings for him."

The words tripped out and felt foreign for me to say.

Amelia cursed under her breath. "Fuck. Nyla, no."

"Yes. I thought you'd be happy for me. You, of all people, wanted me to get in touch with my yang."

"No, Nyla, it's not that. Look, that's another reason I was trying to call you last night. Remember when I told you a few days ago that I was going to follow the money trail? That whatever the London Lords were up to, these things usually followed money?"

"Yeah. You said you couldn't find anything."

She shook her head. "No, we couldn't because we were looking at their business. Yes, we had a cursory look at their personal finances, but found nothing untoward. Rich bastards. Money, properties, that kind of thing."

"Yeah, I know."

"But what we didn't do was really pay attention to the finances of people they know. Did you know that they had some kind of monthly dues scenario? I didn't flag it immediately because it was made up of one lump payment, going back five years. All three of the London Lords made the same payment to Elite Pops Ltd. Care to hear how much their membership dues are?"

I winced. "I'm pretty sure I don't want to know."

"Each of them paid a lump sum of one million pounds."

My eyes went wide. "Jesus Christ. What was it for?"

"Well, at first, I didn't know. But since they all made the same payment in the exact same amount, I figured maybe some blackmail scheme. Some underhanded deal. After all, they paid it through a shell company. I hit dead end after dead end. And then it occurred to me, when you want to know something, just ask."

I frowned. "You went to one of the London Lords?"

"No. I went to someone who I know hates them. Bram Van Linsted. Obviously, I knew it would be flagged if I went to visit old man Van Linsted because of all his sex trafficking crimes, but the younger Van Linsted is in prison only for fraud. Much easier and less visible to go chat. He hates the London Lords, the lot of them. He insists that they set him up."

My heart started to race. "What do you mean he insists?"

"He insists that he and his family had the original Canary Jewel. That Ben Covington and his friends stole it from his family."

My brow furrowed. "What do you mean stole it?"

"I'm just telling you what he told me. He said that they stole it from his family, and that if we can locate it, we'll know that they're the ones who belong in jail. I asked him about the finances and if he had any idea what the hell Elite Pops Ltd. was, and you know what? He started talking a mile a minute. He said he'd been abandoned by the people he called his brothers so he owed them no loyalty."

"Jesus Christ." I couldn't breathe. This was it. This was what I'd been looking for.

"He said they are all part of a secret group, like the Illuminati or whatever. This is huge."

"Easy does it. We're not going to jump into conspiracy theories here, but what do you mean a secret group?"

"Okay, you know how Eton has the Pops, right?"

I nodded. "That's no secret. Everyone knows most prime ministers come from Eton and were part of their elite group called the Pops."

"Well, there's an even higher echelon, the cream of the crop, and they are absolutely secret. Until now. They call themselves the Elite. So you first have to be tapped to be Pops, and then you have to be recruited from there to the Elite. He says he and our merry band of billionaires are part of this group. Van Linsted says if we are looking for dirt on them, he's willing to name names. He gave me those three specifically. He said if we can get him out, he's willing to give us more names."

Holy shit.

Amelia was on the cusp, and I didn't know how to stop her.

East

My gut churned. I had known right away that morning that something was off. I could see it in her eyes. Something was bothering her, and she had zero intention of telling me.

Instead, she'd lied. I'd seen the lie in her eyes before she'd even spoken it. When she told me she wanted to go into the office, I knew it was bullshit. Wherever she was going, I knew it wasn't the damn office. So I'd kissed her to make it seem like I was heading back to my car and then followed her.

The tracker I'd placed on her phone when I'd been concerned she was investigating us was still active. The prickle of shame stung. She still didn't know how closely I'd been monitoring her.

I'd promised myself I was going to trust her, but she was lying. Which meant trouble. And as much as I wanted to keep her safe, I had an obligation to my mates first. She couldn't go kicking at the hornet's nest. The CCTV feed on my phone indicated she was going the opposite direction of her office. "Fuck."

Even as I followed her on the cameras, I made a call to Ben. "Hello?"

The three words I spoke had him on high alert. "We've got problems."

"Nyla?"

I sighed. "Yup. Something is up. She just told me an unnecessary bald-faced lie. This is just informational. I'll find out what it is, and let you know."

"Yeah, okay. Thanks, mate."

I checked the GPS location. It had her getting out of the tube and headed to the Doyle Flats. That wasn't too far from where I was, so I drove over and parked. Good thing I had an all-access parking pass. God, I loved that thing. I could park anywhere in London that I wanted and not get a ticket or towed, which was fucking fabulous. I kept an eye on the CCTV to see where she had gone. Some flat nearby. Nice neighborhood. Quiet. I watched as she used a key to enter, and I grabbed my lock picking kit. I just prayed it wasn't rusty. I waited until she came out of the flat. Amelia Jansen was with her.

I climbed out of the car, my gut churning. I didn't want to believe it. I didn't want her to have lied to me. Last night had felt different, like something real. It had been a long time since I'd had something genuine with another person. I *wanted* it to be real.

But you knew the risk.

A neighbor smiled at me as she walked past. Once I was in the main entrance of the building, I frowned, trying to assess which flat it was. But lucky for me, all I had to do was follow her GPS marker. She might not be inside now, but I had everywhere she'd been for the last twenty minutes. I went down the hall to the left and found it easily enough.

I unlocked the door with ease and let myself in. I didn't need to turn on the lights because I could see everything in the main living area of the flat. Kitchen to the side, open concept. Lots of light coming in from the living room. And on the massive wall on the right, were photos of me, Bridge, Ben and Drew. Livy too. Thankfully, none of Lucas or Roone, or Alexi and Xander who had helped us. The London Lords were the focus. But unfortunately, so was Livy. I marched over and followed her little strings of thread. There were notes that followed those, but one caught my eye. And everything sank inside my body, making my legs feel like lead and my lungs feel like incinerated paper.

Elite Pops Ltd.

I staggered backwards. "Christ." Sure, some knew about the Elite. But it was just a handful of people, and that wasn't so much to be concerned about. But she was digging deep. That meant a look at the finances. Hell, she had two members of the Elite in custody they were probably helping her.

Marcus Van Linsted. His own crimes had predicated him being where he was. But Bram...

We had put Bram in jail. He hated us. Just as we hated him. And when all was said and done, he would be joined by two more.

As I stared at the wall, I knew the unmitigated truth. Nyla Kincade was coming for us, and I was the one who had to stop her.

By any means necessary.

To be continued in *East Bound*...

ABOUT THE AUTHOR

USA Today and *Wall Street Journal* Best Seller, Nana Malone's love of all things romance and adventure started with a tattered romantic suspense she "borrowed" from her cousin.

It was a sultry summer afternoon in Ghana, and Nana was a precocious thirteen. She's been in love with kick butt heroines ever since. With her overactive imagination, and channeling her inner Buffy, it was only a matter a time before she started creating her own characters.

Now she writes about sexy royals and smokin' hot bodyguards when she's not hiding her tiara from Kidlet, chasing a puppy who refuses to shake without a treat, or begging her husband to listen to her latest hairbrained idea.

Looking for a few Good Books? Look no Further

FREE
Shameless
Before Sin
Cheeky Royal
Protecting the Heiress

London Lords
SEE NO EVIL
Big Ben
The Benefactor
For Her Benefit

Royals

ROYALS UNDERCOVER
Cheeky Royal
Cheeky King

ROYALS UNDONE
Royal Bastard
Bastard Prince

ROYALS UNITED
Royal Tease
Teasing the Princess

Royal Elite

THE HEIRESS DUET
Protecting the Heiress
Tempting the Heiress

THE PRINCE DUET
Return of the Prince
To Love a Prince

THE BODYGUARD DUET
Billionaire to the Bodyguard
The Billionaire's Secret

London Royals

LONDON ROYAL DUET
London Royal
London Soul

PLAYBOY ROYAL DUET
Royal Playboy
Playboy's Heart

The Donovans Series
Come Home Again (Nate & Delilah)
Love Reality (Ryan & Mia)
Race For Love (Derek & Kisima)
Love in Plain Sight (Dylan and Serafina)
Eye of the Beholder – (Logan & Jezzie)
Love Struck (Zephyr & Malia)

The In Stilettos Series
Sexy in Stilettos (Alec & Jaya)
Sultry in Stilettos (Beckett & Ricca)
Sassy in Stilettos (Caleb & Micha)
Strollers & Stilettos (Alec & Jaya & Alexa)
Seductive in Stilettos (Shane & Tristia)
Stunning in Stilettos (Bryan & Kyra)

In Stilettos Spin off
Tempting in Stilettos (Serena & Tyson)
Teasing in Stilettos (Cara & Tate)
Tantalizing in Stilettos (Jaggar & Griffin)

Love Match Series
*Game Set Match (Jason & Izzy)
Mismatch (Eli & Jessica)